FUN. IMAGINATIVE. MIND-BLOWING.
The Works of Frederik Pohl

The Day the Martians Came
"A clever idea, sure-handedly executed; sure to please!"

—*Kirkus Reviews*

"Not your run-of-the-mill little-green-men sci-fi pulp throwaway...The focus of the novel is the effect...on the people back on Earth."

—*Knoxville News Sentinel*

The Merchants' War
"A new look at the advertising culture... gleefully dissected."

—*Newsday*

"Engagingly hilarious...Pohl launches satiric barbs at his favorite target—mass advertising—consistently hitting the mark."

—*Library Journal*

Midas World
"As this provocative work makes plain, Pohl remains one of SF's all-time masters of satirical extrapolation."

—*Publishers Weekly*

Gateway
"Superlative...A masterpiece by one of SF's greatest talents."

—*Booklist*

S0-AWJ-345

THE DAY THE MARTIANS CAME

FREDERIK POHL

ST. MARTIN'S PRESS/NEW YORK

DISCLAIMER

I have taken the liberty of including a few famous people in the cast of characters of this novel, as appearing on various television programs, being spoken of in published accounts, and so on. However, all the characters who participate in the action of the novel in any way are completely fictitious and do not represent any person, living or dead.

THE DAY THE MARTIANS CAME

Copyright © 1988 by Frederik Pohl.

Library of Congress Catalog Card Number: 88-14780

ISBN: 0-312-91781-3   Can. ISBN: 0-312-91782-1

Printed in the United States of America

St. Martin's Press hardcover edition published 1988
First St. Martin's Press mass market edition/December 1989

10 9 8 7 6 5 4 3 2 1

CONTENTS

ONE

EXTRACT FROM THE
Congressional Record

THE SPEAKER: For what purpose does the gentleman seek recognition?

REP. INGRAM (*Delaware*): I rise for the purpose of speaking in support of the amendment.

THE SPEAKER: The gentleman from Delaware has the floor for five minutes.

REP. INGRAM: I ask unanimous consent to revise and extend my remarks.

THE SPEAKER: Without objection it is so ordered.

REP. INGRAM: Mr. Speaker, honorable members of the House of Representatives, Amendment A3 to the budget bill, H.R. 1107, has the purpose of eliminating all funds for the so-called Mars Colonization Project.

Mr. Speaker, I have sat in this House for eighteen years, and I believe the record will show that I have consistently supported many measures connected with the American space program, even though every dollar spent on space meant a dollar less that could have been devoted to such high national priorities as our schools, our cities, our endangered farm families, and even the health of our senior citizens. The space program, particularly in those applications which can advance our technology and enhance our security, has had no better friend than I. Yet patience must come to an end. A failed venture, however glorious its intent, must be prudently terminated when its pointlessness becomes clear. The day has arrived when we must call a halt.

The Mars Colonization Project is a waste of the treasure entrusted to us by our long-suffering taxpayers. I urge—no, I demand—that this House assert as its will that not one further dollar be squandered on this indefensible waste of our resources.

REP. GAITLIN (*Alabama*): Will the gentleman yield?

REP. INGRAM: I will yield to the gentlelady from Alabama for a question.

REP. GAITLIN: I ask the gentleman from Delaware if it is his intention in this amendment to deny funds to our heroic astronauts, now on the surface of the planet Mars, to insure their safe return.

REP. INGRAM: I thank the gentlelady for the opportunity to clarify that point. The answer is no. Nothing in the language of the amendment would in any way further endanger the safety of Captain Seerseller and the other survivors of his expedition. The amendment deletes all funds for continuing the Mars Colonization Project. It says nothing as to the funds already expended. When, in a few weeks from now, the relationship of the planets is such that the astronauts can commence their long voyage home, the vehicles, fuel, and supplies they will use will be those that are long since paid for and already in their possession, on the surface of Mars and in orbit around it. There will be no need for further expenditures to rescue these unfortunate explorers. Indeed, the purpose of the amendment is not only to stop the further waste of public funds on this ill-conceived venture, but even more to insure that no further American boys and girls will ever find themselves in so tragic a situation.

Mr. Speaker, the House is not in order.

THE SPEAKER: The House will come to order. Will those members in the well please retire to the cloakroom to conduct their conversations? The members will please take their seats.

The gentleman from Delaware may continue.

REP. INGRAM: Mr. Speaker, let us speak plainly here. The Mars Colonization Project is not only a failure, it is a catastrophe. Two hundred and thirty-eight of our people have already lost their lives on that faraway planet. We are told that, tragically, even some of the remaining thirty-eight will perish before the next launch opportunity. And what have we to show for this loss of human life? Do we have new inventions for our industries? Do we have new agricultural methods to help feed our people? Do we have, even, a glorious triumph to inspire us all? We have not. Our people have demonstrated that they are disheartened and chagrined at the failure of the expedition to accomplish any worthwhile purpose.

THE SPEAKER: The gentleman will please suspend. The House is still not in order.

I ask the House to remember that we have three other amendments to consider before we can adjourn. If the House wishes to conclude its business before the Christmas break we will have to come to order.

The gentleman may continue.

REP. INGRAM: I would add only one more point. As we all remember, the hearings of the Select Oversight Committee looking into the causes of the tragic accident on Mars have recessed *sine die*, without being able to ascertain the cause of the crash of the supply rocket. This being so, how can we feel safe in assuming that the same fate will not befall any future such venture?

REP. THATCHER (*Illinois*): Will the gentleman yield for a question?

REP. INGRAM: I will yield for a question.

REP. THATCHER: Would the amendment have the effect of halting work on the Mars rockets now being prepared for a future mission?

REP. INGRAM: It would, definitely. It would stop them in their tracks.

REP. D'ITTRIO (New Jersey): Will the gentleman yield?

REP. INGRAM: I will yield for a question.

REP. D'ITTRIO: Since one of the three Martian landing rockets has failed, we should face up to the possibility that the remaining rocket the Seerseller expedition relies on to get home may also malfunction. If no future spacecraft of that capability are to be put in service, how could we then rescue the surviving members of the expedition?

REP. INGRAM: We could not. We can't now. If their return spacecraft should fail, it would take more than three years to complete a rescue ship, secure a favorable launch window, and make the long voyage itself. And, since we do not know what caused the earlier crash, how do we know the new rocket, too, will not fail?

THE SPEAKER: The gentleman's five minutes have expired.

TWO

A
MARTIAN
CHRISTMAS

Millions of miles across space, the Seerseller Martian expedition was getting ready to celebrate Christmas. None of them wrote letters to Santa Claus. None of them had to express a wish for a gift, because every one of them had the same wish: that the days until the minimum-energy return date would pass as quickly as possible, and preferably without any more of them dying off.

While the survivors were counting the days a lot was happening back on Earth. Individual human beings lived their individual lives, no matter what large events were going on around them. In New York City one young man found God. In the suburbs of Chicago, another young man found heroin. In Athens and the East Indies, on L.A.'s Sunset Strip, and on Washington, D.C.'s Beltway, men—and women and children, too—caught glimpses of the magnificent forest only as filtered through their own individual trees. If they noticed the stories about what the Martian expedition was doing at all, it was only with the small fraction of attention they had left over from the headlines about inflation, and what rock star was facing a paternity suit from what underage groupie, and which world leader was one-upping which in the ongoing three-way public-relations contest among Washington, Moscow, and Beijing.

That's the way human beings are.

There's a little bit that's divine in every one of them, but the part that's pure pithecanthropus keeps getting in the way. It's a pity that people aren't more godlike and less apish. But they aren't, and there's nothing much that can be done about it, since they're all we've got.

Meanwhile Christmas was coming closer to all, including the Seerseller expedition on Mars.

Of all the survivors, it was Henry Steegman who thought about it most. It was true that Christmas was only an abstraction on Mars. The calendars didn't match. Earth's winter solstice had nothing to do with Martian seasons. But Captain Seerseller had decreed as soon as they landed—or as soon as they pulled themselves together from the disaster of the landing—that they would stick to the familiar twelve Earthly months. So Henry Steegman marked the days until Christmas, especially since it was certain that it would be the last Christmas he would ever see. He loved to read about children's parties in Dickens, and to watch old tapes like *Miracle on 34th Street*. As the calendar crept past November and Thanksgiving and crawled toward the holiday, Steegman thought more and more about Christmas gift-wrapping paper and Christmas cards and, above all, Christmas trees.

Cards he could make. Wrapping paper could be improvised, if they had had any gifts to give each other. But where on the planet Mars could you find a Christmas tree?

It was the expedition's second Christmas on Mars. The year before the community had pulled itself together and made an effort. Most of them were still alive then, and even fairly healthy; so they flanged together something tree-shaped—sort of tree-shaped—out of foam plastic and transparent piping. After it was sprayed it at least looked green. It didn't smell like a Christmas tree. But once they had hung it with bright red and green micromatrices from the spare-parts bins and festooned it with instrument lights it at least cheered up the common room. They went farther than that, too. They had even made a Santa Claus suit out of somebody's red flannel long johns stuffed with somebody else's sweaters and trimmed with yet another person's curly wig. It made Santa Claus's trimming and beard platinum blond rather than white, but that was the least of the incongruities. Even Santa Claus had very few gifts to give them. For most of them, not even the gift of survival.

Henry Steegman was not an important member of his community of Mars explorers. He was neither a xenoanthropologist nor a xeno-biologist (though that skill had not turned out very useful). Nor did he have any of the special skills that made the lives of the survivors fairly—or barely—tolerable, like the food chemist, power technician, or medic. Steegman was a construction engineer. That is, he drove tractors. He drove interesting kinds of tractors, a nuclear one that crawled through the Martian rock and melted out tunnels, as well as two or three solar-powered models that leveled and shaped the surface of the planet twenty meters up from where they lived. He didn't usually drive any of them in person. The places where his tractors went were not very hospitable to human beings. When his services were needed, which was less and less often, as the captain and the council decided that there was no longer any purpose in building new domes and exploring new anomalies the gravitometers pointed out for them, he sat before a television screen and commanded his tractors by remote control.

That was more or less Christmasy, too. It was like having the world's biggest—anyway, Mars's biggest—set of electric trains to play with. It was about that useful, too, for a community of thirty-eight, once two hundred and seventy-six, mostly sick human beings.

Since there was no necessity for much activity of any kind anymore, Steegman was encouraged to play with his toys whenever he wanted to. It kept him out of the way, and it cost nothing. It didn't cost the community the valuable working time of one of its surviving members, because there wasn't a whole lot Steegman was able to do. Radiation sickness in his case had attacked the nerves. He was likely to spasm when he tried anything very demanding. Since the diggers were nine-tenths automatic he couldn't do much harm there but he couldn't be trusted with anything as delicate as, say, changing bedpans for the dying. And it certainly didn't cost any more than they could afford in power. As long as they were given plenty of time to recharge, the photovoltaic cascades provided plenty of juice for the surface tractors. For the tunneler, there were stocks of fuel rods far beyond any reasonable expectation of need, salvaged from the wreck of the second rocket. The instrumentation that rocket had carried was all mangled, but there's not much harm you can do to stubby, heavily clad rods of radionuclides.

There was also plenty of food, water, heat, and light. In those things the community was well fixed. It was really only short of three things. People. Purpose. And hope.

Hope had vanished for most of them, along with purpose, when the second rocket crashed. The expedition was there to conduct scientific investigations. When the drone rocket toppled off its axis of thrust it split open, blew its fuel tanks, wrecked every delicate part of the instruments, which was most of their parts, and drenched the surface with radionuclides. Not just the surface. The blunder of misguiding the rocket wasn't the only thing that went wrong. Someone, unforgivably, in the frantic rush to salvage what he could, had brought radioactively hot piping down into the cavern. Someone else had hooked it into the water recirculators, and it had simmered there, seeping powdery fission products into their drinking water for more than a day before any crew member thought to put a dosimeter to his coffee cup.

By then, of course, it was all contaminated.

They couldn't live without water. They drank it, glumly watching the dosimeters go into the black. They drank as little as they could, and as soon as possible they began to melt water out of the permafrost under the Martian Polar Ice Cap, only a dozen kilometers away; but by then the people began to get sick. The dosage was not terribly high. Just enough to kill, but not very quickly.

There was one other bad effect.

NASA's vast and powerful public-relations machine fought for them most courageously, but the odds were too high. No matter how many tear-jerker TV interviews they ran with weeping wives and children, no matter how many presidential proclamations and prayers, the public image of the expedition was robust against propaganda. Bunch of clowns, the public thought. Busted their rocket ship. Ruined their equipment. Got themselves killed.

Fortunately for the American spirit, there was a new black American tennis player who won Wimbledon that year, and a movie star named Maximilian Morgenstern, who actually wrestled grizzly bears in his spare time. The public found new heroes.

And thought rarely, if at all, about the spoiled ones on Mars.

So, on what the calendars said was the twenty-first of December, Henry Steegman got out of his bunk, felt his gums to see if they were bleeding, and went to the common room for a leisurely breakfast. He peered in first to make sure Captain Seerseller wasn't up unusually early. He wasn't. The only other person there was Sharon bas Ramirez, the biochemist, and when he had picked his almost-hash out of the freezer and passed it through the microwave, he joined her. Sharon bas Ramirez was one of the few survivors who treated Steegman like a worthwhile human being, no doubt because it was Steegman who had brought back samples of organic-contaminated rock for her. *Life on Mars!* the headline on their dispatch had read. They had hoped for a wonderful rebirth of excitement back home. But what Steegman had found wasn't really anything alive, only chemicals that might once have been, and besides, that day the movie star had wrestled a female grizzly with cubs.

"Henry," said Sharon bas Ramirez, "do me a favor, will you? See if you can bring back some better samples."

She was looking very tired. He ate his almost-hash slowly, studying her: black patches under her eyes, fatigue in the set of her jaw. "What kind of better samples?" he asked.

She shrugged wearily. "You've been cooking them with the heat of the drill," she complained. "The structure gets degraded."

"I tried using cold rock drills, Sharon! I even went out myself! I even swiped some blasting powder and a detonator and—"

"Don't get excited, Henry," she said sharply, reaching over to wipe some spilled hash off his coverall. He muttered an apology, calming himself down. "Maybe you can find a fissure somewhere," she said. "Try, anyway? Because I'm a biochemist, not a candy striper, and I get real tired of feeding the sick ones because I don't have anything more important to do."

"I'll try," he promised, and thought hard about how he could keep that promise all the way to his handler room.

Usually Henry Steegman spent his hours at the controls making pretty patterns, thrusting the nuclear tunneler out under the Martian rock in long, straight shafts, pausing now and then to spin it on its axis to make bypasses and turnarounds. It was not likely that any of the things he made would ever be used for anything. Or even wanted. But it cost nothing to do the job right. When that became boring he would turn to the surface bulldozers and heap more Martian soil over the foundation of the entrance-lock dome, or man a repair truck and inspect the banks of photocells that gave them interior power. The machines were too well designed to need much maintenance, but that job was, Steegman believed, his major contribution to the welfare of the expedition . . . even though the machines would surely outlast the colony's scheduled stay on Mars.

He decided on the deep tunneler this time, pondering how he could oblige Sharon bas Ramirez. He pushed it through deep Martian rock, twenty kilometers north of the camp. He was not paying strict attention to what he was doing. He was humming "Adeste Fideles," part of his mind thinking about Sharon bas Ramirez, part of it worrying about the latest person to begin to lose blood rapidly—sickly, pale little Terry Kaplan.

Then the instruments revealed a temperature surge before the nose of the borer.

He shut the borer down at once and palped the rock ahead with sonic probes. The dials showed it was very thin. The sonar scan showed a lumpy, mostly ball-shaped patch, quite large, filled with white-traced shadowy shapes.

Henry Steegman grinned suddenly. A cavern! Even better than a fissure in the rock! He could break into the cavern at one end, let the rock cool, bring the borer back home, get in it himself, and ride back to collect all the samples Sharon could want, uncooked. He started the drill again on low power and gentled the tunneler another meter along its course.

The instruments said he had broken through.

Steegman shut it down, and thought for a minute. Good practice required that he let the rock cool for half an hour before opening the shutters over the delicate and rarely used optical system. He could do that. Or he could start the borer back without looking, and then go to the cavern in person, which would take two or three hours, anyway.

He shrugged and stretched and leaned back, waiting for time to pass with a smile on his face. Sharon was going to be real pleased! Especially if there turned out to be anything organic in the rock of the cavern—though of course, he cautioned himself, that wasn't guaranteed. Was pretty damn rare, actually. The crust of the planet Mars was very cold and lifeless; it was only in a few places, where a vagrant stirring of deep-down heat made a patch minutely warmer than what was around it, that you could say it was anything capable of supporting a microbe anyway. Still, they were well under the polar cap with the digger now. There would at least be residual water, here and there. . . .

When the time was up he looked and, in the searchlight beam, saw that the cavern was there, all right, but it wasn't exactly empty. It wasn't natural, either. It was a great bubble laced with what might have been catwalks and what looked like balconies, and all about it were what seemed to be shelves and what could be called tables. Some of them had things on them.

Henry Steegman didn't know what it was he had found, but it had a funnily suggestive look to it. He didn't make the connection for nearly twenty minutes, though. By then his yells had brought others into the control room. They began to yell, too. Captain Seerseller ordered Henry back out of the way, because they were afraid, naturally, that he'd get too excited and knock something over or push the wrong button. Still, even from outside the open door, he could catch glimpses of what was on the screen, and hear what everyone was shouting to each other. He heard perfectly when Marty Lawless yelled, "You know what it is? It's a Martian Macy's!"

It was Captain Seerseller who took the next step; that was what captains were paid for.

"Back up!" he ordered. "Get away from the controls, all you people! Now! Let Henry get that goddam borer out of the way so we can get in there!"

So Henry found himself at the controls again, with the captain hovering over one shoulder and everybody else, it seemed, leaning over the other. Henry put his hands on the start-up lever and then paused, looking around at the captain. "You want me to back it up?" he asked.

"Damn right, back it up! Get it out of the way, dummy!"

Steegman nodded. "All the way back here?" he asked, and hunched his shoulders silently as the captain told him, very explicitly, where he could put the borer—there or anywhere—just to get it out of the way while the first survey party got through to study the find. By the time Steegman had painfully inched it back two or three times its own length and begun to bore a new side tunnel to hide it in he was almost alone. Not quite alone. The walking sick, Terry Kaplan and Bruce DeAngelis and one or two others who were well enough to look but far from well enough to make the trip, were wheezing and gasping behind him, but everyone who could get to the cavern was gone.

The tunnel from the base camp to the "department store" was thirty-three kilometers and a bit, the last five still unlined. Wheeled vehicles couldn't go down the unlined part, but no one was willing to wait for lining. So the first two parties drove, six or eight at a time in the big-wheeled tunnel buggies, as far as the surfaced section of the tunnel went. Then they walked. In air masks and backpacks, tugging barrows or travoises with cameras and tools and instruments, they walked.

They had to. It was a compulsion. Every one of them who could still walk had to get there to see for himself, because the department store was by light-years the most astonishing discovery the expedition had made on Mars, and therefore the thing that most nearly justified the loss of nearly all their lives.

They *almost* all went, all but the ones who were really too sick to make the trip . . . and Henry Steegman. The discoverer of the department store was not allowed to enter it.

It wasn't just that he was needed to get the big borer out of the tunnel so people could clamber through. Captain Seerseller's last order had made that clear. It was, "You stay here, Steegman, you understand? No matter what."

So for the first ten minutes Steegman and his hovering casualties saw nothing on the screen but the sonar scan, reporting on what sorts of rock the drill tractor was nibbling through. Then Steegman turned it off and switched channels to the portable cameras in the first buggy. "Is that it?" little Terry Kaplan asked, hoarding breath to speak. "It looks—looks—" she took a deep breath, "looks different."

"It's only the tunnel," Steegman said absently, watching as the field of view swung dizzyingly around. Then the first party was inside and whoever was carrying that camera was glad to set it down on automatic scan. So Steegman watched jealously as the others piled into the wonderland he had found for them, one more excited than the next. Marty Lawless, six feet six and fifty years old, pulled his spidery body in and out of prism-shaped structures inside the great hollow bubble and cried, "It really is a store! Kind of a store! Like an enclosed market? Like a great big shopping mall, where you can find almost anything."

"It could be a warehouse," objected Manuel Andrew Applegate, senior surviving archeologist, annoyed at the presumption of someone who actually was supposed to be a communications engineer.

"There's nothing on most of the shelves, Manny-Anny," Captain Seerseller pointed out.

Lawless answered that one, too. "The perishables have perished, of course," he cried. "God knows how old this is! But it's a store, all right. A *suk*. A bazaar!"

And back in the control booth Terry Kaplan whispered to Steegman, with what sounded like the last of her breath, "It really is a Macy's, Henry. Oh, how Morton is going to love this!"

And no one answered her, because Terry was a widow. Morton Kaplan had died more than three months before.

And so the expedition began to live again—as much as it could, with most of its people already buried under the Martian soil. Pictures, samples, diagrams, data of all kinds—everyone wanted to put his specialty to work at once. No! Not after the archeological team makes its inventories! Now! Me first! The members of the expedition were being gratified at both ends, in fact, because not only were they thrilled at what they had found, they were actually getting signs of real interest from Earth, for the first time in many months.

That didn't happen right away. The round-trip travel time for talking to NASA Command was less than thirty minutes, but no one at NASA Command was bothering to pay attention when the first excited messages came in. Hours later, some no-doubt bored comm specialist decided he might, after all, earn his day's pay by looking over the last batch of accumulated tapes. And did. And then boredom vanished.

It was a good time for Earth to take an interest in Mars again. The movie star had lost his last bout with a grizzly, terminally; and there was a new Yugoslavian kid burning up the tennis courts. So the network news carried the pictures, and there were special half-hour reports every night after the late news, and NASA's PR people were in heaven. Send us more, they begged. Not just crummy old archeological drawings and photos. Personalities! *Interviews!*

Interviews with, most of all, that one hero of the expedition, whoever he was, who had first discovered the Martian Macy's.

Since the captain was well and truly NASA-trained, he saw his duty and did it. They co-opted Sharon bas Ramirez away from her delightful duties of studying moldering samples of definitely organic substances from the store and put her to work patching the holes in Henry Steegman's old tunic. The one surviving surgeon was taken off the wards of the dying to cut Henry's hair and shave him. Then they put Henry in front of the TV camera.

Captain Seerseller, of course, did the interview himself. He remembered *all* of his training. They found the two best-looking chairs in the colony and planted them before a camera, with a table containing a bizarre sort of metal implement between them. It was the most spectacular piece the archeologists had so far allowed them to bring in. Then the captain gestured the camera to himself. When it was on he smiled directly into the lens. "Hello, my friends," he said. "Mars reporting. Under my leadership the expedition has continued to survey this old planet, on its surface and under, and we have just made the most wonderful discovery in human history. Under my direction, Henry Steegman was extending our network of exploratory tunnels. He broke through into a sealed underground chamber of approximately twenty thousand cubic meters volume. It is divided into five levels. All levels are built over with triangular prism-shaped structures. Each triangular 'booth' contains a different kind of item. Our specialists have made a preliminary inspection, on my orders. Their tentative conclusion is that the objects are merchandise, and that the cavern itself was the equivalent of a Martian department store. This object," he said, picking up the gleaming thing, "was perhaps a scientific instrument, or even a household utensil. Of course, most of the contents of this 'store' are rusted or decayed or have simply vanished—they've been there for a long, long time. So I have ordered our archeologists to exercise extreme care in their handling, so that no valuable data might be lost."

The camera focus had pulled back to show the stand the object had come from, and also Henry Steegman, digging into one ear with a finger while he was listening in fascination to the captain. Steegman was not at all sure what he was supposed to be doing. His instructions had been, *Just relax*. But it was hard to relax with the captain giving him those frosty, sidelong looks. He was feeling that funny buzzy sensation that meant his ruined nervous system was being overstimulated again; he closed his eyes and breathed deeply.

"Now," said the captain, with an edge on his voice, "I want to introduce to you the man who, carrying out my directions, made the first penetration of this Martian marvel, Henry Steegman."

Steegman jerked his eyes open, and blinked at the camera. He didn't like having the camera look at him. His eyes wavered away, but only onto the monitor, which was worse. He could see that he was shaking. He tried to control it, which made it worse. "Henry," said the captain, "tell us how you felt when you broke through into the cavern."

Steegman thought for a moment, and then said uncertainly, "Real good?"

"Real good! Well, we all felt that way, Henry," said the captain with audible forbearance. "But when you completed this task I had assigned you and saw for the first time proof that there had once been life on Mars—even civilized life!—were you surprised? Excited? Happy? Did it make you want to laugh? or cry? or both at once?"

"I guess so," Henry said, pondering.

"And did it make you realize that all the great sacrifices of blood and treasure—the lives of so many of us, and the wonderful support the American people have given us in making this venture possible—did it make you think it was all worth while?"

Henry had figured out a safe response. He said promptly, "I don't exactly remember that, Captain."

The captain swallowed a sigh and motioned to Mina Wandwater, the best looking of the surviving women, who came forward into camera range with a champagne bottle and a glass. "This is for you, Henry," said the captain, leaning forward to stay in range of the camera as Mina poured. "It's your just reward for carrying out my instructions so successfully!"

Henry held the glass carefully while Mina filled it, curtseyed prettily to him and the captain, and withdrew. He looked at the captain for instructions.

The captain said tightly, "Drink it!" There were times, he thought, when the orders of NASA public relations to keep up civilian interest at home cost more than they were worth. "Now!" he ordered, as Henry hesitated.

"Right, Captain," Henry said. He stared at the glass, then suddenly jerked it to his lips. He slobbered half the contents over himself and the floor. Then—because the bottle was champagne but the contents weren't; they were something bubbly the chemists had cooked up to refill the empty—Steegman sputtered and choked. He twitched and dropped the glass, and then sat there, gaping dumbly into the television camera.

It was not only a lot of trouble to keep up the morale back home, it sometimes didn't work at all. The captain gave the camera a great smile and said, "That concludes our interview with Henry Steegman, who under my com—What is it, Henry?" he asked irritably. Steegman had stopped dabbing at the mess on his tunic long enough to wave frantically at the captain.

"I just wanted to say one more thing," he pleaded. "You folks at home? I know it's a little early, but—Merry Christmas!"

They made Steegman take another physical after that, which kept him in the ward overnight, among the immobile and the dying. The surgeon studied his tests and plates and told Henry matter-of-factly, "You're going, I'm afraid. A few more weeks. Your myelin sheaths are rotted away. It's going to get worse pretty soon. That's a nice haircut, though, isn't it?"

When Henry went to the captain's office the captain wasn't there. Neither was the surgeon, but his report had already come over the net and the executive officer was studying it on her screen. "You want what, Henry?" she asked. "You want to go into the *cavern*? Good lord, no! Captain Seerseller would never permit it. The surgeon's report makes it very clear, your motor reflexes are too untrustworthy; that's very delicate stuff in there and we don't want it wrecked."

"I wouldn't hurt anything," he protested, but she wasn't listening any more. She just waved him out.

Nobody else wanted to listen, either, though some of them tried to make it more palatable. "You wouldn't want to spoil your own discovery, would you?" Mina Wandwater asked. Steegman conceded he would not. "Then wouldn't it be silly for you to go in there and be messing things up? Breaking irreplaceable artifacts? Getting things out of order, so the archeologists can't complete their studies?" He frowned, and Mina added reasonably, "You know, Henry, how important it is to the archeologists and the anthropologists to study the site exactly as it was left."

"I wouldn't hurt anything," Steegman pleaded.

"Of course you wouldn't *mean* to. No," she said kindly, "you just stay out of there, okay? We just can't afford any more accidents on our record, you know."

She was gone before Steegman remembered to point out that he wasn't the one who had crashed the instrument rocket, or let the fission products into the water. Sharon bas Ramirez was kinder, but also busier. She looked up from the tubes of samples long enough to say, "I really can't talk to you now, Henry, but don't worry. They'll let you in sooner or later, you know."

But if it weren't sooner, it couldn't be later. Steegman said absently, "You know it's Christmas Eve?"

"Oh. So it is. Merry Christmas, Henry," she said, turning back to her lab bench.

Steegman limped and stilted his way back along the drilled corridors of the camp to his control booth. It was a longer walk than it used to be. He thought briefly of what the surgeon had told him about his life expectancy. Then he dismissed the thought; since he couldn't do anything about it, it didn't need to be mulled over.

The corridor not only seemed longer than usual, it certainly was longer than it had any real reason to be. It was a quarter of a kilometer from end to end, punctuated every five or six meters by a door to someone's private bedroom, or a workshop or a supply chamber. Much of the supplies had been used up. So had most of the people. For that reason, more than half the doors were now nailed shut.

Steegman listlessly activated his tunneling machine. Then he sat moping before the screen without sending it forward. Sometimes he got pleasure out of executing circles and figure eights under the surface of Mars, drilling the old planet hollow, lacing it with wormholes and channels the likes of which it had never known. Would never know again, most likely, but would also never forget. The Martian crust was too thick and too old and too cold to squeeze itself seamless again. The arteries Steegman gouged would stay there forever.

He turned the tunneler off and thought about the surface tractors. But he didn't like working on the surface much. Oh, in those first weeks after landing—in spite of the deaths and the doom that hung over most of the survivors—what a thrill it had been! He had delighted in bulldozing ageless, eternally untrodden Martian sand and gravel into flat bases for the huge dish transmitter that sent their signals back to Earth, or in roaming out fifty or a hundred kilometers to pick up samples and bring them back for testing. Just to gaze at the dwarfed, distant sun was a thrill. The tiny points of hot light that were the stars were a delight. The queerly close horizon was an astonishment—they were marvels, all of them, all the time. On the other side of every hummock, there was the mystery of what Mars was all about. What would they find when they crossed it? A city? An oasis? A . . . *Martian*?

Or, as hopes for any of those dwindled, a tree?

Or a bush?

Or a thin patch of moss on a rock?

They had found none of them. There was nothing except the same sterile sand and rock, or sandy ice at the beginning of the cap. Even the tiny sun and the white-hot stars weren't exciting anymore.

Steegman kicked against the rock wall under his control desk.

Then he brightened.

It was, after all, Christmas Eve!

So Henry Steegman made the long trek back to the captain's office again, pausing on the way in his own chamber. The Santa Claus suit was still there in the locker under his cot! He pulled out a knapsack, stuffed the suit in, and hurried down the corridor. Captain Seerseller was not there, and Lieutenant Tesca was not encouraging. "He's at the Macy's," she said, "and really very busy, and so am I—I'm going there myself. What, a Christmas party? No, no, I can't authorize that—really, Henry," she said patiently—fairly patiently. "I don't think you understand what finding this means to us. We just don't have time for nonsense right now."

But she let Steegman hitch a ride with her. The big-wheeled buggy slid smoothly down the tunnel until they reached the unlined part, then the executive officer jumped out and left on a run for the last few kilometers. Steegman toiled patiently behind. His gait was getting worse all the time, he knew. His knees were wobbly—not painful, just sort of loosely put together, so that he was never sure his legs would support him at any stride, and his calves were beginning to ache from the unaccustomed strain on the muscles caused by his awkward foot placement. It took him an hour, but by the time he passed the side shaft where he had left the tunneler he could already hear voices up ahead.

The loudest voice was Captain Seerseller's. He was arguing with Manuel Andrew Applegate at the entrance to the cavern. Beyond them Steegman could see the interior of the cavern as he had never seen it before. A score of bright lights had been put in place all around it, throwing shadows, illuminating bright colors and pastels, clusters of long-rusted-away metal things and heaps of heaven knew what, rotted into black grit. When the captain caught sight of Steegman he turned and blazed, "What are you doing here? I've told you to stay out of this place!"

"I wasn't coming in, Captain," Henry said humbly. "I just wanted to ask if we were going to have a Christmas party this year."

"Christmas?" the captain repeated, and Applegate next to him said, "What about Christmas? We don't have time for that, Henry. Everybody's too busy!"

"I'm not too busy, Manny-Anny," Steegman said, and the captain snorted:

"Then *get* busy! Dig something useful!"

"I've already dug six of everything we could ever use."

"Then make some of the things bigger."

"But I've already—" Steegman began, shifting position to back away from the captain, and in the process sliding on the rubble of loose talus from where the drill had broken through. He lurched against the captain. "Oh, sorry," he said, "but nothing needs enlarging. Not even the graveyards."

"Go," snarled the captain. And Steegman went. He hesitated at the tunnel buggy, casting a look at the captain. But the captain was once again deep in argument with Manny-Anny Applegate.

Steegman sighed and started the long, limping walk back to the dome. He could not, after all, just take the buggy and leave those people marooned.

But a dozen meters down the tunnel his face brightened, his stride quickened, and he turned off into the shaft where he had left the tunnel digger. He could drive himself home! Not in that tunnel, of course. But there was nothing to stop him making a new one.

Steegman pressed against the scarred metal of the tunneler, just where it rounded into the straight flank. He found the recessed catch. It had rock chips in it, of course, but he patiently worked them free, opened the hatch, climbed in, and made his way to the driver's seat.

The quarters were cramped, and the cabin was still uncomfortably hot from the last spate of digging. But it was his own. He pulled the Santa Claus suit out of his knapsack and rolled it up behind his head. Then he leaned back and closed his eyes.

He didn't sleep.

After a while, he sat up straight, turned the idling circuits on, checked his instruments. The tunneler had communications as well as control circuits to the campsite, and Steegman considered calling back to let anyone who might care know where he was. He thought he might leave a message about how he felt, too, because in fact he was beginning to feel very peculiar.

Since very few persons would really care, Steegman decided against it. He cut the communications system out entirely. Then he advanced the control for the drills and engaged the tractor motors.

There was a rackcting roar of noise. The cab, and the whole tunneler, shook in short, sharp shocks. It began to move forward, down into virgin Martian rock.

*   *   *

Twenty minutes later Steegman began to throw up for the first time.

Fortunately he had been expecting it. The pounding motion of the tunneler was enough to make anyone queasy, even if he hadn't been drinking the colony's radiation-poisoned water; and Steegman had found a receptacle—actually, it was a case for one of the fuel rods—to throw up in. When he was through vomiting, he was sweating and light-headed, but peaceful.

He advanced the speed of the tunneler a bit and bored on.

He had no particular objective in mind except to go on. He liked having no objectives. It was how you found unexpected things. At the head of the borer, where the immense, terribly hard, tough teeth ground into the rock, were two flush-mounted poppers. Every second each of them emitted a shattering pistol crack of sound, the frequencies just different enough from each other, and sufficiently unlike any of the spectrum of noises the chewing of the borer itself produced, to be distinguishable by the sonar receivers inside the shell. Every second they reached out and felt the echoes for flaws or faults or soft spots and displayed the results on the screen before Steegman. Steegman didn't have a windshield, of course. There was no glass strong enough to fit to the shell of the tunneler, and generally there was nothing to see if there had been. But the sonar screen was as good.

Steegman leaned back, watching the patterns change before him. What he was looking for mostly was soft spots in the rock ahead—an intrusion of lighter rock, maybe, or a lens of clathrate, the ice-and-solids mix that was the closest they'd ever found on Mars to liquid water.

Or—perhaps—another cavern! . . .

It was a pity, Steegman reflected, that he was going to die fairly soon.

It was not a horror to him. The first shock of that sort of realization was long calloused. He had known for a year that his life would be short, and had been certain almost that long that he would not survive to the lift-off, much less through the endless return to low-Earth orbit and home. So there were pleasures he would never have again. Item, he would never see clouds in a blue sky. Item, he would never swim. Item, he would never get a chance to see the marvels he had not got around to—Niagara Falls, Stonehenge, the Great Wall of China. Never again a real full moon, or a rainbow, or a thunderstorm; never hail a taxi on a city street; never walk into a movie theater with a pretty woman; never . . .

Never any of those things. On the other hand, he comforted himself, there was hardly anyone who would ever see the things he had seen on Mars!

Even what he was seeing now on the screen, why, it was wonderful! He was kilometers beyond the "department store" now, far under the thin smear of dry ice and water ice that was the North Polar Cap. The false-color images on the screen formed pretty patterns, constantly changing as the tunneler moved forward and the sonars got better information on what was before them. If there was any tectonic activity at all on Mars it lay not far from here, where echosounders had indicated an occasional plume of warmer, lighter, softer matter—even liquid water in a few sparse, small places. Peter Braganza, the head geologist, had likened some of them to the white smoke/black smoke fountains at the bottom of some of the Earth's seas, slow upwellings of warmth from the tiny residual core heat of the old planet. It was from plumes like those that Steegman had brought back the samples that thrilled Sharon bas Ramirez. Organics! Almost certainly organic matter, she thought, at least—but the heat of the tunneler had boiled the water out of the minerals and cooked the carbon compounds as well. If they had had some of the instruments they should have had, the nuclear magnetic resonance scanner in particular, she could have been sure . . . but the NMR equipment had been on the crashed rocket.

Steegman leaned forward, peering at the screen.

A gray blob on the lower right-hand corner had changed to pale blue, as the sonars got a better reading on it. Clathrate? Not exactly. Liquid water? Perhaps. Steegman couldn't get a temperature reading that meant anything while the drills were going, but things did warm up a little as one approached the plumes. It was quite possible that water could be liquid here. He was humming "Silent Night" to himself as he studied the screen.

The picture was unusually pretty now. It was almost a hologram, or at least it gave the illusion of depth. What the poppers scanned, the sonar computers examined and analyzed and sculpted into the scene before him. What they displayed was almost always more intricate and beautiful than anything he would have seen drilling through the crust of the Earth. Even the most homogeneous of Earthly rock shows differences of texture and density. On Mars, where almost all the crust had been cold for almost forever, there were countless splits and cracks and fault lines to make a pleasing tracery of color streaks and blobs.

It was funny, Steegman thought, that they didn't look really random.

He had to pause for another seizure of vomiting, holding the canister close to his lips against the cruelly short lurches of the tunneler. When he was through he put it aside, still staring at the screen. He tried to make sense of what he was seeing.

Almost ahead, a little below the level he was drilling through, there was a prism-shaped tubular structure that was displayed in golden yellow. That was not clathrate! It wasn't even liquid water. It stretched off to the left and as far away as the sound probe could reach in one direction. In the other direction, it extended for a hundred meters or so back toward the "department store" he had long ago passed, until it came up against a hard, new—geologically new—intrusion.

Smiling to himself in pleasure, Steegman inched the nose of the borer down and around to intersect it.

When it was huge before him there was a lurch and the cutting nose spun madly. The tunneler had hit empty space.

That was a surprise! There were not many caverns under the Martian surface. Steegman quickly shut the blades off. On the tractor treads alone, dead slow, the tunneler shoved its way through a few crumbling edges of rock. When it was free he turned everything off and paused to consider.

He was really very tired, he realized. Although he was glad that the painful jolting of the tunneler had stopped, he was still very queasy.

He cautiously allowed himself a few sips of water from the tunneler's supplies. When he did not immediately throw them up again he felt more cheerful.

He thought for a moment of opening the communications link again to report his find. The geologists would surely want to investigate this unusual structure. . . .

But Steegman wanted to investigate it alone.

He pulled on his air mask and, with less strength than he had expected, was finally able to force the front hatch open against the gravel that had accumulated outside it. It was hot. When he stepped cautiously out onto the talus it burned his feet. He hopped back into the tunneler, rubbing one foot and looking around for what he needed. Lights. There was a shoulder pack of batteries and a hand lamp. Clothing, too, because apart from the rock heated by the drill the tunnel was quite cold.

He grinned to himself, took the red-dyed garments from the back of the seat and pulled them on, even the platinum-blond beard.

He engaged the tractor treads and inched forward, past the rubble where he had broken through, as far as he could until the motionless drill teeth crunched against the far wall.

Then he stepped out onto the smooth, flat floor of the tunnel, which was not any kind of a geologic feature at all.

Although his vision was blurring and his breathing had become painful, Steegman was sure that the tunnel was as much an artifact as the "department store." Crystalline walls, undimmed by the millennia, bounced back the light of his hand lamp. The cross section of the tunnel was triangular, with rounded corners.

Natural formations did not come in such shapes.

What price Niagara Falls now! Steegman laughed out loud in triumph. His duty was clear. He should jump back in the tunneler and tell the rest of the expedition what he had found. They would want to come rushing, to explore this tunnel, to see what it led to—

But so did he.

Without looking back he turned left, settled the battery pack better on his shoulder straps, and began limping down the tunnel. When he had his next spasm of vomiting he had no handy canister to fill. (On the other hand, there was not much left in him to throw up, so the mess was minimal.) When at last he could walk no longer, he sat down, his fingers fumbling with crumbled bits of what might have been broken porcelain or might have been some kind of stone.

He closed his eyes, perfectly happy.

It was a long time before he opened them again, and he wouldn't have except that he felt as though his old dog was nuzzling at his fingers.

When he woke the sensation remained. Something was nuzzling at his hand. It wasn't a dog. When he stirred it flinched away from the light, but with the last of his vision he got a good look at it. More than anything else, it looked like one of those baby harp seals the fur hunters clubbed, only with skinny, stiltlike legs. "Merry Christmas," Henry Steegman whispered, and died.

When at last someone noticed that Steegman was missing, the captain ordered Manuel Andrew Applegate to follow the new tunnel and retrieve, at least, the borer itself—whether Steegman were retrieved or not, he declared, he didn't at all care.

When Applegate reached the borer, and saw what it had broken into, his almost incoherent message back brought half the colony there on as close to a run as they could manage.

When they finally saw the dimming glow of Steegman's hand lamp far down the corridor and hurried toward it, they saw that Steegman was not alone. He was dead, propped against the wall, in his Santa Claus suit. Even under the fake beard they could see he was smiling; and around him, whistling in distress as they tried to avoid the harsh glare of the approaching lights, were eight unbelievably, wholly unexpected, unarguably living and breathing Martians. And when at last the survivors of the expedition came home to a presidential reception and a New York ticker-tape parade, Broadway was not renamed Captain Seerseller Avenue for the occasion. It was called Henry Steegman Boulevard.

THREE

From *The New York Times*
"MARTIANS LACK LANGUAGE BUT POSSESS ORGANIZED SOCIETY"

by Walter Sullivan, Science Editor

Dr. Manuel A. Applegate, senior archeologist of the Seerseller Martian expedition, has discovered that the living autochthons discovered by the expedition on December 24th have a well-organized social structure, based on family relationships very like human institutions. They do not, however, possess a spoken language, Dr. Applegate reports, and the question of how they manage their affairs is still a perplexing one.

Preliminary estimates show a surviving population of living Martians of between 650 and 700 individuals, most of them adults. All known Martians live in the complex of tunnels and caverns just discovered, although there is evidence that within relatively recent times—perhaps only a matter of centuries, Dr. Applegate suggests—there were other colonies maintaining contact with the group discovered by the Seerseller expedition.

Reaction from Earth scientists is a mixture of incredulity and joy. Dr. Carl Sagan, reached at his office at Cornell University, describes the data as, "Wonderful! The most exciting event in my life—maybe in the human race's lifetime," and chides those colleagues who accepted the Martian lander findings that seemed to indicate Mars was a lifeless planet as "born pessimists who fear the new and strange." At the Jet Propulsion Laboratories in Pasadena, California, senior scientist Dr. Tom McDonough agreed with Dr. Sagan, adding, "This is just the jolt we need to get our stalled space-exploration program back on track," while a highly placed source at the National Science Foundation predicted that ways would be found to bring a few of the Martians to Earth to represent their dwindling people in our more hospitable environment.

Even Senator Warren Breckmeister (R., R.I.), chairman of the committee investigating the crash of the original supply ship of the Seerseller expedition, describes the new discoveries as "a welcome change from the long list of NASA failures and disasters." Questioned about the future course of his investigation, presently in indefinite recess, the senator stated that a meeting of the committee members would be called shortly to decide whether to go on with its probe into possible derelictions or blunders in the space program.

As the time for the return of the Seerseller expedition's survivors is growing short, decisions must be made soon about whether in fact any of the Martians will be brought back. Captain Seerseller himself is known to be urging this step. A source close to him says that his reasons are that it would now be inexcusable to abandon the studies of the expedition, and that, as no new expedition could be organized and transported to Mars for perhaps four years at best, the surviving Martians might well be extinct before they could be visited again.

FOUR

SAD SCREENWRITER SAM

The story about the Martians the Seerseller expedition had found on Mars took Sam Harcourt by surprise, because he wasn't the kind of person who followed interplanetary affairs.

The fact of the matter was that Sam wasn't the kind of person who followed the news much at all. He figured he didn't have to be. Sam had found out, long since, that most of the people he dealt with already thought they knew everything there was to know. So why should he bother? It was easy to get along following two simple rules. Rule One, you listened to whatever the guy had to say. Rule Two, you then played it back to him, ornamented with a few plot twists and bits of business you remembered from old movies. That was all there was to it; and then your agent took care of the rest.

Sam was twenty-seven years old and five feet three inches tall. His sex life was aggressive and his fortune precarious. But one of these days, he was certain, one of these days he would get The Big One. Major theater releases. Top of the chart in the Hollywood *Variety*. Solo writing credit, *before* the title, with his name as big as the star's.

Then Sam would be ten feet tall and the chicks would have to hustle *him*.

Meanwhile he was driving his classic old Mustang with the top down from his agent's home on Gower to The World's Biggest Drugstore, practicing racing starts as the traffic lights changed and frowning when his Top 40 station on the car radio began an interview with a rock star he'd never heard of . . . .

And then, switching channels, he heard this congresswoman from Alabama telling the people of the United States, and most of all her constituents, that the Seerseller expedition's discovery of living Martian beings—"creatures like ourselves," she was saying, "with the intelligence and civilization to construct great underground cities"— was the most important event in human history since, well, the Declaration of Independence, anyway, and could not have been achieved without the great work of those dedicated scientists in Huntsville, whom she was proud to call her constituents.

Sam did not usually waste his time on talk-talk-talk, but the word *Martians* stopped him.

Even Sam Harcourt had heard about the funny department store kind of thing the guys from NASA had turned up on Mars, because you couldn't help it. He even remembered, thinking hard, that, yeah, sure, there had been something about finding Martians there, only he hadn't really been paying much attention to anything when that happened, because it was around Christmas and that was when Deirdre told him she thought she was pregnant, and then there was all that bad time when she was trying to get him to admit he was the father. Well, that had stopped being really urgent when she found that, after all, she wasn't. But then she'd been really uptight about the things he'd said and, all in all, who had time to watch the news then?

Anyway, this was new. It wasn't just, like, Martian *fossils*. It was *live* Martians! Right now, at this very minute, getting ready to get into a spaceship on their way back to Earth!

Sam Harcourt immediately fell into a deep study. He knew the feeling. He was Getting an Idea.

Sam knew all about Martians, although, to be sure, he hadn't thought much about them since he was thirteen. But he remembered all those marvelous old stories, and it came to him, as the light turned green and the driver of the big Coca-Cola semi behind him began to blast his horn, that that knowledge had a cash value to him right now.

Sam gave the truck driver the finger, scooted across the intersection, pulled into a zone marked No Parking, and set his hand brake. He picked up his car phone and dialed his agent's number. "Jesus H. Christ, Oleg," he shouted when the phone was answered, "have I got an idea! *Barsoom.*"

His agent's voice was thinly patient. "I wish you wouldn't keep calling me up all the time, Sam. You just left here, and anyway you're supposed to be seeing Chavez right now."

"I've got plenty of time to see Chavez, and besides this is probably a lot too big for him. He's a wimp, Oleg, and this is *vast*. All Chavez's blood-and-demon stuff is out the window now. Don't you know what's happening? Don't you ever turn on your radio, watch TV, open the door and listen to what people are talking about? It's *Martians*, Oleg. They found live Martians and they're bringing them back!"

The agent said, "Yes, I did see something in the trades." Cautiously: "What about it?"

"I want to do a film about *Barsoom*, Oleg! That's the native name for Mars. Do you see the potential? I thought at first of maybe Spielberg or, I don't know, one of the big studios, but they move too slow. They'd miss the timely quality, you know what I'm saying? There's twenty million dollars worth of free publicity right there to pick up, so it has to be *now*."

"What has to be now, Sam?"

"My story! I've got the whole thing worked out in my head. A gorgeous red-skinned Martian princess. A big aerial fight, like the Battle of Britain, only with swords. Comedy. Sex! Oleg," Sam cried into his phone, one eye on the police car that was moving slowly toward him along the Strip, "I have to hang up in a minute, but you haven't heard the best part. This isn't a Sam Harcourt original. It's from a *best-seller*. It's a classic that every boy has read, and the beauty is, it's maybe in the public domain, because somebody didn't renew the copyright."

"Maybe, Sam?"

"Well," Sam said, "I'm pretty sure I remember seeing something about that. It was some time ago, but your legal department could check it out."

"My legal department," said the agent, "gets a hundred and a half every time I ask him a question and I have better questions to ask him than did somebody forget to renew a copyright. Anyway, *you* forgot something. Please let me remind you. Chavez made a special trip in from the Valley to hear what you're going to write for him, and Sam, please, Chavez is eighteen thousand dollars cash if he bites, a guaranteed sale once it gets past the front office. Come out of the clouds, Sam, with your twenty million dollars' worth of public domain. If it's in the public domain nobody owns it, right, so what have you got to sell anyway?"

"That's what I have an agent for," Sam said. "Call you back." And he hung up, released the brake, and was in motion, nodding pleasantly to the cop behind the wheel of the black-and-white before it reached him.

To horror films Daniel Chavez was what Mack Sennett had been to comedy. He was fast and cheap.

He had not always specialized in horror films, just whatever was selling that week. His first big box-office success, *Monster of the Maelstrom*, had been a sci-fi shocker shot principally in his brother-in-law's backyard swimming pool, which had a center-draining plug. It had cost him fifty-two thousand dollars to make (of his brother-in-law's money, mostly; the man was a plastic surgeon, after all), and Chavez had sold it from the negative to a major studio for two hundred thousand even.

Counting his profits, he saw that this was a magic money machine. He looked for fuel to keep it running. It happened that his next-door neighbor was a collie breeder. One morning, listening to the yelping from the neighbor's yard and remembering some special-effects footage he had paid for but never used, Daniel Chavez came up with his next triumph, *Lassie Meets the Maelstrom Monster*. He sold that one from the negative, too, but then he got tired of letting the studios make all his money when it was just as easy to sign a distribution contract himself.

He sensed that sci-fi had had its day, and moved on. He successively rode the crest of the surfer wave, flew with the drug scene, swung with Kung Fu, bared all in the nudies, and found his true home in the horror flick. He even got a small critical reputation for cinema-verité auteurism. He appreciated the attention, especially since, finance-wise, hand-held cameras and somebody's rented house in Westwood were a lot more attractive than union crews and rented studio space. One of his principles was low overhead. He saw no reason to maintain an office while there were booths in soda fountains.

As Sam Harcourt came into The World's Biggest Drugstore, Chavez was casting his next picture. "You'll do, my dear," he said, patting the behind of the young girl in hip-huggers as she rose from the seat next to him. "Don't forget, I'll pick you up tonight so we can go over your characterization. Around nine-thirty," he explained, "because I have a business dinner date." She peered impassively at Harcourt through two feet of cascading honey-blond hair and rolled away.

Harcourt took her seat and, for openers, said, "Chavez, the horror flick is dead."

"Funny you should say that," Chavez said. "I agree with you. I'm getting into relevant films, and I'm putting that kid in my next picture: *Up Against the Wall, Cardinal Bernardin!* I think it has the potential of a modern *Keys of the Kingdom*."

"How would she look in brick-red body makeup, Chavez?"

"No, no. She's playing a young nun who wants to be a priest."

"No good," Harcourt said, shaking his head. "Relevant flicks aren't going anywhere, either. I'm talking about Martians."

"Oh, my God," said Chavez, looking at him with loathing. "I told

Oleg I didn't want any more crap from you. I didn't even want to talk to you, but he said you had a fresh concept about how somebody would put a demon through a Cuisinart."

"That was then. I did. You would have loved it. But now I've got something better."

Chavez sighed. "I got to listen to this? All right, but hold it while I get something to drink. You want a vanilla malted?"

"Chocolate. I guess you didn't hear the news, so I have to tell you. It was on the radio. The astronauts are going to take off from Mars, you know? And they've got real, live Martians with them. And what I have to offer you today is a story about Martians that, with any luck at all, you can have in release before they're out of quarantine."

Chavez sat down again. He stroked his sideburns, looking at Sam, who rushed on: "They're real Martians, Chavez! Authentic. I'm not talking about some dude in a crappy monster suit, I'm talking about the big one you've been getting ready for all your life."

Chavez had begun to shake his head. "Sci-fi," he said. "You know what the special-effects stuff costs?" But he was listening.

"Who said anything about special effects? You aren't listening, Chavez. Now we've got the real Martians. Everybody's talking about it. I'm actually astonished you haven't heard."

Chavez meditated for a moment, rousing himself as the waitress came by. "Two malts, honey. One black, one white. Sam? I like it a little bit."

"Not just a little bit. You like it a lot."

"I like it well enough to ask you how you're going to get the real Martians signed up. For openers, do they speak English, do you know?"

"Details, Chavez! We could dub it, couldn't we? Anyway, listen, let me tell you the story. It's got everything. The man's a war hero to start out. So now he's trapped in a cave, and he's got these Indians —no, wait a minute, these Cuban soldiers—and they're waiting outside. They want to kill him. But he gets out in the open for a minute, and—we'll call him John Carter—and Carter stares up at the stars, and he sees this one big star, Mars. He stretches his arms out to it. So tell me, Chavez, do you see any big costs so far?"

"I don't even see any story so far, Sam. Why do you want to call him John Carter? I'd like a grabbier name—let's see, something like Rick Carstairs?"

Elated, Harcourt cried, "That's great! Rick Carstairs!" When the customer began suggesting details the hook was entering his heart. "I see him as a real macho guy—maybe we could get, you know, the guy that wrestles bears for the lead?"

"Not from what the hospital says, Sam. Don't do casting. Do story."

"Right. So Carstairs stretches out his arms, like I say, and somehow, mysteriously, he's drawn to Mars. Right out of his body. Right into space, *psssschwt*, speed of light, he's zooming past the stars; and all of a sudden we cut to him falling to the ground on Mars, and this great big ugly green Martian is poking him with a sword. So Cart— so Carstairs jumps up, and what do you know? He jumps right over the big boy. Now, this is kind of a tricky technical point to grasp, but Mars has this different gravity so he can jump like crazy because—"

"Sam, Sam," chided Chavez. "Don't you remember I produced *Worlds at War*? You don't have to explain that kind of thing to me. They're on a planet beyond the pull of gravity, so go on."

"Right, Chavez. So they have this terrible sword fight, and, uh, Carstairs is winning. But then along comes another Martian. This one's green, with four arms—no, wait," he said hastily, as Chavez began to scowl. "It doesn't have to be four arms. It could be only two, in a regular Martian suit, if you don't want to have too much special effects. Anyway, Carstairs licks them all, and he rescues this girl they've kept prisoner. Now, she's *beautiful*, Chavez! A real looker. Red skin. Maybe that kid could play her. Her name's Dejah, wait a minute, Dejah Thoris. She looks at Carstairs like she's grateful, and besides he's quite a hunk, and she says, '*Ikky-pikky hoo-hah Barsoom.*' Carstairs is giving her eyes too, and he says, 'I don't understand your language, madam, but in tribute to your loveliness I cast my sword at your feet.' And he does. Well, she blushes all over. He doesn't know why, but —what's the matter?"

"I don't get something there. You said she had red skin, right? How can you tell she's blushing?"

Sam hesitated. The waitress brought their malteds, and he unzipped his straws from their wrappers and took a long pull before he answered. "You got a good point there," he said. "I think I can handle it, but let's pass it for now. Anyway, she picks up his sword and hands it to him. Then she acts like she's waiting for something, but he doesn't know what. Some other enemy Martians come running up at them right then, and he picks her up and jumps the hell away with her over the roof of the breeding shed—I didn't tell you that part yet. Where he landed's near a breeding shed where those green Martians lay their eggs. That's only a detail, but there's good values in it. I mean, comedy. Maybe there's this one Martian that's a sort of a dope, and he drops this egg, and it's his own little boy—"

Chavez finished his malted, wiped his lips, and said courteously, "Let's pass that part about the eggs for now, too, although I ought to tell you that I think it sucks."

Sam Harcourt shrugged. "Well, anyway. So then Carter and the girl get away to where she had her airship, and they're chased and there's this hell of a big aerial battle—what is it?"

Chavez waggled a finger. "Carter, Sam?"

"Yeah, all right, Carstairs. But what comes next is the big part. An aerial battle in the thin air of dying Mars! This is the only place where you'll need a lot of special-effects stuff, but it's going to be worth it. And listen, I have an idea that could help out with the money part. How'd you like to get the whole shooting script for nothing? I mean, not a nickel, Chavez, except maybe a few grand to help cover expenses—maybe not even that," he said, watching Chavez's face. "Let's say even no cash at all up front, just a cut of the producer's net."

Chavez's lips were compressed now, the fingertips of his joined hands pressed against them in thought. He parted the fingers long enough to ask, "How big a cut, Sam?"

"We'll work it out. Hell. Even fifteen percent. I don't care, as long as it makes a good picture—twelve and a half, maybe," he amended as he saw Chavez's scowl. "I'd frankly prefer not to discuss money with you. Oleg doesn't like his clients doing that."

"Yeah, I know what Oleg doesn't like." Chavez stroked his left sideburn very hard for a moment. Then he pulled back his coat sleeve to examine the three-dialed skin diver's watch on his left wrist and said, "I'll be open with you, Sam, and tell you that with costs the way they are now, that kind of deal could put me right through the wringer. Still, maybe we can work something out. Not on those lines, exactly."

Sam protested, "I was only trying to help you out with front money. Anyway, here's the rest of it. They win the air battle. So Carstairs takes the girl back to her father. He's a local king; and the girl talks to him, all upset and worried and kind of crying, and then Carstairs sees there's something wrong. The girl's gone all sort of ticked off and sad, and her father the king's yelling and fingering his ray gun. Carstairs can't figure it out. What'd he do? The father the king says, '*Huppeta-huppeta cranberries!*,' and some soldiers come running in, and it looks like there's going to be another fight. But then the girl—he's taught her a little English by now—she says, 'Rick, I can't figure you out.' And he says, 'Why, what's the matter?' And then it comes out. It's like he broke her heart. That business where he threw his sword in front of her? On Mars, that's like a proposal of marriage. When he didn't follow through after she handed it back to him, that's like treating her like a tramp. So anyway, they clear that up and—and that's all. Clinch. Music up and out. Final bit of comedy with this mind-reading kind of dog she's got—I left that out, but there's good values there, too. Chavez," he said earnestly, "I can see every frame of this film. I only hope I've been able to make you see it, too."

Chavez meditatively sipped the last of his ice water. When he looked up Sam steeled himself, but what Chavez said was, "Sam, I like it."

"A little bit, Chavez?"

"Maybe more than a little bit. I got to think. Also I've got to dig a little more about these real Martians. No offense, Sam, but I haven't had a chance to keep up with the news much lately, so I want to take a look for myself. But—"

He shrugged winningly, smiled, and beckoned to the waitress. He offered her his Visa card to cover the two malteds, the two earlier iced teas, and the cheese Danish he'd split with the girl.

Then, "Let me sleep on it, okay?" he said. "I'll call Oleg in the morning. I mean that, Sam. Don't go calling him up to call me the minute you get out of here, you know what I'm saying? It's possible that there's something here, so don't crap it up." And they parted, each, in his way, well pleased.

Sam's mind was flashing fireworks with thoughts of screen credits and residuals and—well, who the hell could tell?—a table at the Oscar ceremonies even, as he drove out of the parking lot and around the corner. He ducked into a Phillips 66 filling station, waved away the pump attendant as he parked, and picked up his car phone.

"Now what, for Chrissake?" his agent asked irritably when Sam had identified himself. "Don't tell me. Chavez laughed in your face and you want me to find you another live one, right?"

Sam chortled. "You couldn't be more wrong. He's hooked. H-o-o-ooked, hooked. He practically promised fifteen percent of the net, in fact, only he wants me to turn in the script free and I can't go for that without at least ten or twenty thousand up front. I count on you to firm up the details."

There was silence on the car phone, except for the raspberry noise of static from someone, somewhere, racing his car engine. Sam grinned. "You having a heart attack, Oleg? Surprised I pulled off a deal you couldn't make in a million years?"

Cautiously, "I have to admit," the agent said, "that I didn't really anticipate this outcome, exactly. When you say practically promised, Sam, exactly how practically are we talking?"

"Come on, Oleg! The details are your problem, right? That's what you always tell me: 'Let me be the one that puts on the screws, dummy.' But he definitely didn't say no."

"Yeah, bullshit, boy." But the agent's tone was reluctantly admiring. "So you'll call him?"

The agent rallied his skepticism, which had always served him well.

"Maybe I'll call him. Probably. Listen, I already called some people, and you've maybe got a couple of little problems you don't know about. You know there's a Senate committee looking into all this stuff, and somebody's ass is in a crack?"

"Aw, no! Anyway, look, they aren't blaming anything on the Martians, are they?"

"Maybe not, but there's something else. That Barsoom stuff? I talked to a fellow that knows, and he tells me they straightened out that copyright business long ago."

"Christ, Oleg!" Sam howled. "If you blow this deal—"

"What blow? It's all on the public record, no problem finding it out. I'm just telling you that the story isn't public domain, like you thought."

"All right," Sam said, refusing to come down. "That's not a problem. What can it cost? Offer them fifty per—Offer them twenty-five percent of my take. Five hundred dollars for an option—tell Chavez he's got to get that part up. They'll go for it. If you're the contracts man you're always telling me you are, they will. Anyway," he said, picking up speed again, "this is only for openers. What do we need Chavez for? If Chavez'll go for it, one of the big boys will. Spielberg. Kubrick. With the values this thing has got, capitalizing on a hundred million dollars' worth of free publicity—"

"Yeah, yeah," Oleg interrupted him, sounding as though he were grinning at the phone. "Look at this guy! One 'maybe' from a Daniel Chavez and he's telling me the agency business!" But his tone was not hostile; in fact it became definitely ingratiating. "All right, Sam, we're in this together and I'll roll the dice with you. And listen, I've got something that can help out. You know Dorfmann, the naturalist? Best seal man in the country. He used to train for Marineland of the Pacific. Well, I happen to have the representation for him."

"Hold it there for a minute," said Sam. An unreasoning alarm began to seep through his veins. "Oleg, why are you telling me about this crappy animal act?"

"I mean, for your Martians."

"I don't get what you're talking about."

"Well, don't you get it, Sam? Suppose, maybe, you can't get the real ones off the ship, right? But I see a solution. I was just looking at the pictures on the TV. Take away those funny little arms and the teeth and what have you got? A regular seal! Now, if there's anybody who can dress up a seal to look like a Martian I assure you, Sam, Hersch Dorfmann is the guy."

"Oleg!" Sam screamed in torment.

There was a pause.

Then, "Oh," the agent said. "I think I'm getting a picture. You mean you didn't see what the Martians looked like yet, right?"

There was another pause. Sam couldn't fill it. His throat was dry with fear. Then, with the normal irritation back in his voice, the agent said, "Sam, look, I got to take a meeting. Tell you what to do. You go home and turn on a TV set and look at your Martians. Then call me back. I mean, if you've got anything to call me about."

If some ancient samurai had been in Sam's place—that is to say, in the place of a gallant warrior defeated by a base trick of fate in a battle that had seemed won—he would have sliced his belly in *sep-puku*. A traveling salesman who had seen the Big Order get away might have drowned himself in an evening of blondes and booze.

Harcourt did neither. He sat stricken in front of his twenty-seven-inch TV screen, staring with rage and loathing at what he saw. A forgotten can of Pepsi-Cola had gone warm and flat in his hand.

Seals? But the Martians weren't *even* seals!

He glared at the picture from the Seerseller expedition. It was in full living color, a miracle of technology to bring it into his living room from forty million miles away, with a picture as sharp as eighteen hundred dollars and a satellite dish in his backyard could make it. He hated what he saw. The ship was being readied for takeoff. The survivors of the expedition, haggard and sickly, were nevertheless grinning into the cameras. Harcourt could see no reason to grin. With everything the television technicians could do to enhance their images, on the screen of the best television set in Brentwood Heights, the Martians looked like fat, stupid, charcoal-gray slugs.

"Dejah Thoris," Sam sobbed. "Oh, you *bastards.*"

If only they had been simply ugly—

If only they had been merely strange—

But what they were was nasty, disgusting, and, worst of all, dull.

Sam Harcourt set down the can of Pepsi, thumbed the remote button, and watched the picture shrink away. With it went all his dreams of red-skinned princesses and immense battles in the Barsoomian skies.

He cried out to the blank screen, "Couldn't you at least look like *something?*"

But, really, they couldn't.

The Martians had no say in how they looked. They had evolved to fit an environment orders of magnitude harsher than our own. They were slow, dull, and ugly, not because they had chosen to be, but because they could not be anything but what their environment had made them . . . any more than could Sam Harcourt.

FIVE

"NBC Nightly News": "FERDIE DEAD"

BROKAW & RP: MARTIAN	FERDIE IS DEAD.
	THE SEVEN MARTIANS ABOARD THE SPACECRAFT "ALGONQUIN 9" HAVE NOW BEEN REDUCED TO SIX, AS THE AILING MARTIAN CALLED "FERDIE" DIED OF INJURIES RECEIVED IN THE TAKEOFF FROM THE PLANET ELEVEN DAYS AGO.
	NASA ADMINISTRATOR CARLETON MAYFIELD RELEASED A SHORT STATEMENT THIS AFTERNOON TO CONFIRM THE SAD NEWS:
VT: MAYFIELD *(Transcript)*	IN CUE: CAPTAIN HARRY SEERSELLER ON THE SPACECRAFT "ALGONQUIN 9 . . ."

in his broadcast this morning told us that "Martian F," whom we have all come to love as "Ferdie," failed to respond to medical treatment and was declared dead by the expedition's remaining medical officer, Dr. Clara Pettigrew.

The cause of death, Dr. Pettigrew believes, was traumatic pneumonia, a consequence of injuries received during the lift-off period, when "Ferdie" is believed to have wriggled free of the safety straps in his restraining couch and suffered several fractures and perhaps internal injuries in his respiratory system.

Captain Seerseller's words were, "Everything possible was done. Ferdie was just too weak to make it. We feel as bad about it as if he was human."

I know I speak for everyone in the National Aeronautics and Space Administration, and for every American from the President down . . .

	OUT CUE: WHEN I SAY THAT WE SHARE HIS GRIEF.
BROKAW	ALTHOUGH ADMINISTRATOR MAYFIELD IS OBVIOUSLY DEEPLY SADDENED—NASA SOURCES SAY HE WAS IN TEARS BEFORE DELIVERING HIS STATEMENT—HE DECLINED TO RESPOND TO QUESTIONS.
	AND THERE ARE QUESTIONS.
	PROTESTS HAVE BEEN RECEIVED IN THE WHITE HOUSE, IN THE HOUSES OF CONGRESS, AND ELSEWHERE FROM A VARIETY OF INSTITUTIONS AND GROUPS. THEY INCLUDE ALLEGATIONS THAT THE MARTIANS WERE COERCED INTO COMING TO EARTH AND THAT THEIR SURVIVAL IS AT CONSIDERABLE RISK, BECAUSE OF THE FRAILTY OF THEIR BODIES.
	PROTESTORS INCLUDE THE AMERICAN SOCIETY FOR THE PREVENTION OF CRUELTY TO ANIMALS, THE L-5 SOCIETY, AND THE ROMANIAN DELEGATION TO THE UNITED NATIONS, AS WELL AS ALL THE

MEMBERS OF A KINDERGARTEN CLASS IN WACO, TEXAS, . . . AND SOME OF THE PROTESTORS ARE DOING SOMETHING ABOUT IT.

FOR A REPORT WE GO TO NBC CORRESPONDENT TOM PETTIT AT THE HOUSTON SPACE CENTER:

VT: PETTIT

IN CUE: THE PEOPLE YOU SEE BEHIND ME. . .

. . . ARE MARCHING IN PROTEST AGAINST THE ACTIONS WHICH LED TO THE DEATH OF THE MARTIAN, FERDIE. IT IS AN ORDERLY CROWD, AS YOU SEE—THERE HAVE BEEN NO ARRESTS AND NO VIOLENCE— BUT THE NUMBER IS ASTONISHING. POLICE ESTIMATE THERE ARE MORE THAN THREE THOUSAND PEOPLE MARCHING, CHANTING, AND WAVING BANNERS.

NASA AUTHORITIES HAVE ISSUED TO THE PROTESTORS COPIES OF THEIR RELEASE AT THE TIME OF TAKEOFF, EXPLAINING IN DETAIL THE MEASURES THAT WERE TAKEN TO PROTECT THE MARTIAN BODILY STRUCTURES AGAINST THE CRUSHING PRESSURES OF ACCELERATION.

THE PRECAUTIONS WERE CARRIED EVEN TO THE POINT OF WRAPPING THEM IN PLASTIC AND IMMERSING THEM IN TANKS OF WATER TO ACT AS CUSHIONS.

YET OBVIOUSLY THEY WERE NOT ENOUGH. FERDIE'S INJURIES WERE ALMOST CERTAINLY WHAT LED TO HIS DEATH.

THE OTHER INJURED MARTIAN, "MAR-

TIAN G," OR GRETEL, IS REPORTED TO HAVE
FRACTURED TWO LIMBS AT THAT TIME,
BUT IS NOW RESTING COMFORTABLY AND
EATING ONCE AGAIN.

SOME OF THESE DEMONSTRATORS
WARN THAT THE WORST IS YET TO COME.
THIS IS MME. RACHEL D'ALEMBERT, REP-
RESENTING THE SOCIETE DES EXPLORA-
TIONS ASTRONAUTIQUE OF LYONS,
FRANCE:

VT: D'ALEMBERT   IN CUE: IT IS SIMPLY A FARCE TO PRETEND
(Transcript)   . . .

that the Martians had the capability to comprehend the dangers and
injuries that would confront them in this space voyage. It is not even
ascertained that they have a proper language, so how is it possible that
they could consent?

In any event one must remember that the surface gravity of Mars
is far less than that of Earth, and thus the acceleration that was required
for lift-off from Mars was substantially less than the similar forces they
will encounter on the proposed landing on Earth. What will happen
to Gretel, Alexander, Bob, Christopher, Doris, and Edward then?

I say nothing of the fact that they are simply not strong enough to
live without great discomfort and even danger on the surface of our
planet, for the same reason. Nor do I speak of the fact that their entire
lives have been spent in near-darkness, so that they have no known
natural protection against the possibly harmful rays of sunlight.

If the Martians came from our own planet they would without
doubt be declared an endangered species and every effort would be
made to preserve them.

This whole episode is disgraceful, and cannot help but endanger
any future Franco-American . . .

OUT CUE: . . . COOPERATION IN SPACE
VENTURES.

VT: PETTIT

A NASA OFFICIAL, WHO DOESN'T WISH TO SPEAK FOR ATTRIBUTION, PROMISES THAT THE PROBLEM OF LANDING THE MARTIANS ON THIS HEAVIER AND LARGER PLANET IS UNDER CLOSE STUDY, AND THAT IN THE TIME BEFORE THE LANDING OCCURS ADEQUATE MEASURES WILL BE PROVIDED FOR THEIR SAFETY AND WELL-BEING.

ZOOM TO
DEMONSTRATORS

BUT THESE DEMONSTRATORS ARE OBVIOUSLY NOT CONVINCED . . .

OUT CUE: . . . THIS IS TOM PETTIT FOR NBC, REPORTING FROM THE HOUSTON SPACE CENTER.

BROKAW

THE HUMAN BEINGS RETURNING ON SPACECRAFT "ALGONQUIN 9" ARE ALL WELL, THOUGH THE MOOD IS ONE OF WORRY OVER THE MARTIANS.

RP: MAP
(SOLAR SYSTEM)

THE SPACESHIP IS NOW JUST BEGINNING ITS RETURN FLIGHT TO EARTH. ITS PRESENT POSITION, LIKE THAT OF THE PLANET MARS ITSELF, IS ON THE FAR SIDE OF THE SUN. IT IS BECAUSE OF INTERFERENCE FROM THE INTENSE SOLAR RADIATION THAT THE TELEVISION PICTURES FROM THE SPACECRAFT ARE SKETCHY AND UNCLEAR, SO THAT COMMUNICATION NOW AND FOR THE NEXT WEEK OR SO IS LIMITED ALMOST ENTIRELY TO VOICE RADIO.

POP ON:
SPACECRAFT
ORBIT

MORE NEWS AFTER THIS MESSAGE.

six

THE VIEW
FROM MARS HILL

Because he had stayed late in his room, listening to the news on the American armed forces radio until the very last minute, Vladimir Malzhenitser hadn't had any breakfast. He didn't mind. The news from the *Algonquin* 9 was better food than any he could buy in Athens. He was buoyed up by excitement. There was more happiness and hope effervescing like bubbles of champagne in the arteries of his dumpy, soft body than he had felt in almost any of his sixty-odd years—many more than sixty, if one were to tell the truth, but he didn't have to tell the truth. When you were a refugee with no proper papers you could say what you liked about how old you were. How could anyone know if you lied?

Malzhenitser got off the bus at the tour headquarters, still buoyant. When the tour dispatcher, Stratos, told him that he was assigned to guide Germans that day, even that did not dampen his mood, though it came close. It was not what he wanted. What he wanted was a busload of Americans. Rich Americans, probably. Certainly the kind of Americans who would share his excitement over the word from

Mars with him. Especially Americans who were willing to accept praise for the wonderful American exploit of sending spaceships to Mars and bringing them back with live Martians incredibly aboard. On any other day, Germans might not be a bad second-best, he reflected as he peered over the tour manager's shoulder to steal a glimpse at the day's assignment sheet. Germans too could be rich, and they too were interested in space. Unfortunately they seemed to be convinced that their Opel and their Von Braun had invented it, with no assistance needed from expatriate Russian nationals.

Americans would be best.

He saw that his closest friend among the other guides, Theodora Senhilos—not really that close, and not always a friend, actually— had had the luck to draw that day's English-speaking group.

That could be corrected. Malzhenitser knew where Theodora would be at that moment. She too would have got up too late for breakfast. Undoubtedly she would now be swallowing a last cup of coffee in the little taverna around the corner. So Malzhenitser flipped a cheery wave to the tour manager and hurried there. He shook off the waiter who wanted to sell him the genuine American French toast breakfast and sank down next to the old woman. "Will you trade with me today, please?" he coaxed. "Remember, three weeks ago when your grandson became ill in school I took your people back to their hotels for you."

"And three times since three weeks ago I have done the same for you," the woman returned. Her tone was waspish, but then it always was. "How many favors must repay one favor? In any case, my English is better than yours."

"Your German is also better than mine," Malzhenitser wheedled. That was pure flattery, and quite untruthful. He had learned German very well, in a place where learning to speak German quickly and completely meant greatly increasing one's chances of remaining alive.

Theodora recognized the flattery. She also enjoyed it; she snorted, but didn't deny what he said. "For that reason," he went on, "I need the practice in English so that when my visa is approved I will be ready."

"In that case, you have plenty of time," she said. She wasn't being unusually disagreeable. She was only stating what she believed to be a fact. Malzhenitser, unfortunately, often believed the same thing; but not today. Today the news from the Martian expedition was too exciting for such doubts.

"It will come! Have you heard the news broadcasts? They will need me, Theodora. Where else will they find people with expert knowledge of the Soviet space program?"

"In Moscow, of course! Not here in Athens."

"But in Moscow the people they would like cannot leave," Malzhenitser pointed out.

"And without a visa neither can you," she said, but she was softening. She shook her head. "Always these dreams, Volya. If the Americans wanted you, you would have been there twenty years ago when you first defected. You would not now be a starving tour guide in Greece, especially in Athens, about which you know so little." But then she relented; Americans or Germans, what did it signify? It was, after all, a matter of indifference to a woman who spoke six languages colloquially. She said grudgingly, "Very well, we will exchange. I will notify Stratos. But in return you may pay for my coffee."

Stratos was annoyed about the switch of assignments: "It is I who prepares the assignments!" he shouted, as he always did. But, as always, he let it stand. Stratos didn't much like Malzhenitser anyway—probably, Malzhenitser believed, because of Stratos's lifelong membership in the Greek Communist Party, which caused him not to care for Russians who had fled their country for the decadent West. However, for that same reason Stratos was determined to have at least one Russian-speaking guide on the roster. That was politics, not business. It would have harmed the tourist agency's finances very little to pretend that Russians didn't even exist, since not enough of them came as tourists to Athens to fill a bus even once a month. But the tour director had concerns beyond mere money. So Stratos put up with Malzhenitser's accented German and English, and even with the fact that Malzhenitser wasn't Greek, just so that when a trade mission from Kiev or Leningrad allowed its members a few hours off to study the cultural history of the ancient Greeks they would have faultless (and, above all, politics-free) Russian spoken to them on the tour.

In those respects, Malzhenitser was perfect. When he guided Russians, the rage and resentment that his heart held against the Soviets never got past the smile on his lips. He knew that if he displeased Stratos his job was lost. Then worse would almost certainly follow, because then it was very likely that the Greek government might stop turning a blind eye to his irregular status.

In matters like the concealment of feelings Malzhenitser was quite skilled, because those skills, too, had contributed to the survival of a young man who had been so unfortunate as to be captured by the Germans in their 1942 offensive . . . and so foolish as to take what had seemed the best way out of the Nazi wartime extermination camps.

Malzhenitser had never had good luck with governments. The Russians had sent him off to get captured. The Germans had done their best to kill him. The Greeks tolerated him only because he meticulously kept a low profile. He didn't like any of them. That made him, Malzhenitser believed, a perfect candidate for American citizenship, because he had observed that Americans never got along with their government, either, but managed to remain free and rich anyhow.

He would, Malzhenitser was confident, fit right in in the US of A—if he could ever get that fool in the consulate to give him his visa.

So while the tour bus was ponderously squeezing through Athens's choked streets, Malzhenitser was studying his clients of the day.

He did his job while he was assessing them. He did not fail to point out Hadrian's Arch and the Temple of Olympian Zeus—or what was left of them after a couple millennia of neglect and a couple decades of acid air. He indicated the best restaurants and pastry shops, and the most fashionable shopping streets. He showed the passengers where *evzones* were changing the guard, and the Parliament building and all the other buildings of state. But all the while he was canvassing the occupants of every seat, trying to locate his quarry.

There were no suitable people in the first three rows; those were filled by a party of Australians on a package tour. There was nothing to be gained from those at the back of the bus, either. They were all Americans, all right. But none of them seemed to be over the age of twenty-five, and certainly none of them looked like the sort of person who might have any influence with the American state department.

The only other Americans were, surprisingly, three black couples. Malzhenitser studied them as he moved along the aisle, handhold by handhold. The blacks seemed to be traveling together; well, one would expect that. Perhaps. Malzhenitser was not very sure of what one might expect, since he had never had much experience with blacks. At least these particular specimens did not seem to be the kind one saw at the cinema, which was to say the kind who carried portable tape-players on their shoulders and jived as they walked. Nor did they look likely to mug anyone. He observed that they were fashionably dressed, in the style of American tourists in a hot climate—all three of the women, and one of the men, were wearing shorts, and all had sunglasses. Still, he was far less hopeful than he might have been. Out of his limited knowledge he conjectured they would not be likely to be very useful to him. They would probably be either dentists or clergymen of some kind, since no other American blacks seemed wealthy enough to travel as far as Greece. In either case, they were not likely to be influential where it mattered.

The situation did not look promising. Malzhenitser's mood began to sink slowly from the morning high.

Still, one must not give up. So, while the bus was groaning up the hill toward the steps that led to the Parthenon, Malzhenitser cruised the aisle. He should have been staying up front with the microphone, and in the mirror the driver was staring curiously at his back. But Malzhenitser chose to do now what he would normally have left till almost the end. He made his way along the bus from seat to seat, asking which hotel each couple wanted to be returned to, listening carefully to accents in case he had overlooked a chance. He hadn't; but God was good to him that morning.

One of the black men was scowling over an *International Herald-Tribune*, open to a headline that read:

PRESIDENT ENDORSES SECOND MARS MISSION PLAN

while his wife, twisted around over the back of the seat to talk to one of the other wives, was complaining, "I don't expect *favors* just because Jeffrey's brother is in Congress, but I do think the embassy here could give us at least *consideration* like any other American citizen in a strange country when the airlines have smashed a suitcase."

A congressman's brother!

It was the closest Malzhenitser had ever come to anyone with real power in America—and on the very day the American president had announced a new Mars program. Just the day when it could be most useful!

Vladimir Malzhenitser had not started out to be a traitor to his country.

For that matter, he didn't even think he was now. In Malzhenitser's view it was his country that had been traitor to him. First it had drafted him into the Red Army, a child of sixteen, to fight in the Great Patriotic War against Adolf Hitler. Well, you could understand that, he acknowledged fairly. Hitler had certainly invaded the USSR with tanks and planes and armies of very efficient slaughterers, and the need was great. Young Volodya Malzhenitser had been glad enough to fight. If being a Russian had not been reason enough, then being a Russian Jew—even a nonpracticing, nonbelieving, even noncircumcised one—certainly was.

But then the high command of the Red Army, following whatever strategic devices no one could imagine, had thrown Malzhenitser's single division against a German armored thrust of two entire assault armies. The orders were to hold fast at any cost, and a bullet in the head for the first Soviet soldier who took a step in retreat. They could not retreat. They also could not contain the crushing power of the German juggernaut; so there were only two possibilities for any soldier in Malzhenitser's division. He could surrender. Or he could die.

Malzhenitser chose not to die.

A little later, when he found that the German prisoner-of-war camp for Red Army soldiers was no more merciful than Auschwitz, if a little less efficient, he was far from sure he had made the right choice.

But then, one winter day when the future looked painfully terminal, a delegation came to the POW camp. They were uniformed, well fed, strutting about with officers' insignia on their well-tailored uniforms—and they spoke in Russian! They *were* Russian. They came from the headquarters of General Vlasov, and they had a thrilling message to deliver.

"Brave Russian soldiers!" went their call to arms. "Join with us! We will form a Free Russian Army! We will fight against the Bolsheviks who have betrayed us until we overthrow their evil regime. Then we will liberate our homes and make our beloved Russia free!"

It had sounded very plausible, not to say glorious.

This General Vlasov, as every Red Army soldier knew, was neither hooligan nor Trotskyist. General Vlasov had been decorated with Stalin's own medal, earned by courage and skill. If in his last campaign he had been captured by the Germans, well, so had Malzhenitser and every other prisoner of war in the camp.

So young Malzhenitser, by then all of nineteen years old, almost, had joined Vlasov's armies of Russian prisoners signed up to fight on the German side against their brothers.

At least there he was fed. At least there he got a uniform to replace the rags he had surrendered in, even if it was a German uniform. At least when the war ended Vladimir Malzhenitser was still alive, and in that way far luckier than twenty million of his countrymen.

Then the luck ran out.

When the Germans surrendered, the Vlasovites had to surrender too. That time the luck went all to the Germans. They were rounded up to be put in prisoner-of-war camps, and then, after actually quite a short time, perhaps no more than a year or two, they were allowed to return to their homes. On the other hand, when Vlasov's Russians were rounded up the place they went to was the Gulag.

So nineteen-year-old Malzhenitser became thirty-year-old Malzhenitser before Khrushchev's amnesty emptied some of the camps and, all unready, he found himself a free man again—or as free as any Soviet citizen with a blemished record was likely to be.

The years in the Gulag camps had not been a total loss for Malzhenitser. Early on he had found a valuable friend in the person of an old man named Kostya Gershuni.

Kostya was ancient but strong; moreover, he had once been a rocket scientist. He had actually known Tsiolkovsky. He had been allowed to travel outside the Soviet Union! Kostya, in the long nights in the camps, boasted to wistful, yearning young Malzhenitser of those wonderful days. He had been allowed to visit Berlin's fledgling German Rocket Society. He had even crossed the Atlantic Ocean—once—to interview the American, Goddard, at his tinker-toy rocket proving ground in Worcester, Massachusetts, USA. The travels had been *wonderful*, the old man told Malzhenitser with a smile and a tear, but they had turned out to be expensive. Those Western contacts had been what had put him in the camps in the first place, in the paranoid Stalin purge days of the 1930s.

Then that same record made the camps bearable for the old man. When in 1947 the Great Patriotic War was over, and the Leader decided that to keep the Soviet Union's wonderful new status as a superpower it must ready itself for missiles and space travel, it was his background in rocketry and allied sciences that had got Kostya Gershuni out of the soul-destroying physical labor of the tundra camps to a new assignment, to help build from scratch the new Space City at Baikanur.

And because Malzhenitser had excelled at mathematics in school, the old man was able to take the young one with him.

So for a couple of decades after he got his freedom, Malzhenitser slowly worked his way back to a position almost of respect. He was never a big figure in the Soviet space program. But he was on the scene from its beginnings. Since he had helped build Baikanur, he was kept on to work there. He once did some computations for Shklovsky. He helped prepare orbits for a dozen cosmonauts. He was entrusted with checking the programs that sent the first Venera probe to

Venus—he and many others, because there was invariably someone to check the checkers. Finally he was even allowed to attend a meeting of the International Astronautical Federation in Vienna, and that was the chance he had been waiting for. He slipped out of his pension and made his way to the American embassy to defect.

The Americans wouldn't have him.

It was a matter of regulations, they told him; their hands were tied. He admitted being a member of Vlasov's army, didn't he? And the Vlasov armies were actually Nazi SS units, were they not? Well, then. The immigration laws were very strict. No ex-Nazi, or a person who had served in a Nazi *party* fighting force, could be accepted into the puritanically clean United States . . . unless, of course, some well-connected person really wanted him there, in which case the hell with the immigration laws. But no one wanted so small a fish as Malzhenitser that much. Go away, they told him. Aren't you Jewish? Then try Israel; they have to take you.

And so Israel did; but after Malzhenitser had found out that former SS troopers were not beloved in Israel, even if they happened to have had Jewish parents, he was happy to be allowed to slip into Greece on a tourist visa.

He had been there ever since.

There weren't any jobs for space scientists in Greece. On the other hand the Greeks did have jobs, though not the kind of jobs that paid very well, for multilingual persons capable of memorizing the history of the Golden Age of Pericles for tourists.

So Malzhenitser became a tour guide. And thought he would die a tour guide. Until the Martians showed up.

Abominable little ugly creatures they were, Malzhenitser thought affectionately; hardly intelligent; homely organisms the size of terriers, with bodies like seals and legs like spiders—but what did that matter?

They were Martians!

They had revived the flagging American interest in space exploration as nothing else since that first walk on the surface of the Moon. Now the President of the United States had definitely stated—it was right there in the newspapers—that another Martian expedition would be launched! Within a few years at the most, another fleet of ships would lift themselves off the scorched pads of Cape Canaveral into orbit—

And they would—*perhaps* they would—also lift Vladimir Malzhenitser right out of Athens.

On the venerable but uneven pavement at the summit of the Acropolis Malzhenitser gathered his flock together, just as the Apostle Paul had done on the Areopagus just across the way. "This temple, the Parthenon," he droned, "which was designed by the great artist Phidias two thousand five hundred years ago, was severely damaged in the war of liberation against the Turks. Then it was loot—then further damaged," he corrected himself swiftly; these were not Germans or Russians he was speaking to and some of them might not be pleased to hear Lord Elgin referred to as a looter—"when many of its most valuable pieces of sculpture were taken to museums all over the world. All of this marble was quarried from the mountains you see behind me and then brought here to be fitted together, without mortar, in a way that has lasted all these centuries. Why is this temple called the Parthenon? Because it was dedicated to the goddess Athena Parthenos, which means *virgin*. And why is the hill we are standing on called the Acropolis? Because those are the Greek words for *high place*; this was the highest point in ancient Athens. Now," he finished, "you have forty-five minutes to walk by yourselves, take photographs, perhaps have a cooling drink at the cantina at the bottom of the steps. We will meet again at the bus. . . ." The programmed lecture wasn't finished; he went on with the standard pleas to be on time and threats that the bus would leave without anyone who wasn't; but these were experienced tourists who knew that page of the script as well as he did, and the group had already begun to dissolve.

That was fine with Malzhenitser. He had his eye on the three black couples. As they turned and strolled away he neatly intersected their path, smiled, and said to the black congressman's brother, "If you would care to walk with me? Just over there are some particularly good points to take pictures from—perhaps you would like me to snap all six of you, with the temple just behind?"

And, of course, they would.

Among the things Malzhenitser knew best was how to charm tourists—that was what brought the tips in. He gave them one of the finest private lectures of his career: about Phidias and the great statue that had disappeared; about the ruined structure that had been the gate one approached the Parthenon by—about the Areopagus. That was the make-or-break point. He performed with exquisite skill. "It was on that rock," he said, pointing, "that St. Paul preached to the Athenians, and on that same rock where Orestes was condemned for his crime. Do you know what Areopagus is named for? It might be called 'Mars Hill.' Perhaps," he said, twinkling, "some rich American might buy it and move it to the States, because certainly the Americans have a right to anything concerning Mars now! Oh, I do admire the skill of your scientists. I myself spent many years in the Soviet space program before I was able to escape—participated in many Soyuz launches, in the planning for the Mars orbiter. I suppose you could say," he added deprecatingly, "that I was perhaps their principal expert on Mars studies for a time. But now—"

He smiled and shrugged and went on to the other glories of Greece.

But he knew that he had tweaked their interest.

By the time the bus was ready he had exchanged commiserations with them on the failings of the slovenly, time-serving diplomats at the American embassy; he had dazzled them with a capsule history of the Soviet, German, and American space efforts; he had ascertained that the tall, forbidding one, Bayard, was a lawyer; the plump one with the silly little beard and the wife who looked almost white was a real-estate operator; and the one named Thatcher, praise God!, was indeed a brother of a real American congressman from the state of Illinois! And he had received an only slightly grudging invitation to join them at their hotel for a drink that evening.

When the tour was finished Malzhenitser's heart sang. America was possible at last. Ugly and wretched as those Martians were, they had served his purpose: The Americans would launch their next Martian expedition, and now that he had a possible ally to help him he might yet become part of it!

* * *

In the hotel Georgette Thatcher declared, "I don't like getting involved with this man, Jeffrey. He could be a spy or something."

"Honey," her husband said reasonably, "what do we know to spy on?"

"I don't mean a Russian spy. He could be CIA, maybe. Or IRS."

She caught her husband taking a sip of his drink, and the involuntary twitch of the American businessman who hears the initials IRS made it look as though his Scotch had spoiled. It was only momentary. "There is nothing to worry about," he declared.

"Yeah," said Georgette Thatcher; and then, executing a swift reversal, "Well, anyway, it could be really interesting to find out more about this man. Maybe I could even give a talk at the church about him."

"You certainly could," Thatcher agreed. He was used to his wife's way of stating diametrically opposed arguments for and against anything new—but then almost always opting for the novelty. Georgette might confuse her husband, but she seldom bored him.

Jeff Thatcher was neither a dentist nor a minister, but his father had been the one, and Georgette's father had been the other. The Thatchers had married and started their adult lives just in time for the benefits of the civil rights revolution. The dentist's savings, and the minister's skills at wangling scholarships, had got the two of them into Northwestern University, where they met and after which they married. Neither Thatcher nor his brother had chosen to follow their father into tooth repair. The older brother, Walter, had opted for law, and then politics. He was in his second term in the House of Representatives, and his name was sometimes talked about for U.S. Senator from Illinois. Financially, Jeffrey had done even better than his brother. He had majored in business administration. Because they were born when they were born, to the people they were born to, both brothers had distanced their parents with ease. Jeffrey had signed with a headhunter the day before his commencement and wound up with a first-rate job with a major corporation that wanted to improve its image, racial equality-wise.

That had been the watershed event. In ways that neither Harriet Beecher Stowe nor John Brown could ever have imagined, everything else followed for the Thatchers. The FHA loaned them the eighty thousand dollars to buy a four-bedroom house in the northwestern suburbs—now, with swimming pool, sun deck, and inflation, probably worth more like a quarter of a million. When Jeffrey decided to strike out on his own, the Small Business Administration had advanced the capital; and now he was president of an insurance business that grossed six million dollars a year in premiums. Their suburban Methodist church, broad-mindedly accepting into its congregation this first (but very respectable) black couple in the neighborhood, had quickly made Georgette their Social Action chairperson, and shortly after that a member of the local school board. They had no children. But they had prosperity—and two late-model BMWs in the garage, and an annual trip to Europe.

As they sat in the hotel bar, waiting for Malzhenitser to show up, they were a distinguished couple of middle years—too young for golf, too old to listen to funky music—and they were aware of it. Jeffrey was drinking Chivas on the rocks, Georgette was experimenting with ouzo. With her pale blue silk suit and his bleached-sand safari jacket, they were as tastefully dressed as any other couple in sight. "We're going to miss the floor show," Georgette said, pouring in a little water to watch the ouzo turn milky; she wasn't complaining, only setting out the possibilities again.

"But we'll be in time for the bouzouki dancing," her husband said peaceably. They were signed up, not with Malzhenitser's tour promoters, for an Athens at Night package, a Greek taverna dinner with music, to be followed by a *son et lumière* at one of the old amphitheaters. It had seemed more interesting to Jeffrey than a drink with this ugly old foreigner, until he had got to talking with Bayard and Swanson.

"He's just coming in the door," said Georgette Thatcher, gazing into her milky drink.

"Let him come to us," said Jeff. He didn't look around. He wondered a little bit about this man, who had made it clear that he didn't expect to be paid for the evening, but would doubtless want a tip. Or something; in Jeffrey's experience everybody always wanted something.

But that was all right, because so did Jeff Thatcher.

At one time or another Vladimir Malzhenitser had been in every big hotel in Athens, not just fancy chain tourist traps, but the really elegant ones that tour brokers never booked. Generally speaking, he was bored with such decadent opulence. This time was different. He looked around the lobby with delight. He wasn't impressed by the mirrored walls or the great golden Foucault pendulum that swung from the six-story roof. What impressed Malzhenitser was money. He knew to the penny what the rooms, the meals, the drinks in these places cost. Americans! How wonderful, how *American*, to be able to be gouged so extortionately and even, almost, enjoy it!

He looked around, scowled at the bell captain who was about to greet him by name, and bustled over to the bar tables on the far side of the lobby. "Mrs. Thatcher, Mr. Thatcher," he beamed, trying to smile without showing the gold teeth which, he knew, Americans considered vulgar. He produced the tiny box of chocolates with a flourish. "A small thing to add to your enjoyment of Athens," he said as he handed it over.

"How very thoughtful," said the black woman, sliding the coppery ribbon off the box without harming the little sprig of lilac under the bow. Malzhenitser approved. She was opening it with care; as he had paid eight hundred and fifty drachmae for the eight chocolates in the box, he appreciated the care. "Look, Jeff," she said. "It's candy."

"Real nice of you," said Thatcher. "Mind coming upstairs, Mr. Solzhenitsyn? Our friends wouldn't forgive us if we kept you to ourselves."

"Certainly!" cried Malzhenitser, delighted to be asked into a room of the hotel—it was almost like being invited into someone's home. "May I? It is *Malzhenitser*, not *Solzhenitsyn*—though, to be sure," he twinkled, "one must be flattered to be associated in any way with so great a Russian as the world's greatest author!"

"You bet," said Thatcher. He scribbled his name on the check and led the way to an elevator which moved so gently that Malzhenitser hardly knew they had left one floor before it arrived at another. "It's way at the end of the hall," he said, leading on.

"Yes, fine," said Malzhenitser, with pleasure. Better and better! The rooms at the ends of the halls were not rooms; they were suites. Oh, he had made no mistake in seeking out these black Americans, he assured himself, smiling and chattering as they strolled the hall.

A suite it was. Not one of the *big* suites that the really rich used, or the politically powerful, but still a living room and bedroom that cost more per night than Malzhenitser earned in a month. The other couples were there, rising gracefully as Malzhenitser and the Thatchers entered, the men shaking hands. "What you need," said the one called Bayard, "is a drink." He waved at a sideboard. Malzhenitser recognized Scotch, bourbon, a couple of kinds of liqueurs, half a dozen of those sweet American soda-pop drinks, and next to them platters of canapés, wafers of toast, even a pot of caviar. "Say what you'd like. Seven and seven be all right, Mr. Mal . . . Malzen. . . ."

"Malzhenitser, please, sorry, it is such a difficult name," Malzhenitser apologized. "Could you possibly call me Volya? It is the intimate form of my given name, Vladimir."

"Sure," said Bayard cordially, but his wife said:

"But isn't that, well, like addressing you as a servant?" Gwen Bayard had taught French in the Chicago high-school system before her husband's real-estate business began to prosper, and she well understood the difference between *tu* and *vous*.

"But I am your servant, my dear lady," Malzhenitser said gallantly. "In any case, I am after all only a humble tour guide here in Greece, although in my own country's space program I was for many years something perhaps more distinguished."

"Yeah," said Thatcher. "I wanted to ask you about that. Sit down, why don't you? Ready for Ted to freshen your drink?"

Malzhenitser blinked. He hadn't tasted it yet. Was that offensive by the standard of American manners, to fail to drink what you were given at once? He took a swallow, almost gagged on the sticky-sweet soda that diluted the whiskey, but not very much, and managed to say, "Yes? You wish to know about the Soviet space program? Well, I have been away from it for some time now, but my work in the calculation of ballistic orbits—oh, I assure you, only for nonmilitary purposes—"

Bayard cut in, "You said Mars."

"Mars? Yes. Yes, I was deeply involved in the Mars orbiter—"

"Mars *Hill*, I mean."

"Mars Hill?" Malzhenitser had lost the thread of the conversation. He took another sip of the drink, frowning.

"You told us about it today. That little hill by the Acropolis. You called it by some other name—"

"Oh, of course," Malzhenitser cried, enlightened. "Mars Hill. Or, as it is called, the Areopagus. The hill where St. Paul preached. Of course," he added, trying to decipher what these black people were getting at, "in this case the word *Mars* does not refer to the planet, but to the ancient god."

"But that's the right name for it? In English, I mean?" Bayard pressed. He seemed actually worried for a moment. When Malzhenitser reluctantly assented, Bayard relaxed and gazed around at his friends triumphantly. "Trouble with you, Mr.—Volya, is we're a couple of drinks ahead of you. Finish it up and let me make you another!"

"They have such pretty names, don't they?" said Mrs. Swanson, offering Malzhenitser the canapé tray while Bayard was refilling the drinks.

"Of course," said Malzhenitser. He was not at all sure what she was talking about, but "of course" could have been taken to mean of course he would like one of the canapés. He acted it out by taking the nearest one. It turned out to be some sort of soft, sweet cheese with a slice of pale and nearly tasteless pepper of some kind on top. He would have much preferred the caviar, even though it was the big red kind, but wasn't sure how to ask. He took refuge in his refilled drink. It was sticky and sweet, like a child's drink, but it had an alcoholic bite, and Malzhenitser realized he was beginning to feel the effects.

"Let's talk business," said Jeff Thatcher affably.

Malzhenitser took refuge in another polite "Of course." He managed to keep the question out of his voice, though he could not imagine what business they had in mind, unless . . . unless. . . . He could not let himself believe that the "unless" could possibly be the thing he so desperately hoped it would be.

"I think you said you were a specialist on Mars for the Russian space program, right?" Thatcher inquired briskly, almost in the manner of a prosecuting attorney getting the basic facts on record before moving in for the kill.

"Oh, yes?" And then, collecting himself, "Yes, of course. In Baikanur. For many years. I was working on the Soviet space program in many matters, but in particular the Mars orbiter. You recall our orbiter project?" It was obvious they didn't. Malzhenitser sighed internally but kept the narrow smile on his lips and his tone light. "Our Martia spacecraft was required to enter a high-inclination orbit around the planet. It could not be truly polar—we did not have the maneuverability of your wonderful American spacecraft!—but it was so calculated that, over a period of seven weeks, the orbiter was able to map some 93.8 percent of the planet's surface. By *mapping*," he explained, "I do not just mean taking pictures with just an ordinary camera, of course. No, certainly not! In addition to the optical systems we had also infrared and ultraviolet frequencies, as well as contour-mapping radar, magnetometers, all those fine instruments. And," he added with a shrug of deprecation, "yes, it was I who calculated the orbit and the course corrections." *I and forty-five others, to be sure.* Yet it was not a lie. Malzhenitser was determined not to lie, at least not in any way that could possibly be discovered against him. Still, the risk was small. How could any American know exactly who had done what at Baikanur, when the Soviets would not even identify all of their crews by name? "—What?" he asked, surprised, as Mr. Swanson pulled something out of a dispatch case and handed it to him.

"If you know about Mars," Swanson said, "do you know what these places are?"

Malzhenitser peered at the paper. It was a map of Mars. It was not a very good map; it had been torn from an issue of the international edition of *Newsweek*, it appeared. But it did have the whole face of the planet—two faces, laid out in Mercator projection.

He glanced around at the intent faces watching him, then took his pince-nez out of his pocket. He wiped the lenses with the little cocktail napkin Mrs. Bayard had given him and studied the map. "Yes, I know this is Mars," he said uncertainly, wondering what was expected of him.

"But the particular *places*," Swanson said insistently. "Do you know what they are?"

"He means the ones with the pretty names, Volya," Swanson's wife said helpfully. "Like, here's one that says Lacus Solis, you see?"

Malzhenitser gazed at her, then bent to the map. "Yes, Lacus Solis," he said. "As you would say in English, Lake of the Sun. Of course, it is not truly a lake, you understand. All these major features were given names long ago by astronomers who did not possess very good telescopes. They thought, perhaps, that this was an actual lake, then, but we are now certain there is no free water of any kind, much less so large a lake!"

"Lake of the Sun," said Bayard thoughtfully. "Sun Lake. Sun Lake Drive?" He shrugged and pointed. "What about this here?"

Malzhenitser followed his finger, then said, "Yes, that is Olympus Mons. It is a mountain—a volcano, in fact; indeed, it is the most huge volcano ever discovered, anywhere in the solar system. Extinct now, of course—"

Mrs. Swanson was pursing her lips. "I don't know about that 'Mons. It sounds, well, you know, sort of, uh, sexy."

Her husband said, "We could call it Olympus Mountain. Olympus Mountain Parkway? Mount Olympus Drive?"

"That's two drives already, honey," Mrs. Swanson pointed out.

"Write down the names and we'll figure that part out later," her husband commanded. "Okay, Volya. What're these other names?"

"Get the man another drink first," said Thatcher genially. "Can't you see you're working him too hard?"

Drink or no drink, Malzhenitser decided, they really were working him too hard, and the worrisome thing was that he didn't know what he was working at. Each new name he read from the map got a reaction. He did not comprehend what the reactions added up to. Valles Marineris bored them, though it immensely surpassed the Grand Canyon in size. Utopia Planita got a shake of the head—"Tried a *Utopia* in Schaumburg," said Bayard cryptically—and when he seized on Chryse Planita and told them about how the American Viking lander had set down there all Bayard said was, "Sounds kind of religious."

Then the men sat back, looking at each other. Bayard nodded to Swanson. Swanson nodded to Thatcher. Thatcher said:

"I think it's time for another drink." He sounded pleased, though Malzhenitser could not guess at the reason. So did Swanson, who chuckled as he got up to fix the new round of drinks; and so did Bayard as he rose to help him.

"I hope I have been of service," Malzhenitser said dismally.

"Oh, you really have, Volya," beamed Bayard. "Here you are. Now let's talk business. I think you can help us with a little project we've got going near Chicago."

There had been moments of triumph in Malzhenitser's life before this—not many, true—certainly not *any* to compare with this! He felt himself glowing as he struggled forward from the deep armchair to accept his "freshener"—was it, he thought wonderingly, his fourth already? But what did that matter? Was there ever a better time than this to celebrate? *Chicago!* He rolled the word around the inside of his mouth as he took a deep swallow of the new drink. He no longer even tasted the sugary, lemony flavor of the drink. He only tasted the delicious word. Chicago was in *America*.

It was true, he told himself with puzzlement, that he had not heard of any space facilities in *Chicago*. No. Such things were in Houston, or Canaveral, or Vandenberg in California, or Huntsville in Alabama.

Chicago, Malzhenitser was nearly sure, was perhaps farther north than any of these, so it could not be a launch site, at least; only Russians launched spacecraft where the weather was cold, and only because they had no choice.

Malzhenitser felt a slight touch of disappointment. He had seen so many pictures of the Cape, with its sands and crocodiles and palm trees and the blue Atlantic off to the east—fool, he told himself, amused at his reaction; there are palm trees here in Athens, America means *space*! America means *America*.

He became aware he was sweating with joy.

Malzhenitser furtively wiped his forehead with his cocktail napkin, wondering if anyone had noticed. He tried to sit up straight, paying attention to what was going on. The black man named Swanson was taking some typed pages out of a folder that bore the imprint of the hotel's public stenographer, speaking earnestly as he did. Malzhenitser thrilled as he caught the wonderful word *consultant*.

"Yes, yes," he said, beaming, "a consultant, of course. Where my experience could be put to use. I would be honored to work on the American space program in any capacity. It has been my dream!"

He stopped. Swanson was shaking his head. "It isn't the space program, Mr.—Volya. We're talking about a private business venture. I thought I made that clear."

"Oh," said Malzhenitser. "Ah." He took another swallow of the drink. "Yes, I see. One has heard of these American private space ventures—marvelous that they should exist. Of course, since my background is in the Soviet Union I know little of such private projects. Still, if I can be part of a space program of any sort at all—"

"Not space. Real estate."

Malzhenitser blinked at him.

"It's a real estate development," Bayard explained patiently. "Swanson here is a developer."

"Ah," nodded Malzhenitser faintly. "A developer. Of real estate."

"The three of us have formed a sort of consultancy, you see. To help get it going."

Bayard put in, "It's a first-class tract, out near Barrington. Thirty-one acres of farmland, but it's got all city utilities, lake water, storm sewers. Everything. Mostly three-bedroom houses, you know, with nearly half an acre each. The model homes are almost ready and the streets are in. But, you see, I didn't know what to name them."

"Yes, of course," said Malzhenitscr, who didn't really see at all. He took the papers Swanson was thrusting at him and glanced at the top. It was headed:

MEMORANDUM OF AGREEMENT

between Theodore Bayard, Victor S. Swanson, and Jeffrey Thatcher, d/b/a Mars Hill Associates, an unincorporated limited partnership, and (BLANK) Solzhenitser, a Russian national currently residing in Athens, Greece.

"You'll have to change where your name is on the contract," Swanson apologized. "I wasn't sure of the spelling when I dictated it."

"To be sure," Malzhenitser nodded, trying to make sense of the document.

"But this is perfect," Bayard went on. "We'll call the whole development Mars Hill! We'll name the streets after Martian geography—I don't think anybody's thought of that before!"

"And it's so timely," his wife added. "And anyway, you can't keep on with streets like Harvard, Princeton, Yale, or the names of the presidents, or birds, or trees. We wanted something really different."

"And because we never would have thought of this without you," Thatcher finished virtuously, "we decided it was only fair to make you a consultant. With a royalty on every house sold. And an advance against royalties."

"So," said Swanson, "if you'd just care to sign the agreement—"

"And I'll give you your advance in cash right now," smiled Bayard, opening his wallet. "Two hundred dollars American. Let's see, the rate they gave us this morning was about a hundred and thirty pesetas to the dollar—"

"Drachmae, dear," chided his wife.

"I mean drachmae." Bayard counted out twenty-six thousand-drachmae notes. "And we're very grateful to you, Mr.—Volya. Be sure to put your address on the contract, so we'll know where to send your royalties. And, gee, I wish we could ask you to stay with us for dinner, but we've made these other plans—"

"But first," beamed Thatcher, "one final drink. To Mars Hill! To the finest new development in northwest Cook County!"

As he stepped unsteadily off the dizzyingly gentle elevator Malzhenitser realized he had an urgent need to urinate. He walked with unsteady dignity across the lobby, nodding frostily to the night bell captain, and entered the men's room.

He did have twenty-six thousand drachmae, that was sure. It was nearly a month's pay. It was worth having.

But he did not have the visa.

On the other hand, he thought, leaning one hand against the cold, hard enamel top of the urinal to steady himself, he had certainly done a favor, some sort of favor, for the actual brother of an actual U.S. congressman. It was not at all unreasonable to think that he could, perhaps, use the congressman as a reference when next he visited the American consulate. It was even possible that that stony-hearted woman, the vice-consul, might even listen.

As he hurried out of the hotel toward the place where he could catch his bus home he thought, *First a new suit. The money will be useful for that! Then a letter to the congressman. Then when I get an answer, for certainly he will be polite enough to send me an answer, I go to the consulate once more. And then—*

He could not see beyond that final "and then," but as he walked rapidly through the hot, soggy streets of Athens toward the bus stop, he decided that perhaps, after all, his luck might yet be turning.

When the three black couples got down to the lobby ten minutes later, they were very pleased with themselves. There wasn't room for all six of them in one of the tiny Greek taxis, so they split up. The wives went first. The men, grinning, jostled around the doorman as he whistled frantically for another cab. They had not matched Malzhenitser drink for drink, but they had each had a few, and they were very cheerful.

"I think it's going to rain," observed Swanson.

"Doesn't matter," said Thatcher, "because tomorrow we'll be in Cairo. Anyway, what's a little rain when we've just beat the Feds out of a lot of money?"

They all laughed good-naturedly, and Swanson said in admiration, "And all it cost us was two hundred bucks. Don't forget to kick in your share, you two."

"Any time," said Thatcher, "but don't forget we have to pay old Volya his royalty yet—what was it, five dollars a house?"

"I only said three," argued Swanson, turning to the lawyer.

"Don't be greedy," Bayard reproved. "I made it five when I dictated the contract. Otherwise he wouldn't get any royalties at all, and it wouldn't look legitimate."

"Well—" the builder said doubtfully. Then he grinned. "What the heck! Sixty-six houses. So we're talking about a little over a hundred each. You're sure this is okay, Ted?"

"Positively," said the lawyer. "Look at the facts. The development is real. You're really going to follow the advice of us consultants. We've made this trip to Athens to engage this other consultant. We devoted an entire day to him, all of us, wives and all. We even signed the contract—no, it's ironclad; I'll handle the audit for you guys personally, if they argue it."

"A hundred and change each, and we get to write off the whole trip," said Swanson admiringly. "Jeff, that was a brainstorm!"

"Damn brilliant," Bayard agreed. And Thatcher, basking in their respect, shrugged deprecatingly.

"Every little tax deduction helps," he said. "Especially when it's like a couple thousand dollars each!" And then, as the cab finally showed up and the perspiring doorman opened the door for them, "Hey!"

The others paused, looking at him. "Forget your wallet?" Swanson asked.

"No! Remembered something! Cairo!"

"Yes, sure, we're going there tomorrow. What about it?"

Thatcher's grin was heavenly. "The Pyramids! The Sphinx! All that Egyptian stuff, you know? Don't you have a different development going in after Mars Hill? Maybe we can find a camel driver or somebody—"

"And set up another consultancy? Oh, Ted," Swanson cried, "*Listen.* Do you know what you've got here? Every year! China! India! *Rio de Janeiro,* for God's sake—fellows, if we work it right, we've got tax deductions for the next ten years' vacations taken care of!"

"And," said Bayard virtuously, "every dollar of it perfectly legal!"

SEVEN

Scientific American: "MARTIAN POLAR WANDERINGS"

The astonishing discovery of living Martians by the Seerseller expedition is surely the most unexpected development to have come from the NASA project, but there is much more. The expedition's data have forced a revision of some well-respected theories about the crustal structure of the planet, while lending fresh support to others.

Even the preliminary findings, which are limited to an unfortunately short-term exploration of the tunnels and enlarged spaces inhabited by the Martians themselves, have provided rock samples and stratum observations far more complete and detailed than the borings of the expedition prior to the discovery.

The crustal structure under the cap reveals many old (up to 1 billion years B.P.) fractures and faults, many of them extending vertically for perhaps two or more kilometers, according to seismic soundings. Some of the fractures contain liquid water. Others, shallower and nearer the surface, are filled with ices and clathrate slush. Where did the water come from? The North Polar Ice Cap itself contains a substantial amount of water ice, although it is generally covered by seasonal accumulations of frozen carbon dioxide, but nowhere else in the atmosphere or surface features of Mars can water be found. In any case, the water in the Martian catacombs is old water. Although dating of the ice, liquid water, and clathrates will not be conclusive until the expedition's samples are returned for detailed analysis on Earth, the preliminary study suggests that the fossil water is of approximately the same age as the fractures. So the creation of the fractures, and their filling with water, must both have taken place at least some hundreds of millions of years Before Present.

There is a second puzzle on Mars equal to the one of where this water came from. It has long been known that there are formations in many places on Mars which appear almost identical with scoured-out flood valleys on Earth, in particular those in the northwest United States, but there is no known water or mud source nearby on Mars. If these are indeed fluvial features, where did the water go?

Fortunately a theory already exists to account for some of these observations.

In the 1980s Anne B. Lutz and Peter H. Schultz proposed that the Martian poles of relation, relative to surface features, have wandered extensively over the surface of the planet for the past two billion years. The driving force behind the movements of the crust is not known, although the Lutz-Schultz model suggests it may have been the extrusion of large lava flows or volcano-building. According to their scenario, the north pole of Mars began, two billion years ago or more, at what is now approximately 150° W and 5° N. It then described a loop around the present position of Olympus Mons before reaching its current location. This implies that Olympus Mons, which is now not far from Mars's equator, was at one time near its pole. Correspondingly, the area of the present North Polar Ice Cap must at one time have been relatively near the equator. If it is supposed that all surface water evaporates on Mars except at the poles, and that all water vapor in the air condenses at the poles to render the atmosphere as dry as it is known to be, then water accumulations at the poles may account for ancient floods in regions now totally dehydrated.

The Seerseller expedition has provided a neat bit of evidence to support this model. That is in the many fractures and faults discovered by Henry Steegman and others of the expedition. The argument is basically geometrical. The equatorial region of Mars, like that of the Earth, bulges out because of the planet's rotation. This implies that if a solid crust is dragged over the equatorial region, with its different radius of curvature, it will be stressed to the point of splitting and fracturing, and these fractures will remain after it moves on to another part of the planet's surface. Indeed, this is exactly what the Seerseller expedition has found.

The polar-wandering model accounts for many things. It predicts that the sources of water and the ultimate destination of it may be at considerable distances from the surface features that display water erosion, exactly as observed. The cracks and faults are accounted for. Even the observed statistical fact that meteor craterings of relatively recent date display east-west orientation, while earlier ones tend to be oriented north and south, can now be explained: The direction of meteor impacts was always predominantly east-west, but since then the surface has rotated as the poles moved. It is an elegant solution to many problems, though it casts no light at all on the great and as yet unclarified question of the existence of the Martians themselves, and the disparity between their present, and apparently rather primitive, state of culture and the artifacts that, presumably, they once produced, such as the "department store" and the network of tunnels.

EIGHT

SAUCERY

The young talent-booker behind the desk was slim, quick, heavily eye-shadowed and, Marchese Boccanegra decided, quite ugly, and he hated her.

He didn't much like her office, either. It was tiny and bare. It didn't do justice to one of the richest television networks in the world, and besides the woman was watching the wrong program. All of this displeased Marchese Boccanegra. Not that he cared that somebody on the NBC payroll was sneaking looks at an offering of CBS, but the program the confounded woman was watching was a pickup from the spaceship *Algonquin*, on its way back from Mars with a bunch of those equally confounded Martians aboard. Nasty-looking things! People said they looked a little bit like seals, but seals at least didn't have spindly legs. No, they were definitely hideous, although it wasn't their looks that made Boccanegra dislike them.

The woman giggled. "They're cute," she said, to Boccanegra or to no one.

Boccanegra sighed—silently. He sat erect in his far from comfortable wooden chair, his hands folded reposefully on his lap, his expression unchanging, and his eyes half-closed. He could see her well enough. Her nose was hardly more than a pug and her teeth, although white enough and bright enough, were unacceptably long. She was at least as unattractive as the Martians, not to mention that she wasn't treating him right. First he had been kept sitting for forty-five minutes in the waiting room outside, with all the jugglers and struggling comics and publicity agents for people who had just written a book. Then when she did let him in most of her attention was on the TV screen, when what she should properly have been doing was deciding exactly when—Boccanegra did not allow himself to say *whether*—he would appear again on the "Today" show.

Boccanegra didn't realize his half-closed eyes had closed all the way until he heard her say irritably, "What's the matter, are you asleep?"

He opened his eyes slowly and gazed at her with the unfathomable look that had always gone so well on television. "I am not asleep," he said austerely.

She was looking less attractive than ever, because she was scowling at him, but at least she had turned off the television set. "I hope you wouldn't fall asleep on the air," she sniffed. "Sorry about that, but I had to watch. Anyway, how do you say your name?"

"Mar-KAY-say BOH-ka-NAY-gra."

"You can really get screwed up trying to say those foreign names on the air," she said pensively. "What's that first part, a title or a name?"

He allowed himself to twinkle. "It is the name my parents bestowed on me," he said, not truthfully. "It does in fact mean *marquis*, but my family have not used a title for more than a hundred years." That was not untruthful, technically, for they certainly hadn't. Or before then, either, because grape growers hardly ever had one.

"In any case," he went on smoothly, "I don't know if you have had an opportunity to study my sitrep. This latest contact—"

"What in the world is a sitrep?"

"The situation report, that is. It details my latest contact with the Great Galactics, which is actually far more exciting than any I have experienced before. I was meditating before the fireplace in my summer home at Aspen when suddenly the flames of the fire seemed to die away and a great golden presence emerged to—"

"You told me," she said. "They talked to you. What I need to find out is what they said about the Martians."

"Martians? My dear woman, they aren't *Martians*. The Great Galactics come from so far beyond Mars that they are in another universe entirely, which we call the theta band of consciousness—"

"Uh-uh. The people aren't interested in other universes right now, Mr.—" she glanced at her notes and pronounced it, for a wonder, almost correctly "—Boccanegra. I'm booking a particular show. I've got one three-and-a-half-minute spot open, and the show's about Mars. We've already got Sagan, Bradbury, and some woman from NASA and we need a— we need somebody like you, I mean. Now, you've had other experiences with flying saucers, right?"

He said patiently, "*Flying saucers* is a newspaper term. I don't care for it. In my book, *Ultimate Truth: The Amazing Riddle Behind the 'Saucer' Flaps*, I expose the falsity of the so-called flying-saucer stories. On the theta level of reality, what we human beings perceive as 'saucers' are really—"

"No, but, hey, whatever they were, did any of them come from Mars?"

"Of course not!" Then he added hastily, "Naturally, on the other hand, most of the so-called Martian mysteries are explained in my book, as for example the huge stone sculpture of a human face which appears on Mars in—"

"No, no, no face. We've already got the guy who wrote the book doing that on the eight-eighteen spot on Tuesday. Anything else about Mars?" she asked, glancing at her watch.

"No," said Boccanegra, coming to a decision. He had been in the business long enough to know when to cut his losses. She wasn't buying. He would not do the "Today" show on the basis of this interview. All he could do was to try to keep the lines open for the future.

As she was opening her mouth for the don't-call-us-we'll-call-you, he widened his eyes and said quickly, "Oh, just a moment, do you mean *next* week? I am so terribly sorry! My staff must have got the dates wrong, because next week I have to be at a conference in Washington." He gave the woman a meager forbearing smile as he stood up and shrugged apologetically.

As he picked up the gray suede gloves and gold-handled walking stick the woman said, "Well, actually I don't think we could've—"

"No, I insist," Boccanegra cut in. "It's entirely my fault. Good day!" And he was gone, not even pausing to admire his reflection in the full-length mirror on the back of her door. It was just as it ought to be anyway. Tall, spare figure in the severely cut black suit, the moon-white stock gleaming at his throat, and the white carnation in his lapel, he was exactly as striking and vaguely sinister a spectacle as he set out to be. *Color*, the well-meaning experts had said to him. *It's all color on the TV now*. And it was; but for exactly that reason Marchese Boccanegra had stood out in his stark black and white on the talk shows and the panels.

Had once, anyway. There weren't as many of them for him to do anymore. You could put it even more strongly: There were practically none at all, and the big reason for that was the Martians. How they had ruined it for everybody!

Passing through the waiting room, Boccanegra gave the receptionist a quick four-fingered wave—it was the benediction and greeting of the Great Galactics, as he had demonstrated it for more than thirty years in the field. But she didn't seem to recognize it. No matter. Boccanegra took the carnation from his buttonhole and laid it caressingly before her (a receptionist who remembered you could make all the difference!) before pacing out to the hall, where he tapped the elevator button with the head of his cane.

Only when the door had opened and he stepped inside did he say in surprise, "Anthony! I didn't expect to see you here!"

The month was June and the day warm, but Anthony Makepeace Moore wore full regalia: fur-collared coat and black slouch hat. His expression was more startled than pleased—so was Boccanegra's own—but the two men greeted each other with the effusion of colleagues and competitors. "Marchese!" Moore cried, wringing his hand. "It's been too long, hasn't it? I suppose you've been granting interviews, too?"

Boccanegra permitted himself a wry smile. "I had intended to appear on the 'Today' show," he said, "but the appearance they wanted me to make is unfortunately out of the question. And you?"

"Oh, nothing as glamorous as the 'Today' show," smiled Moore. "I was just taping a few radio bits for the network news."

"I'll be sure to listen," Boccanegra promised, the generosity of his tone almost completely concealing the envy. The network! It had been at least two years since any network news organization had cared to have Marchese Boccanegra say anything for their listeners—and now that they'd done Moore it would certainly be a while before they wanted anyone else. There was a time—a pretty long-ago time, now—when the two of them had done publicity appearances together. But that was when the alien-encounter business was booming. The fact was, now there just wasn't enough to share.

So Boccanegra was surprised when Moore looked at his watch and said diffidently, "I suppose you're in a great hurry to get to your next engagement?"

"As a matter of fact," Boccanegra began, and then hesitated. He finished, "As a matter of fact, I'm a bit hungry. I was thinking of a sandwich somewhere—would you care to join me?"

Moore courteously bowed him out first as the elevator reached the ground floor. "I'd like that a lot, Marchese," he said warmly. "Any place in particular? Something ethnic, perhaps? You know how I like odd foods, and we don't get much of them in Oklahoma."

"I know just the place!" cried Boccanegra.

The very place was the Carnegie Delicatessen, half a dozen blocks from the RCA Building, and both of them had known it well.

As they walked up Seventh Avenue people glanced at them curiously. Where Boccanegra was tall, hawklike, and aloof, Anthony Makepeace Moore was short and round. He wore bushy white sideburns on a head that had no other hair but bushy white eyebrows.

He would have been plump even in a bathing suit—so one supposed; no one had ever seen him in one—but his standard costume, winter, spring, and fall, was a bulky coat trimmed with what might well pass for ermine. It made him appear even rounder. As much as anything, Moore resembled a fat leprechaun.

What he wore in the summer was quite different, because in the summer he spent his time on the five hundred acres of his Eudorpan Astral Retreat, just outside of Enid, Oklahoma. There he wore the robes of the Eudorpan Masters. So did everyone else on the premises, though not all in the same colors. Seekers (the paying guests) wore lavender. Adepts (the staff) wore gold. Moore himself, taking a cue from the Pope at Rome, never appeared in anything but spotless and freshly laundered white.

At the delicatessen, Boccanegra stepped courteously aside to let Moore go first through the door. It was midafternoon but there was a short line waiting, and the two men exchanged amused glances. "Fame," whispered Moore, and Boccanegra nodded.

"Your picture used to hang right there, next to the fan," he said.

"And yours over by the door," Moore recalled, "and now they don't even remember who we are." The cashier, overhearing, looked at them curiously, but no identification came before their table was ready.

When Moore took off his coat he revealed a red and white checked sport shirt underneath. "No robes today?" Boccanegra asked. The only answer he got was a frosty look. Then Moore began to pore over the menu and his expression softened.

"That good old pastrami," he said sentimentally. "Remember how they used to send tons of it over to us at WOR? And Long John begging us to take some home because there'd be a new batch the next night?"

"That's where we met, isn't it?" Boccanegra asked, knowing exactly that it was. The all-night "Long John Nebel Show" had, in fact, given both of them their start in the alien-contact industry. "Remember the Mystic Barber, with that tinfoil crown he always wore?"

"And Barney and Betty Hill, and the Two Men in Black, and Will

Oursler, and—oh, God, Marco," Moore said, rolling his eyes, "we didn't know when we had it good, did we? We were so young!"

"And no damned Martians to take people's minds off us," Boccanegra grumbled. "Are you ready to order?"

They passed reminiscences back and forth while they were waiting for their food to arrive—Long John and his wonderful scams, the revolving Empire State Building, the bridge off the RCA tower, and all; and not only Long John but every other broadcast medium. They all seemed willing to give air time to talk about intelligences from other worlds, network TV and little local radio stations where you had to crouch between record turntables and hand a single microphone around the guests.

"We were all so young," Moore repeated dreamily, pouring ketchup on his French fries.

"Remember Lonny Zamorra?" Boccanegra asked.

"And the spaceport at Giant Rock?"

"And the mutilated cows? And the car engines that got stopped? And, oh, God, the Bermuda Triangle! Good lord," said Boccanegra earnestly, "I can think of at least a dozen people that lived for years on just the Bermuda Triangle. You know what they were getting for a single *lecture*? Not counting the books and the workshops and. . . ." He trailed off.

"And everything," said Moore somberly. They ate in silence for a moment, thinking of the days when the world had been so eager to hear what they had to say.

In those days everyone wanted to give them a voice. Radio, television, press coverage; there was nothing anyone might say about flying saucers, or men from another planet, or mysterious revelations received in a trance, or astral voyages to other worlds that did not get an audience. A *paying* audience. Both Moore and Boccanegra had had their pick of college lecture dates and handsome honoraria —enough for Boccanegra to start The Press of Ultimate Truth, Inc., to print his books; enough for Moore to buy the tract of played-out Oklahoma grazing land that became the Eudorpan Astral Retreat. Both had flourished wildly. There was no end to the customers for Boccanegra's books, more than fifteen titles in all, or to the Seekers who gladly paid a month's wages to spend a week in their lavender robes, eating lentils and raw onions out of EAR's wooden bowls (and sneaking off to the truck stop just outside the Retreat for hamburgers and sinful beer), and listening worshipfully to Moore's revelations.

When the last of the pastrami and fries was gone, Moore leaned back and signaled for a coffee refill. He looked thoughtfully at Boccanegra and said, "I've been looking forward to your new book. Is it out yet?"

"It's been held up," Boccanegra explained. Actually it was a year overdue, and the new book wasn't going to appear until the bills for the last one were paid, and that didn't seem likely in the near future. "Of course," he added with as near a smile as he ever allowed himself in public, "the timing might be better later on. It's all Martians now, isn't it?"

Moore was startled. "Are you writing a book about the Martians?" he demanded.

"Me? Of course not," Boccanegra said virtuously. "Oh, there are charlatans who'll be doing that, no doubt. I'll bet there are a dozen of the old guard trying to change their stories around to cash in on the Martians."

"Shocking," Moore agreed with a straight face.

"Anyway, I've about decided to take a sort of sabbatical. This fad will run its course. Perhaps in a few months it'll be the right time for my book, which tells how the Great Galactics have provided us with the genetic code that explains all of the mysteries of—"

"Yeah," said Moore, staring into space. His expression did not suggest that he liked what he was seeing.

Boccanegra studied his ancient adversary. It didn't look like a very good time to bring up the sudden inspiration that had come to him in the elevator. Moore sounded depressed.

But there would never be a better time, so Boccanegra plunged in. "I've been thinking," he said.

Moore focused on him. "Yes?"

Boccanegra waved a deprecating hand. "I'll probably have some free time for a while. Perhaps the whole summer. So, I wonder—would you be interested in having me as a sort of guest lecturer at the Retreat?" Moore's eyes widened under the bushy eyebrows, but he didn't speak. Boccanegra went on ingratiatingly, "Since I'm at liberty, I mean. Of course, we'd have to make some special arrangement. It wouldn't be appropriate for me to be there just as part of your staff. Some new position? Perhaps I could wear black robes? Naturally the financial arrangements could be worked out—professional courtesy and all that," he finished with a twinkle.

The twinkle dried up. Moore's expression was stony. "No chance," he said.

Boccanegra felt the muscles in his throat begin to tighten. "No chance," he repeated, trying to keep the sudden anger out of his voice. "Well, if it's the robes—"

"It isn't the robes," said Anthony Makepeace Moore.

"No, it wouldn't be that. I suppose, since you and I have been pretty much opponents for so long—"

"Marco," said Moore sadly, "I don't give a shit about that. I can't take you on at the Retreat because there isn't going to be any Retreat this year. I haven't got the customers. By this time I should have had forty or fifty people registered—some years I've had a hundred! You know how many I've got now? Two. And one of those is only a maybe." He shook his head. "The whole thing's down the tube if something good doesn't happen. The bank's been on my back about the mortgage, and they put in that damn interstate and even the truck stop's losing money every week—"

Boccanegra was startled. "I didn't know you owned the truck stop!"

"Well, this time next month I probably won't. They even took out the Coke machine."

Boccanegra sat in thoughtful silence for a moment. Then he laughed out loud and waved to the grouchy waitress for more coffee.

"You, too," he said. "Well, let's put our heads together and see if we can figure something out."

* * *

By the time of the fourth refill the waitress was muttering audibly to herself.

The problem wasn't just the fickle tastes of the public. It was the Martians. There simply was no room for imaginary wonders in the public attention when the real thing was getting a few hundred thousand miles closer to Earth every day. And the unfair part of it was that the Martians were so damned *dull*. They didn't have spiritual counseling for the troubled billions of Earth. They didn't warn of impending disasters, or offer hope of salvation. They just stood there in their stalls on the spaceship *Algonquin* 9, swilling down their scummy soup.

"I guess you've gone over all your books to see if there's anything about Martians in them?" Moore said hopefully.

Boccanegra shook his head. "I mean, yes, I looked. Nothing."

"Me, too," Moore sighed. "I'll tell you the truth, Marco, I never for one minute considered the possibility that when we were visited by creatures from outer space they would be *stupid*. Say!" he cried, sitting up. "What if we say they aren't real? I mean, they're like the household pets of the real Eudorpans?"

"The Great Galactics," Boccanegra corrected eagerly. "Or maybe not pets but, you know, like false clues the superior space beings put there to throw us off the trail?"

"And we can say we've had revelations about it, and—well, hell, Marco," said Moore, suddenly facing reality. "Would anybody believe us?"

"Has that ever made any difference?"

"No, but really, it'd be good if we had some kind of, you know, evidence."

"Evidence," Boccanegra said thoughtfully.

"See, these Martians will actually be here in a few months, right? Next thing you know they'll be landing, and they'll be in a zoo or something, and people can see them for themselves. They don't talk, but they might, you know, communicate something that could blow us right out of the water."

"They really *are* stupid, Tony."

"Yes, but, Marco, if they've got some kind of writings that we don't know about, because all we've ever seen is what they sent on the TV from the spaceship—"

"But maybe they're degenerate," Boccanegra cried, "so they don't know what the stuff *really* means!"

"Well," Moore said doggedly, "there might be a real problem there, all the same. If we wait until they land. . . ." Then he shook his head. "Scratch that. We can't wait that long, at least I can't. I could stall the creditors for maybe a month or two, but the spaceship isn't going to land till nearly Christmas."

"And this is only June." Boccanegra puzzled for a moment; there had been, he was almost sure, something good they had come quite close to. But what was it?

"How about," said Moore, "if we found some *other* Martians?"

Boccanegra frowned. "Besides the ones they've found, you mean? Somewhere else on Mars?"

"Not necessarily on Mars. But the same sort of creatures, maybe on Venus, maybe on the Moon—we say they live in caves, see? So nobody's seen them? I mean, they do live in caves on Mars, right? There could even have been some long ago on, what's its name, that moon of Jupiter that's always having volcanic eruptions, only the volcanoes killed them off."

"Um," said Boccanegra. "Yeah, maybe." He was scowling in concentration, because that faint ringing of cash registers was still in his ears, only he couldn't quite tell where it came from. "I don't see where we get any kind of evidence that way, though," he pointed out. "I'd like it if we had something right here on Earth about that."

"Okay, Antarctica! There's a colony of them on Antarctica, or at least there used to be, but they died of cold after the continents migrated."

"There are people all over Antarctica, Tony. Scientific camps. Russians and Americans and everybody."

"Well, could they be at the bottom of the sea?"

"They've got those robot submarines going down there all the time."

"Sure," Moore said, improvising, "but those are all U.S. Navy or something, aren't they? The subs have seen all the proof in the world, but the government's covering up."

"That's good," Boccanegra said thoughtfully. "Let's see if I've got the picture. There were beings like these Martians all over the solar system once. Of course, they're not really 'Martians.' It's just that the first live specimens that turned up were on Mars, all right? They've been on Earth, too, ever since the time the Great Galactics came— the people from Planet Theta, too," he added quickly. "And all these years they've been hiding down there, exerting an influence on what has happened to the human race. It hasn't all been good: wars, depressions—"

"Crazy fads. Narcotics," Moore put in.

"Right! All the things that have gone wrong, it's because these Martians have been willing it; they've degenerated and become evil. We don't call them Martians, of course. We call them something like Emissaries, or Guardians, or—what's a bad kind of guardian?"

"Dead Souls," said Moore triumphantly.

"Sure, they're Dead Souls. Sounds kind of Russian, but that's not bad, either. And they've been in Antarctica under the ice and. . . . Aw, no," he said, disappointed. "It won't work. We can't get to Antarctica."

"So?"

"So how do we get evidence that there really are Dead Souls there?"

"I don't really see why you keep harping on evidence," Moore said irritably.

"I don't mean evidence like finding a real, live Dead Soul kind of Martian," Boccanegra explained. "You know. We need some sort of message. Mystic drawings. Carvings. Something like the Nazco lines, or whatever they call them, or the rune stone in Minnesota. Of course," he explained, "they wouldn't be in any Earthly language. We work out translations. *Partial* translations, because we don't give the whole thing at once; we keep translating new sections as we go along."

"We get the key from Planet Theta in a trance," Moore said helpfully.

"Or astral projection," Boccanegra nodded, "from the Great Galactics." He thought for a moment, and then said wistfully, "But it would be better if we had something to take photographs of. I always put photographs in my books; they really make a difference, Tony."

"Maybe we could crack open some rocks, like Richard Shaver? And find mystic drawings in the markings?"

"I don't like to repeat what anybody else has done," Boccanegra said virtuously. "And I don't know where Shaver got the rocks, either. Maybe in a cave, or—"

He stopped in midsentence, the ringing of the cash bells now loud and clear. They stared at each other.

"A cave," Moore whispered.

"Not under the ocean. Under the ground! Tony! Are there any caves under the Retreat?"

"Not a one," Moore said regretfully. "I didn't think of that when I bought the tract. But, listen, there are millions of caves all over. All we have to do is find one big one with a lot of passages no one ever goes into—"

"There are lots right along the Mississippi River," Boccanegra chimed in. "There's even the Mammoth Cave, or Carlsbad—why, there are some in Pennsylvania that haven't even been explored much."

"And then maybe I can say I've seen the carvings while I was in astral projection—"

"And then I can actually go there and discover them and take pictures!" Boccanegra finished triumphantly. "I wouldn't say where they came from at first—"

"—until we got a chance to put the drawings there—"

"—and nobody would argue, because everybody knows you and I have never worked together—"

"—and they'd be kind of like Shaver's Deros—"

"—only not deranged robots; they'll look kind of like the Martians, because they're the same Dead Souls, and they mess everything up for humanity because they're evil—"

"And we'll split the money!" Moore cried. "You do your books. I'll do the Retreats. Maybe along about Labor Day you and I can have a public reconciliation, submerging our old differences because now we've discovered this ultimate reality not even we suspected before—"

"—and I can come to the Retreat—"

"And, sure, you can have black robes," Moore said generously. "Marco, it's doable! The good old days are coming back, for sure!"

The two men smiled at each other, their minds racing. Then Moore said, "What about the "Today" show? That'd be a great place to start, if you can get in."

Boccanegra pursed his lips. Thank heaven he'd sweetened the receptionist; she'd let him in, probably, and then he could just walk in on the booking woman; then it would just be a matter of how fast he could talk. "At least fifty-fifty," he estimated, "if I get back to NBC before the offices close."

"And I'll go right down to the library and start looking up caves," Moore said. "And we don't want to be seen too much together, so what do you say we just get together for a minute later on tonight, say about seven?"

"Lobby of the Grand Hyatt," Boccanegra agreed. He clapped his hands imperiously at the waitress, sulking by the kitchen door. She came over and dropped the check in front of him.

"I'll get the tip," Moore offered, pulling out a handful of silver. Boccanegra, back in character, merely inclined his head in silent agreement, although inside he was marking up the mental ledger: $9.50 for the pastrami sandwiches, and only five quarters for the tip; next time they would eat in a better place and *he* would take care of the tip. As he waited for the cashier to fill out the slip on the one remaining valid credit card he possessed, Boccanegra said suddenly, "My cane!" He hurried back to the table before the waitress got there and picked up two of the quarters. Then he rejoined Anthony Makepeace Moore at the door and the two prophets went out into the world they were about to conquer.

NINE

New Scientist:
"MARS AT THE
BRITISH ASS."

Next to the packed, but discouraging, seminars on possible future
high-tech employment opportunities in the UK, far the best attended
sessions at last month's Chester meeting of the British Association for
the Advancement of Science were the panels on Mars, the Martians,
and related subjects.

There were a few embarrassing moments. One of them came when
Superstar Carl Sagan turned up as an unexpected keynoter at the
seminar, causing several staid British scientists to retreat early to their
digs. "One can stand just so much gloating," one groaned as he fled.
But even the most senior of the scientists gave him credit, however
grudging, for having consistently maintained the possibility of life on
Mars against all challenges of the past decades.

The biggest hit of the convention was a paper with the forbidding
title of "Report on the chirality of previously unstudied optical isomers." It was not the subject matter, but the author, that caused even
hardened British Association attenders to glow as they heard it read
—not by the author, as she was unavoidably not present. It was, in

fact, the first paper at any meeting of the British Association (perhaps anywhere in the world) which was not only based on extra-terrestrial data, but had been completed and written in space! It had been specially written by Dr. Sharon bas Ramirez for the occasion, in (as she said) appreciation of pleasant memories of BAAS meetings she had attended while a post-doctoral student at London University.

The "chirality of the optical isomers" refers to the phenomenon of "left-handed" and "right-handed" organic compounds—the difference, say, between the two sugars levulose and dextrose, which are chemically identical but whose molecules are mirror images of each other. This chirality appears to be the same on Mars as on Earth, and this fact has two significant consequences according to bas Ramirez. First, biochemists who have previously thought that the predominant "right-handedness" of terrestrial organic chemicals was only a matter of original chance and later evolutionary victories in the struggle for survival must now explain how the same chance event occurred on Mars, the only other major independent observable source of organochemistry. And, second, bas Ramirez says, it means that we can feed the Martians when they get here!

There were a great many papers on the Martian ecology, perhaps the most outstanding being that presented by two non-British visiting scientists, E. Kampfer and T. Wollenmuth of the Max-Planck Institüt für Geologie in Hamburg, Germany.

On the basis of admittedly preliminary studies of the Martian rock samples carried out by non-specialist members of the Seerseller expedition (its two actual geologists had unfortunately died), the German team claims to have identified examples of "recent" igneous materials of the varieties to be expected in sites that have "recently" (in geological terms) experienced major incidents of vulcanism. They propose that underground reservoirs of hot magma lie not far below the Martian North Polar Ice Cap, and that these provide the energy which not only keeps the underground warrens of the Martians habitable, but even produces sources of living matter.

Their analogy is to the "white smoke/black smoke" thermal springs of hot water found in the East Pacific Rise and other places in the sea bottoms of the Earth. Since sunlight plays no part in the food chain there, it is argued, a similar process can produce organic matter and indeed living organisms at the bottom of the water-filled fractures under the surface of Mars.

We know from the discoveries of the Seerseller expedition that the diet of the living Martians found is derived principally from a sort of pseudo-algal "froth" (and from the lesser creatures that live on it), which appears on the surface of their underground "wells."

Not all of these "wells" have this edible froth. The German team points out that the sonar-reflection observations made by the expedition, although sparse and perhaps inconclusive, do suggest that it is the shallow wells which have only water, while the deeper ones invariably produce the edible scum. These deep water-filled fissures, which are thought to extend as much as 2.5 or even 3 kilometres below the surface, are comparable, the Germans say, to "tall, narrow oceans." It is also suggested that the "shallower" wells, those containing only relatively clear water, correspond with those generally ice-covered, while the deeper ones have a surface temperature of no less than 4°C. This implies a source of heat. Thermal springs at the bottom of the deep ones would account for that, due to convective mixing; and it might also explain the froth of living organisms as what the Germans called "an ocean turned upside down."

Here the reference is to benthic food sources in our own seas. Apart from the rare products of thermal springs, all life at the bottom of earthly oceans survives on the particles of matter, dead animals, and plant substances, etc., that drift down from the surface. Primary food production occurs only in the top few dozen metres of the sea, where light can permit tiny plants to grow. These are eaten by larger, and still larger, organisms. When they die, or when a shark dribbles bits of some smaller fish out of the side of its mouth, crumbs of edible material drift down to the sea bottom, and there they provide sustenance for everything that lives there.

Mars's "seas" may be turned topsy-turvy, the German team says. Sulfur-based organochemistry from their thermal springs produces organic matter, which is fed on by their benthic plants and animals (if these terms are meaningful in Martian biology). Bits of them die and, in decaying, produce gasses that cause them to float to the surface. Thus the organic scum, which Alexander, Doris & Co. eat. (With an occasional treat when they catch one of the smaller creatures that also live on the froth.)

Several other questions about Martian biology were addressed at the meeting in Chester.

A paper by J. T. Naxos of the University of Tyne and Ware calls on data as old as the first *Viking I* lander in 1976 to account for the presence of the air and water the Martians obviously had somehow to retain in order to survive.

According to Naxos's interpretation, Mars is frozen solid just below the surface to a depth of many metres—the so-called permafrost—and there is an additional shell of "hardpan" (the technical term is *caliche*), which is the result of underground water seeping to the surface over the eons. The water evaporates quickly into the thin Martian atmosphere. The inorganic salts it has entrained with it remain. They accumulate, forming a dense, impermeable layer just under the surface which is quite capable of containing substantial pressures. The permafrost-caliche combination, Naxos calculates, would effectively keep enough water (and enough of the gasses that escape with it) just under the surface to supply the observed partial pressures of the Martian tunnels.

This planet-girdling shell would be very effective. Even if it were to be ruptured by, for example, a meteor impact, Naxos says, the permafrost would quickly recur, and the caliche would follow in a period of only months or years thereafter.

A short paper from a team at the University of Edinburgh offered a conjecture about why no fossil remains of the Martians (or, indeed, of any of the other myriad organisms that must at some time have appeared in the planet's long evolutionary history) have been found. Based on preliminary autopsy reports on "Ferdie," the Martian which died of acceleration injuries, the Edinburghers describe the Martian skeletal structure as "extremely spongy, more talc-like than bone-like—if present in a human, it would be diagnosed as fatal osteoporosis." This is, of course, not unexpected in view of Mars's lesser surface gravity; indeed, this may have been an evolutionary advantage to the Martians, since developing hard bones for the skeleton is biologically expensive for Earthly land organisms. So there simply are not enough hard parts in the Martian anatomy to survive as fossils.

Furthermore, the Edinburgh team adds, there is reason to believe the present Martian climate is unusually severe. They point to long-accepted analyses of Mars's orbit and polar inclinations. Both vary with time, as do Earth's. (However, the Martian variations are more extreme—the polar inclination varies from 10° to 30° over million-year cycles.)

If they are correct in thinking this is an unusually stressful age for Martian organisms, then it follows that many species which may have been abundant, and may even have found it possible to live on the surface of Mars, at least in deep valleys where the air pressure increases by a factor of two or more, may over the past million years have gone extinct, or possibly retreated inside the caverns. It is also possible, one team member added during the discussion, that the dominant Martians may simply have eaten all the others.

The same member contributed to the discussion after the report immediately following, in which a Cardiff paleontologist proposed that the "punctuated-equilibrium" theory of evolution allowed for devolution as well as improvement, and so the apparent relatively primitive state of the Martians (which contrasts seriously with their elaborate tunnel network, for example) may simply have been a natural consequence of random evolutionary change. The Edinburgh scientist then said, "Nonsense! Things simply got too tough for them, as with the Inuits and the Aleuts."

It was the papers on the Martians themselves that drew the biggest crowds, especially among the fourteen-year-olds of the Junior BAAS.

The hottest scientific quarrel, however, was between the opposing parties of the Tectonics and the Anti-Tectonics at the final session.

Those who believe that the crust of Mars shows evidence of tectonic motion, as for example in the "loose and slipping shell" theory of Martian polar wandering, defended their views fervently. While those who declare that Mars shows no more crustal shifting than a cabbage pointed to the evident datum that "hot spots" on Mars remain in the same position for millions, and perhaps for thousands of millions, of years.

Since no new evidence was forthcoming on either side, both parties simply rehashed old matters. The hot-spot evidence was particularly argued. No one seriously questioned the existence of stationary hot spots on Earth. The one that caused the "island arc" of the Hawaiian archipelago, for instance, has evidently remained in the same place for at least some tens of millions of years. It produced vents (which became volcanoes, and then islands) one after another as the great Pacific tectonic plate sailed past it overhead, toward the north and west. On the other hand, Mars appears different. The hot spot that created the solar system's largest volcano, the Martian Olympus Mons (not to mention the hot spot that may currently keep the Martian race alive), has apparently nourished only one continuing eruption, in-dicating no motion of the crust relative to the inside of the planet. But in response to this the Tectonics speculated that the Martian crust is much thicker than Earth's, and possibly entrains a good bit of magma as it slides about—including the as yet not understood sources of "hot spots" in general, on whatever planet they may be found.

What both sides appear to agree on, however, is that such hot spots are rare on Mars—suggesting that the Martians found by the Seerseller expedition may well be the only Martians there are.

TEN

THE
BELTWAY
BANDIT

The word that caught Bernard Sampson's ear on the network news was *Martians*.

What Dan Rather had said was only that one of the surviving Martians on the *Algonquin 9* spaceship seemed to be recovering from a slight case of sniffles, but that didn't matter. The word *Martians* was guaranteed always to get Sampson's attention, wherever he heard it, in spite of the fact that everybody was hearing it all the time these days, because that was the kind of thing that Sampson's life was all about. He was a space nut.

The great good thing about Sampson's life was that, these days, people were willing to pay him to be a space nut—some of the time, anyway. True, in order to spend some of his working life on space he was compelled to spend a whole lot more of it on mundane things like public health and urban renewal and traffic flows. True, he didn't work on space in the way he really would have preferred. "Consultant" wasn't bad. "Astronaut" would have been about a million times better.

All the same, if there was any justification Sampson could claim for living, it was the part he and his Washington Beltway consulting firm had played in the Seerseller expedition to Mars. That was S*P*A*C*E. It didn't even matter that so much of the Seerseller expedition had turned sour. What was sweet enough to flood his heart with joy was that it had *happened*, and the expedition was coming back, and with it were coming Real, Live M*A*R*T*I*A*N*S.

And a tiny bit of the credit for that belonged to Bernard Sampson. . . . Unfortunately, so did a tiny bit of the blame. But he tried not to think of that part.

Until Rather showed the film of the Martians in their pens Sampson hadn't really been seeing the picture on his bedroom TV screen, though his eyes had been more or less focused on it. He hadn't even been hearing the sound, because his ears were exclusively tuned to the distant splashing sounds made by his pretty wife, Sheila, as she showered before going out for the evening.

Those sounds registered loudly in Sampson's thoughts. It took a lot to distract him from them, but he was glad enough to be distracted by Rather's story about the Martians. And glad that, when the story was over, Sampson's phone rang.

"That you, Benny?" snapped the voice on the other end of the phone.

Sampson didn't have to ask who it was. Only his business partner, Van Poppliner, called him Benny. "Of course it's me," he said. "What other man would be answering the phone in my wife's bedroom?"

"Don't joke," Poppliner ordered. "Benny, did you catch the story on ABC? They've got a new thing for the Martians. About the acceleration, I mean. They're putting them all in Styrofoam or something."

"I guess I was watching CBS," Sampson apologized. "I did see something about it, I think."

"You got to be on your toes, Benny," Poppliner said reproachfully. "Anyway, it gave me an idea. Do you see the angle? Medical care for Martians. Medical care for people. I figure there's a connection there for us. Health and Human Services probably needs to know what the implications of this kind of health care for Martians would be for, let's say, old ladies with fractured hips and so on, do you know what I'm saying? A brittle bone is a brittle bone, right? And it goes the other way, too. Like, NASA ought to have an update on all that kind of stuff that's been done for human beings."

"I see what you mean, Van," Sampson said cautiously. "Sure, I guess we could put together a couple of reports, but wouldn't we be going pretty far outside our regular area of expertise?"

Poppliner said with patience, "Benny, our regular area of expertise is whatever we can make a buck out of. Also the kind of reports we've been selling aren't bringing in the kind of bottom line that we need to go public. You hear what I'm saying?"

"Oh, sure I do, Van," Sampson agreed.

"Right. So here's the thing. I think we need to develop some new areas. There's big money in health care, and we aren't getting our piece of it. This thing with the Martians could be the way we get in. So drop whatever you're doing. I want you to listen in on MacNeil-Lehrer, they'll have something on it in depth, and then start figuring out where our databases are and how we can package the reports. Got that? And I'd like to have a preliminary project appreciation sitting on my desk by the time I get to the office tomorrow morning."

"Tomorrow morning? Well," said Sampson, thinking about it, "I suppose I could do that. I'm not real busy tonight. Tell you what. I'll start making some preliminary notes, and I'll give you a call later—"

"No, you won't do that," said Poppliner, "because I've got a couple of congressmen to see tonight. Tomorrow morning is time enough. But get on it, Benny, because I think this one could do a lot for us."

"All right," Sampson agreed, listening to the sounds from the bathroom. The splashing of the shower had stopped. Sheila would be coming out of it now. "I'll talk to you tomorrow," he said hastily, and hung up.

He sat on the edge of the king-size bed he shared with his pretty wife—at least on the nights when she didn't simply bunk in on the couch downstairs, so as not to disturb him—and turned the bedroom television back on with the remote. The MacNeil-Lehrer program hadn't yet started on the PBS station. He pushed the mute button on the remote and went back to listening attentively to the sounds of his wife in the bathroom.

They weren't hard to hear. The kind of house you got for two hundred and twenty-five thousand dollars in one of Maryland's fastest-growing residential suburbs did not include soundproof doors. He could identify every sound. Opening and closing of the medicine-chest door: That was Sheila getting out her deodorant. Faint *wiss, wiss, wiss*: That was Sheila spraying perfume inside her bra, in the waistline of her panties, against the small of her back. Rub-a-dub sound: That was Sheila brushing her teeth. Moment of silence: Sheila, studying every inch of her face and throat in the three-way mirror, looking for a wrinkle, a sag, any kind of a blemish. Loud motor sound that kept going for a long time: the hair dryer. That was the final step in the process, Sampson knew, but it would take five minutes at least to get every strand perfectly in place, and besides MacNeil and Lehrer were indeed getting ready to talk about what had happened to the Martian named Grace.

Bernard Sampson's dedication to space had started with "Star Trek" when he was ten, and it had never stopped.

He still kept up his memberships in both the L-5ers and the British Interplanetary Society, though by now he was also a full-fledged fellow in both the American Astronautical Society and the American Institute of Aeronautics and Astronautics, among many others. At the age of twenty he had made himself swallow the truth that he himself was never going to go Out There. But there was a big need for right-minded people to do the drudgery work for space right on the surface of the Earth. There were about five thousand of those planet-dwellers for every hero (or heroine) who ever got to sit on top of a thousand tons of high explosive at a lift-off. So he stuck out the courses in astronomy and physics and wound up with the doctorate that said he was employable.

And, in fact, he even got employed. Not, unfortunately, by NASA. Not even by one of the big contractors who made the fuel tanks and the rocket motors and the life-support systems and the electronics. But he wound up as a partner in an authentic space consultancy on Washington's Beltway; and, yes, they had provided studies for the optimal orbits to Mars, and, yes, they had done peer review on other people's studies for the Seerseller expedition's lander systems (pity about that part, of course, but they'd done their best—hadn't they?), and, yes, that expedition was well on its way home. It was limping a little, all right, but still it was coming home—and with *Martians*.

Sampson even got the privilege of appearing on television now and then, when the news departments cast their nets for ten-second sound bites from one expert or another. Actually, it was usually Van Poppliner they wanted, because he was the partner who did the talking. But Van didn't like appearing before the public for some reason, so now and then Sampson had had the thrill of seeing himself on the screen, standing in front of the launch pad at the Cape and explaining something like why it took ten and a half months to get to Mars but only eight to return, and that wasn't bad. In fact, that, all of that, was the luckiest thing that had ever happened to him. . . .

Except, of course (at least, he always used to think it was the exception), his incredible luck in marrying pretty, sexy, bright-haired Sheila.

What Sampson wished, almost as much as he wished that he could have gone Out There, was that he was still sure his marriage had been good luck.

By the time Sheila came out of the bathroom her husband was making notes on a yellow pad, hunched up against the satin pillows at the head of the bed. As she slipped blouse and skirt over her underwear she gave him a friendly, disparaging smile. "That's my old workaholic, Bernard," she sighed forgivingly, and added, "Don't wait up for me. After I see what the stores are giving away I think I'll take in a flick."

"Anything I might like to see with you?" he asked experimentally. It wasn't the kind of experiment they did at MIT or Fermilab or one of the big biochemistry places. It was more like the kind the teacher did for his high-school science class, where you knew in advance exactly how it was going to come out. Sure enough, the experiment had the predicted result.

"You know you don't like to go to the movies," she reminded him, sitting on the chaise longue on the far side of the room to pull on her open-toed slippers. "There's a new Sissy Spacek movie, I think it is, that's supposed to be good. Anyway, you look like you're all set for the rest of the night." She rummaged around in her pocketbook until she found her car keys. "Who was on the phone?" she asked, holding the keys up to show she had succeeded.

"Van Poppliner. He's got something he wants me to do for him for tomorrow morning."

"Slave driver. Still, you'd better do it," she said practically, leaning over to kiss the top of his head. She smelled wonderful, he thought wistfully. "Have a good one," she said, and was gone.

Bernard Sampson was well off in his possessions. He had an expensive house (though with eighty percent of the mortgage still unpaid.) He had a BMW of his own in their two-car garage, with room for a zippy little Nissan for his wife—and a neat, if aging, Econoline van parked in the spread of the driveway in case they ever got around to taking weekend trips again. He had no children—but that was a plus, his wife explained to him, because children would be sure to interfere with their busy lives. He had twenty-five percent of the shares in a privately held high-tech research corporation called Macro-DyneTristix, Ltd., with expensive space-age offices located on Washington's Beltway, and of which he was both Executive Vice-President and Chief Executive Officer. (Van Poppliner didn't like titles, he said. Of course, he was still the one who made the decisions.) And, most of all, Sampson had a wife—a markedly beautiful one—who cooked his meals and washed his laundry and never complained about the fact that she had given up her own career as an interpretive dancer when she married him . . . and was out of the house shopping (she *said* she was shopping) five nights of every seven.

He had all those things. What he didn't have was peace of mind.

It was after ten by the time Sampson finished keyboarding the preliminary notes for the new projects into his PC. He pulled the floppy disk out, marked its sleeve *Martians,* and put it in his dispatch case to take to the office in the morning.

Then he made himself a cup of cocoa. He drank it thoughtfully in the kitchen, staring into space. As he rinsed out the cup and saucepan, he wondered just where his wife was.

When Sampson turned off the Carson show after the monologue and put his head down to sleep, he squinted for a moment at the empty pillow next to his own. "You know what Sheila's doing? She's fooling around," he said out loud.

But that was just another experiment. He was only trying it out to see how the words would sound. He didn't for one minute believe it was true, not then, not even the next morning when he woke up and found the right-hand pillows still unoccupied, because he heard Sheila singing to herself in the kitchen. "Hon, hon," she said, kissing him fondly with the spatula still in her hand, "you looked so sweet last night when I came in I didn't have the heart to disturb you. So I slept on the couch in the living room. The movie? Oh, it was all right, I guess—but you better get your act cleaned up, because the griddle cakes are just about ready and my little genius has to get out there and revolutionize the world all over again this morning!"

Revolutionizing the world was not actually a good description of what Sampson did for a living, although there had been a time when he sort of hoped it might turn out that way.

He parked the BMW in the slot marked *MacroDyneTristix— Sampson* and climbed the wide steps with the palm tree growing alongside out of a pot to the company's clean, bright, handsome offices.

Sampson looked at the carved oak plaque over the door, with the name of their corporation. They had labored long and hard to choose the right name. The formula was simple enough; you took something like *Compu* or *Tech* or *Poly* or *Macro,* married it with something like *Data* or *Syn* or *Temp* or *Omni,* and finished it off with an *Istics* or a *Dyne* or a *Tronics.* The big problem was making sure nobody else had come up with that particular combination before you. That had done in their first inspiration, PolySynTronics, when the lawyers had reported a corporation with the same name on Route 128 in Massachusetts. Then Sampson had solved the problem. He treated it as a simple project in mathematical conjugation. Their resident hacker, Mickey Vorobyev, put it all on the computer and randomized all the possible components. Then all they had to do was pick out the best-looking and make a few little editing improvements to produce their corporate name, MacroDyneTristix.

Poppliner wasn't in yet, but Rose, the receptionist, told Sampson that all the researchers had arrived. "I want a meeting in my office in ten minutes," said Sampson. "Bring in a pot of coffee, will you?"

Although Sampson was the chief executive officer of the little corporation on the Beltway, it was Poppliner who made the money come in. Like most of its neighbors, MacroDyneTristix, Ltd., lived by government handouts.

Nominally, of course, the company was private industry. That was to say, Sampson owned a quarter of it and Poppliner owned an equal share, and the other half of the stock was held by "The Backers," the shadowy group of investors Poppliner had persuaded to put in the start-up money that had got the thing going in the first place. Sometimes Sampson wondered just who The Backers were, but Poppliner was very discouraging about any possible contact with them.

MacroDyneTristix was not *real* private, though, since every dime the company took in came out of the pockets of the U.S. taxpayers. The hardest work Poppliner and Sampson ever did was dreaming up new grant proposals. It was a pity that the projects couldn't all be about space, but Poppliner explained there were times when nobody wanted to hear anything about space and you had to keep the cash flow up regardless. Thinking up new research topics was normally Sampson's job. Then, if Poppliner approved them—which he did maybe one time out of five with the brightest of Sampson's ideas—Poppliner himself went around to somebody he knew in, oh, let's say the Department of Transportation and said, "Listen, I've been meaning to tell you that Benny—you know my partner, Benny Sampson, he did that great urban-renewal study for Baltimore—Benny's got a new procedure that lets us model traffic flows as an input-output matrix, so you could pick out right away the factors that can lead to unacceptable congestion or even gridlock. It's cheap, it's fast, it's *good*, and we could do a study for you for, really, tiny money."

And then, if things were going right, the Department of Transportation guy would say, "Okay, Van. We're in for, oh, hell, let's say two hundred K." Government people always said *K* instead of *thousand* when they were talking about technology, so they would sound technological themselves. What that meant was that MacroDyneTristix, Ltd., had a firm commitment of two hundred thousand dollars, which with overruns could almost always go to two and a half or even three.

That was the hardest part of what they did for a living, getting the grants approved. The rest was easy. All they had left to do after that was to write a fifty-five-page report, the last ten pages or so requiring very little effort because it was just bibliography, and bind it up with some color glossies in one of MacroDyneTristix's expensive—and expensive-looking—custom-designed plastic binders.

That was it. All of it. What the report said was of no importance at all.

Once the procurement office at the DoT checked it over for compliance with the purchase order no one would ever look at it again.

Nevertheless, it did have to get by the people at the procurement office, and every once in a while one of them might actually read one. Even worse, one of those damned Budget people might check it out, or some congressman's aide could snoop around, looking for something for the congressman to give a nasty award to. So the report had to say *something*. That was what MacroDyneTristix's four resident researchers were for. One of them would go hotfooting over to the Library of Congress to pick up copies of the last five or six papers that had been written on the subject of traffic congestion—not so much for the studies themselves, but to pick up a nice, long bibliography. Another would produce a few pages of "context"—meaning, in this case, the history of the computer, from Babbage on. A third would catalogue all the methodologies he could find for predicting statistical problems, with special emphasis on trend-line extrapolation, morphological mapping, relevance-tree studies, and DELPHI. When all that was done, the preliminary papers went to Bernard Sampson.

Sampson's own job was to discuss what the literature searches had turned up, and then write a conclusion. The conclusion was the easiest part. Generally speaking, he could write his conclusions long before the literature searches were complete. The final paragraph of each report, at least, was foreordained. It would always say something like, "It is clear that the potential offered through Computer-Modeled Optimization Techniques (CMOT) will be of increasing importance over the decade's time-frame, though the present state of the art does not yet permit real-time interactive model-to-street dynamics."

Thus warned against imputing any reality to the paper, no one would try to do anything with the report. That was all right; everyone understood that by its means MacroDyneTristix had been kept in business for another couple of months. That gave time for Poppliner to go to the Pentagon and say, "Look, our resident genius, Benny Sampson—you know him, he's the one who got the Man of the Year award from the data-retrieval people—has just done some pretty interesting stuff on traffic flows, and we think it has applications for outbreak-of-war mobilization and logistics problems."

And then, with any luck at all, the Pentagon guy would say, "Okay, we're in for four hundred K," and Poppliner would see clearly where the next dividend was coming from for the money men in the background. Pentagon grants were just about the best, anyway. You could always get in a few paragraphs about something like the implications of traffic flow on the randomization of nuclear-missile silo siting. Then, when Poppliner delivered the report, he could point out that there was obviously a lot of material there that they wouldn't want the Russians to know about. That meant that, with any luck, he could get the whole document classified secret, and no unfriendly eye would ever see it at all.

It was a harmless exercise, as Van Poppliner had explained. It didn't hurt anybody. It provided a lot of jobs for people with advanced degrees, who might have had to work for a living if they hadn't managed to get taken on in one or another of the private "research" companies lining the highway that girdled Washington, D.C., known collectively as "the Beltway Bandits." It even gave people like Bernard Sampson himself BMWs in the garage and business-expense-deductible first-class airline tickets to professional meetings all over the world. And the money that kept MacroDyneTristix Ltd.'s cash flow going was no problem. It came spilling out of the limitless cornucopia called the United States Treasury. The taxpayer paid for it all—and, after all, wasn't that what taxpayers were for?

Sampson fed the floppy into his terminal, logging it in as *Martians*, and waited for his staff to show up.

MacroDyneTristix had nine people on its payroll, including Sampson himself and Van Poppliner. There were two secretaries, one for Van Poppliner and the other for everybody else who needed to write a letter, plus one receptionist–coffee maker. The other four were the "research staff."

All four of them straggled in to Sampson's office, more or less within the ten minutes he had specified, ready for the day's assignment. They were a good crew. There was Mikhail Vorobyev, fresh out of Leningrad by way of Vienna and Israel, thirty-one years old and a statistical mathematician just waiting for one of the universities to waive his broken English so he could teach in Cambridge or California. There was Jack Horgan, still pimply at twenty-seven, tall and skinny and the only person the University of Chicago had ever graduated with three concurrent bachelor's degrees. There was the token black, Randy Murfree, who wore gray three-piece suits when he wasn't wearing white suede jackets and Adidas—this was a white suede day—and the token woman, Mildred McClurg Lippauer.

Mickey Vorobyev was eating a Twinkie as he came in, but he crammed the last of it into his mouth and licked his fingers apologetically as Sampson began to speak.

"Right, gang, we've got a big one. You know about the Martians and their physical problems," Sampson said. "We're going to develop some proposals about them. Especially about their skeletal weaknesses as they relate to human beings—flimsy bones because of low gravity as against osteoporosis, and so on." He was roaming around the room as he spoke. When he approached the couch where Randy Murfree and Mildred McClurg Lippauer were sitting he got strong whiffs of musk oil and cigar smoke—the musk from Randy, the cigar smoke from Mildred. "So what we need today," he finished, "is abstracts. We need to dig up everything that's been written about the Martians in this area. That means all the sources cited in the papers, if they're relevant to (a), Martian physiology, (b), resemblances to human problems, (c), technology dealing with them in either case. That's for openers. After I see the abstracts we'll get together again and I'll hand out specific assignments. Got it? The file is *Martians*. Divide it up among you, and see if you can get back to me after lunch."

That was already a pretty good day's work, but for some reason Sampson could not feel much pleasure in it. His wife was on his mind.

He made the effort to think of other things. There was, after all, work still to do. He made himself spend the next hour editing the conclusions for the study, the roughs for which were on his computer, on the economic implications of possible extensions of the Washington subway system. "The validity of cost-benefit analysis (CBA)," he wrote, "has been established in similar contexts, and it is likely that its findings will become applicable to this question within the five-year time horizon. However, it will be essential to input new data as available, and a follow-up study is recommended within eighteen months."

He scrolled back to the beginning of the paragraph and read the whole thing over. He decided it was all right. Then he saved it, got up, and drank the rest of the cold cup of coffee on his windowsill, thinking about what he had just done.

It was an adequate study. It would get them the balance of the ninety-five-thousand-dollar grant Poppliner had wheedled out of the always pinch-penny District of Columbia administration.

But it wasn't, he thought, really very much for a guy who had been one of MIT's brightest graduating students to show for all his skill and smartness. And it had nothing to do with S*P*A*C*E.

There was a little litmus test Sampson applied to measure his accomplishments now and then. Maybe it was time to do it again.

He thought for a moment, then sat down again at his work station. He sighed, squeezed his eyes closed unhappily, wriggled his fingers over the computer keypad, and then logged in with the Science Citation Index in Philadelphia. *CA CITESEARCH*, he typed, and then, *AUTHOR CITE*, and then his own name.

It had been a while since the last time Sampson had done this particular thing. It was a form of self-checking, like an aging jock seeing how many pushups he could still do, in the privacy of his own bedroom. The test of a scientific career wasn't how much money you made. It wasn't even how many awards you received. There was always somebody ready to give you a plaque or a framed certificate, because whatever the award did for the person getting it, it did a lot more for the donors—it showed they were important enough to give awards. No, the real measure of scientific achievement was in the number of other scientists who thought what you had done was important enough to cite it in their own work. If you were cited, you mattered. If you weren't, you didn't.

The Science Citation Index was the best way, really almost the only way, to keep score.

When the SCI display popped up, Sampson gazed at it glumly.

It hadn't changed, not in over a year. The numbers were the same. A total of three people had cited the paper on *False-color interpretation: The validity of NOAA imaging for resource location*, written seven years earlier, when he was a postdoctoral fellow back on Boston's Route 128. A fourth person had actually cited his doctoral dissertation, but there wasn't much comfort in that: The man had been his dissertation adviser, and the subject was tailor-made to fill in some trivial gaps in his own ongoing study.

That was it.

Of the twenty-five reports produced under his name by Macro-DyneTristix, not one had been cited by anyone, anywhere, ever.

Sampson confessed unhappily to himself that there was a reason for that. It was that none of these reports represented any real original research at all. They had about as much significance, in the grand, universal scientific effort to increase Man's knowledge of the world, as a sophomore's American Lit. term paper titled "A Comparison of the Literary Significance of *Huckleberry Finn* and *Moby Dick*: Which Is the 'Great American Novel'?"

It was a relief when his phone rang.

And a surprise when he answered it, too, because the voice was his wife's. "Hon?" Sheila said. "I've been thinking. I haven't really seen a lot of you lately, you know? I kind of miss you. How'd you like to buy your bride a lunch today? About twenty minutes? Wonderful; I'll bring my appetite along!"

What Sheila was wearing when she arrived was a frilly white blouse and a pale blue skirt. She had been to the hairdresser some time that morning. She looked great. She was smiling as she sailed into Sampson's office and planted a kiss on his cheek. "I'm starving, love," she announced, "but let's take a look around the shop first, can we? It's been a while, and besides I'm desperate to see this great new girl Van's got working for him."

It was a great lunch; they split a bottle of wine and, for the first time in many months, Sampson found his wife paying undiverted attention to him for an hour and a half straight. He kissed her good-bye in the parking lot, and watched her tootle off in the Nissan with a bemused smile.

The smile didn't last. When Sampson got back to the office that afternoon Randy Murfree was sitting on the edge of the couch in the office, looking unhappy. He had taken off the white suede jacket, and the pink shirt underneath was looking rumpled.

"You've got a problem," Sampson diagnosed.

"It doesn't come out right," Murfree said, waving at a stack of Xeroxes on Sampson's desk. "The first thing I did was pull the medical reports on the Martians. Look at them, will you?"

"Sure I will, but tell me what they say."

Murfree hesitated. "What they add up to is, everybody knew the Martians had soft bones and kind of, you know, loose anatomy. It figured. They never experienced more than Martian gravity. That's what they evolved for, you know what I'm saying? And there wasn't any doubt from the beginning that putting them through a space voyage was risky—no, I don't mean risky, I mean dumb. *Dangerous* dumb. They just couldn't handle it." He scowled at the Xeroxes. "It's a wonder they didn't all die on the takeoff."

"Ah," said Sampson. "I see. That's, uh, interesting."

Murfree said, "All I do is dig up data for you, Bernard, and if you want more of this stuff I'll get more. Only the way it looks to me, you aren't going to make NASA happy by pulling it all out. It makes them look pretty bad."

"That's nasty," Sampson agreed.

"Yeah," said Murfree vaguely. "Well." Then he said, "The thing is, some of that material could be our baby, you know? At least, we did peer review on it. I mean, somebody could say we should've been a little tougher on it, you know?"

Something like an electric shock went through Sampson. "I'll read the papers," he promised.

But when he did, it was even worse than Murfree had indicated.

Then he went next door to Van Poppliner's office.

Poppliner was dictating letters to his new secretary, Marian, who was by all odds the best-looking woman in the office, if not the best in the state of Maryland. She was even better looking than the last three secretaries Poppliner had had; to put it even more precisely, she was very nearly as good looking as Sampson's wife had been when he married her, six years before. "Sit down, Benny," Poppliner said without even looking up. "I'll just be a minute."

Actually, and surprisingly, he was. When Marian had swayed out the door Poppliner gazed thoughtfully after. Then he said, "The funny thing is, she can type, too. I hear Sheila came by."

"What? Oh, Sheila. Yes, she wanted to see what your new girl looked like."

"I hope she was impressed," Poppliner said with a scowl. "How's the Martian thing going?"

"Well," Sampson said cautiously, "going fine, I guess. Partly it is anyway. I sent all the people off to get started, and Randy Murfree's already come back with a lot of stuff."

"Yes?" said Poppliner, looking at him narrowly. "What's the other part of the partly?"

"Some of Randy's stuff doesn't look too good for NASA. If you were thinking of selling them a report—"

"I am damn well *going* to sell them a report."

"Yeah, that's what I thought. Well, we're going to have to watch what we say; the basic documents say they should've known the Martians were bound to get damaged by the launch. Not to mention what will happen to them on Earth."

Poppliner shrugged. "What you're telling me," he said, "is that there's a real need for this report. Like, NASA ought to know all this stuff."

"NASA already did know it," Sampson protested. "They even transmitted copies of all the reports to Captain Seerseller's expedition. He just went ahead and took off with them anyway." He hesitated. "I feel a little responsible myself," he confessed.

"For what? Because NASA dropped the ball?"

"Because my company was supposed to review all this stuff. Just as we did on the landing-orbit simulations; I still feel a little guilty about—"

"Benny," Poppliner commanded, "shut up about that, will you? It's history. We've got no problems with it."

"Yes, but now here's this new thing—"

"Handle it, Benny!"

When Poppliner squinted his eyes and scowled at his watch, that meant he was getting sore and edgy, and you were supposed to take your cue to leave him alone for a while. Sampson resisted the cue. He said staunchly, "We did peer review on all those reports, Van. I mean, you did."

"Of course I did! I always do the peer-review stuff, don't I? You've got more important things to do with your time."

"But that makes us kind of responsible, doesn't it? I mean, we should have blown a whistle somewhere."

"*Benny*. You know what happens to whistle-blowers."

"But still—"

"Benny," Poppliner said, his tone so markedly patient that it conveyed the fact that the patience was almost run out, "They didn't hire us to tell them it couldn't be done. They wanted to be told it could. We sell the customer what the customer wants to buy; so do like I said and handle it!"

For that Sampson was ready. He went to his second plan of action. "There's something I'd like to try," he said.

Poppliner looked at him warily, waiting.

"I've got a friend," Sampson said. "Did I ever tell you I almost went to work for NASA?"

Poppliner squinted in thought. "Not so far this week, anyway."

"Well, I did. And I still have friends there. One man, Dell Hobart, he's working in the District, and I happen to know he's involved with the Martians."

"Who in NASA isn't?" Poppliner demanded.

"No, I mean, he's been into that from the very beginning. I thought I'd give him a call, maybe take him to lunch—he's a nut for Mexican food and there's a place that's not bad in Georgetown—and I can ask him, man to man, what went on with this fiasco—I mean, this incident."

"Um," said Poppliner dourly, drumming his fingers. He eyed his partner without pleasure. As he had always pointed out, Bernard Sampson was fine for getting product out, but he didn't have the right personality to be client-contact material. "Skip that idea for a minute. What about the flip side? What is there in all this stuff that I can sell to Health and Human Services?"

"That isn't any better for us, I'm afraid. All the studies went the other way; all the recommendations and analyses about the Martians were based on experience with human beings and terrestrial animals."

Poppliner looked thoughtful. "Well," he said, "I've already got a commitment on both reports, so we're going to have to make them come out right. Get on it, Benny; that's your end, isn't it? I'd stay and help you, but I've got a meeting that I've got to get to." He hesitated, then asked diffidently, "What'd she think of her?"

"What do you mean?" Sampson asked, trying to untangle the pronouns.

"Your wife. What did she think of Marian? Did she say anything?"

"Oh, no," said Sampson, trying to remember. Failing. "She said Marian was really good looking, I guess, but you already know that. You know how it is with Sheila. She's always interested in everything that goes on here. She even wondered if maybe we could find something for her to do here in the office. She gets bored, just sitting around the house—"

"Benny," said Poppliner earnestly, "you know that's against company policy. It's pretty close to a conflict of interest, not to mention that I don't know if The Backers would approve of putting family members on the payroll. . . . So," he said meditatively, "Sheila wanted to see the new girl. How'd she know I had one?"

"Didn't you tell her?" Sampson thought for a moment. "No, I guess you couldn't have, you haven't seen her for months, have you?"

But, going back to his office, Sampson thought that was quite peculiar; because, however he searched his memory, he couldn't remember ever mentioning Marian to his wife, either.

In spite of the promise of the luncheon, Sheila regretfully announced that she had one of her really bad headaches that night. She didn't go out shopping. She didn't sleep on the living room sofa, either, but it somehow worked out that Sampson did.

He didn't stay there. When the eleven o'clock news was over, he reached to turn out the light and stopped his hand halfway.

He wasn't sleepy.

What he was was dissatisfied. His soul was not at ease. The person who could have eased it best was already sound asleep in the king-size bed right over his head, but as she wasn't interested in doing that for him he had to find some other avenue to tranquility, or face two or three hours of tossing and turning and hating himself for being unable to get to sleep.

There was an alternative way. A good one, and he hadn't used it for quite some while now.

Ten minutes later Sampson, dressed, was out in his driveway, starting up the old white Ford Econoline that had sat beside the two-car garage, unused, since those days a long time ago when he and Sheila had roamed the mountains and shores of Virginia and the DelMarVa peninsula on long, glad weekends. The picture of the Martian mountain Sheila had painted for him on the side of the van was still bright. The two bunk beds inside were still made up and ready, though it was a long time since they had occupied them—seldom more than one of them, in those days. But the battery was low.

The starter whined a long complaint before the motor started. He craned his neck to see if the sound had—it was barely possible—wakened Sheila and caused her to look out to see what was happening, and then maybe to come down, and then maybe, just possibly—

Nothing like that happened, of course. The window remained dark.

When the motor finally caught he rolled the Econoline a few yards down the driveway, to where there were no trees overhead to block the view, killed the motor, and pulled the old Questar out of its case under the right-hand bunk bed.

For once in the Washington slurbs the sky was pretty nearly clear. The light pollution from bars, highways, and gas stations was as awful as always, but still Sampson was almost sure that he could make out, as the faintest of glimmers, a kind of gegenschein of starlight, the cloudy patch where the Milky Way should have been. Overhead the summer triangle of bright Altair, Deneb, and Vega claimed a major fraction of the sky.

Mars had not yet risen beyond the high-rise office buildings to the east.

It would be along soon enough, and anyway there were other things to look at through the Questar, and anyway before he looked at much of anything he had to mount the telescope and orient it and start the clock drive going. The Econoline had been his birthday present to Sheila the first year they were married, and the telescope mounting on its roof had been hers to him. It was a fine piece of equipment. It would have served for a scope a lot bigger than the Questar, and the plan was that sooner or later it would be used for one. That hadn't happened. Partly because if you lived in the smoky, overilluminated East, what was the point? And partly because—well, partly because there were a lot of things that hadn't happened, for instance, a family.

It didn't take Sampson long to climb up the little metal ladder and fit the Questar in its mount. Although it had been a long time since he did it last, he managed without difficulty to take a sighting on Polaris and start the drive going.

He hadn't brought a star map out with him. He realized wryly that he had forgotten a lot. Even so, he found the pretty double Albireo, between the constellations of Lyra and Aquila, in a few minutes and gazed with pleasure at the twin dots in the eyepiece, one rosy, one ice blue. The planet Jupiter was next, halfway down to the west, and easiest of all to find. Three of the Galilean satellites popped right into view to the left of the planet and one to the right; in the old days he would have known which was which, but it gave him pleasure just to look at them. Saturn would have been nice for an easy practice look, too, but Saturn wasn't in the sky just then; neither was Venus or Mercury, and he didn't have any idea of where to seek for either Uranus or Neptune. It shouldn't have been that hard. Neither planet was one of your near-solar speed demons; they stayed pretty well put from one year to the next, but try as he would Sampson couldn't remember what constellation he had seen either of them in last.

There were lots of other double stars that you could split with a Questar in the summer sky, but Sampson couldn't remember where any of them were, either. He squinted at where he thought M-31 in Andromeda should have been, low down, but there were more high rises along that part of the horizon, and they all had parking lots, and the parking lots kept their lights on all night. He stopped looking for specific things and just looked, for a while aimlessly scanning through the desert within the great square in Hercules, making stars pop out where the naked eye could find no stars at all; and yes, yes, it was as relaxing and calmly simple and placidly satisfying as it ever had been.

He took his face away from the eyepiece and sat back, careful on the narrow roof, contentedly breathing in the night air, honeysuckle, and distant car exhaust and the lingering charred steak smell from somebody's backyard barbecue.

He didn't mind that it was getting chilly. The roof of the Econoline was still warm from the sun, and there wasn't any wind.

He thought: In so great an undertaking as the exploration of space you had to expect accidents. Even bad ones. Even ones caused by mistakes that could have been avoided. People made mistakes; that was the nature of the human condition. You had to get past the mistakes and go on with the work anyway. In a thousand years no one would ever give a thought to the mistakes, but the human race would never forget the Martians.

He reminded himself of these facts as he lay cautiously on his back, fingers linked behind his head, gazing upward at the starry sky as he waited for the planet Mars to lift itself out of the clutter to the east. They were facts, all right. But they were not all that reassuring.

When you picked the arguments into their component pieces, all of those pieces had sharp edges. They cut. *Mistakes* conveyed one thing, but when you defined them as *my mistakes* the term meant something a lot different and a lot more painful.

Fidgeting, Sampson turned restlessly on his side.

There really had to be a better place for him than MacroDyne-Tristix, Ltd. There had to be better things for him to do than invent new suction pumps for the taxpayer cow. There had to be a way for him to serve the cause of space research in a fashion that did not make him an accomplice, at however far remove, to things that wrecked spaceships and killed the first alien creatures ever found.

If only he had sweated it out until NASA had an opening, as Dell Hobart had. . . . Or if only he had taken the offer from Northwestern. . . .

But Sheila thought the money from Northwestern was pitiful, and anyway he hadn't done either of those things.

He opened his eyes, and that was when he saw the tawny, orangey object on the eastern horizon. Mars had risen when he wasn't looking.

Looking at Mars was one of those things that satisfies the eyeballs all by itself. He gazed at it for several minutes, the clock drive keeping it neatly in the center of the field, and grinned to himself as he thought of how John Carter, in a not dissimilar situation, had simply stretched out his arms to the planet and, next thing you know, was lying on his back on the Barsoomian sand, with the four-armed green warrior poking at him with a sword.

That didn't happen this time, nor had he expected it to. He wasn't disappointed. When he had simply allowed the planet to fill his eye for a while he patiently got up, stowed the telescope, and moved the Econoline back to the place where the grass was all dead and brown where it had sat. Then at last he was ready to go to sleep.

A light was on in the kitchen.

Sheila had heard him move the vehicle after all. She had come down, and made herself a cup of cocoa, and drunk it, and gone back to sleep alone, upstairs. If he had been in the house he would have had a chance to talk to her.

He didn't regret it. He stretched out on the sofa happily enough, put one hand under the pillow and his head on top of it, and was asleep at once.

Though the rest of his night's sleep was tranquil, it was also short. When Sampson got to work the next morning he was grumpy, and the word from his research team didn't improve his mood at all.

It wasn't that they couldn't produce the relevant documents. The problem was that the documentation raised more questions than it answered. Why had NASA permitted the Mars expedition to bring some of the funny-looking things back? They must have known it was a death sentence for at least some of the Martians. Poppliner had if anything minimized the clear-cut warnings in the literature; so somebody had goofed. Badly. "I'm seeing somebody for lunch," Sampson promised Mildred McClurg Lippauer. "He'll know more about it than

I do. I'm sure there's a good reason for all this, if we only knew what it was."

Then, when Dell Hobart called him back, there was another disappointment, though not a very big one. Mexican food? Oh, Jesus, no, Hobart said; he had an ulcer, and Mexican food was just out of the question—but the NASA man was agreeable to a quick fast-food lunch somewhere near Sampson's office. "Howard Johnson's? Why not? A malted milk is about the best I can hope for."

So they went into the orange-roofed place on the Beltway, no more than half a mile from the MacroDyneTristix place. They sat in a booth, and it was almost like the old days at MIT, when you dined at either a MacDonald's or a Taco Bell, and going to something like Howard Johnson's was an extravagance you only committed to impress a date.

Only it turned out not to be like the old days at all. Dell Hobart was strangely reserved. He was a fat little man who smiled a lot—the last man you'd expect to have an ulcer—but he didn't smile when they sat down. His ulcer didn't allow him a cocktail, either, not even a Howard Johnson's cocktail, or french fries, or the fried clams he coveted. "It's tough to be on a diet," Sampson said, trying to sympathize.

"That's not what's tough," Hobart replied.

It was said in the kind of tone that lets you know an explanation, or at least an amplification, is on the way, and it was a kind of tone that made Sampson put down his fork. "Is something the matter, Dell?"

Hobart said, his voice low-pitched, "You called me, Bernard. I didn't call you. I've thought about it a hundred times, the last month or two, but I didn't like the way it would look. This way, since you were the one who called, I can always say it would have looked funny if I didn't meet you for lunch, since we're old school chums and all."

"Dell. What the hell are you talking about?"

"The OMB's looking you over," Hobart said. "They've got copies of every report you ever did for us and a lot more. Financial records, too. Lots of them. You didn't hear that from me."

"But, Dell! That's budget stuff—they're not going to come back and claim we charged you too much or anything, are they?"

"The Office of Management and Budget," Dell explained patiently, "isn't just interested in the money. They want to know if what we got for the money is worth it, and they want to know if the money was paid legally, and they want to know if anybody's passing out favors, or bribes, or what."

"We never did that!" said Sampson. And wondered if it were true. "I mean, Van Poppliner's pretty high-pressure sometimes, but he's too smart to cross the line—"

"Is he? I'll tell you about Van Poppliner, Bernard. Did you ever hear of Mid-South Liberty, Inc.?"

"Well, sure. It's a kind of financial thing Van deals with."

"It's a kind of financial thing Van Poppliner *is*. He owns a big piece of it. It owns part of your outfit, and it also owns part of four other think tanks and high-tech management and consultancy things around the Beltway. A couple of them did peer review on your papers, and your place has peer-reviewed them."

"But," Sampson said, dazed, "but that's a kind of conflict of interest."

"Oh, you think that? Well, so does the OMB. And you didn't hear it here."

"My God," Sampson said.

"So if you—" Hobart paused as the waitress came with their lunches. When she was gone again he finished, in a lower tone, "So if you have a paper shredder on the premises you might want to use it. For you personally, I mean. Not for Poppliner. I'd take it as a favor if you didn't alert him, though I guess you'll have to decide that for yourself."

"Dell! I *never*— I mean I never *personally*—"

Hobart waved a hand, embarrassed. "Sure, Bernard. I know that. Why do you think I'm telling you this? But Poppliner did, and he knew what he was doing. It's not just you Beltway guys; Poppliner's connections go right to some of the suppliers. See," he said, looking around, "that's where the cheese begins to bind. One hand washing another, everybody understands that. Hell, half you guys have re-volving-door management, a man works for the government ordering things, and then he takes his retirement and goes to work for the people he's been buying from; and then when he goes back to the government for an order for the new firm the guy who does the buying is the one he himself took on as his assistant. That's the system that made the Pentagon great."

"Oh, *hell*," said Sampson despairingly. "I knew it! That's what I wanted to talk to you about, Dell. We should've yelled when the studies on returning the Martians came along—".

"The Martians? It isn't just the Martians, Bernard. The rocket crashed on landing, remember? And your friend Poppliner owned a piece of the shop that made the landing study, and of the shop that vetted the proposal—your own, as it happens—and of the company that built the landing systems that failed; and that's going a bit far, even for Washington."

"Sweet Jesus," Sampson moaned.

"Yeah, yeah. And nobody blew the whistle; and the people that tried either got fired or were told to shut up. It's the Shuttle all over again," Hobart said drearily. "Aren't you going to eat your London broil?"

Sampson shook his head.

"I kind of don't have much appetite either, Bernard," Hobart said. He picked up a manila envelope from the seat beside him and handed it over. "Look, here's some stuff I came across."

"From the OMB investigation?"

Hobart shook his head. "Stuff the OMB hasn't found out about yet. Just forget where you got it, will you? And, listen, take your hands off that check. I'm paying this time. Don't argue; I don't want to turn up on any MacroDyneTristix expense account right now."

Then, as they were walking out of the restaurant toward the parking lot, Sampson stopped short at the hotel lobby door.

Hobart bumped into him. "What's the matter, Bernard? Did you forget something?"

Sampson turned hastily around, confronting the NASA man—and

blocking his view of the lobby. "I, uh, I'm not sure," he said, improvising. "Did you, ah, didn't you have a briefcase?"

"Me? No. All I had was the envelope I gave you."

"Then maybe I did, don't you think? Ah," he said, smiling with an effort, "maybe I'm just losing my mind, Dell. Forget it. I must've been thinking of someone else." He glanced over his shoulder. "Might as well go on to the parking lot," he said, because the motel elevator had come and gone, and the couple he'd seen waiting for it, on their way to one of the bedrooms on an upper floor, were gone—the couple of which the male member had been his partner, and the female his wife.

That afternoon was one of the busiest of Bernard Sampson's career.

At five that night Van Poppliner looked in on him. "Still here?" he asked cheerily. "That pretty wife of yours is going to forget what you look like."

"Not for a while yet," said Sampson, barely looking up.

Poppliner lingered in the doorway, looking puzzled. "What are you working on now, Benny?" he asked sociably.

"You know. The Mars stuff."

"Oh. How's it going?"

"Why, just fine," Sampson said. "Lot of material here. I want to get it whipped into some kind of shape while I'm on a roll."

"Yeah, that's good," said Poppliner, tarrying. He drummed his fingers on the door frame, blinking. There was something about the situation that he found puzzling, but one of the puzzles was that he couldn't see quite what it was. "Well, good night," he said at last. "Don't work too long, hear?"

Sampson didn't answer. As a matter of fact he was not even thinking of Van Poppliner or, for that matter, the wife who was no doubt arriving home to puzzle over the message on the telephone answering machine. They were not entirely absent from his mind, to be sure. There was one big section of his brain that was mournfully aware of them, but that particular section was walled off for the moment; there would be time enough to confront all of that later on—maybe much later on.

Meanwhile there were the NASA papers. There were a lot of them. There were the ones his staff had turned up for him, the ones in the envelope Dell Hobart had handed him at lunch, . . . and the ones he had printed out on his computer from Van Poppliner's personal datastore, once he figured out (by trying all the most obvious possibilities) that Poppliner's "password" had only been his birth date.

By midnight Sampson had finished Xeroxing eight copies of each of them and the laser printer in Sammie Lou's office was spitting out the last of eight copies of his covering remarks.

The phone had rung six times while he was working, the last time going on for nearly two minutes before the caller gave up. Sampson hadn't answered. He had already addressed eight manila envelopes— to the chairmen of the House and Senate Committees on Space; to the *New York Times* and the *Washington Post*; to the news departments of all three major television networks; and, after a little thought, to the offices of the magazine *The Progressive* in Madison, Wisconsin.

He stopped at the Beltway post office on his way home, bought stamps from a machine and, whistling, dropped all eight of the thick envelopes into the mail chute.

The house was not quite silent when he came in through the garage door. Overhead he could hear the faint mutter of the TV set from the bedroom, where Sheila was, no doubt, fretfully doing her nails in front of the screen. She didn't come down. Sampson didn't go up.

The kitchen table was set for one, with a congealed half of a steak and soggy vegetables left on the table for him as a reproach. He ignored them. He made himself a cup of cocoa, went back to the garage, and once more rolled the Econoline out onto the driveway.

It was nearly an hour before he heard Sheila calling to him from the garage door. "Bernard, for heaven's sake! Where've you been? What are you doing up there?"

He didn't lift his head from the eyepiece of the telescope. "I'm looking at Mars," he said.

"But where the dickens have you *been*? I called and called at the office—"

"I was busy," he said absently. "Important work, but it's all done now."

He could feel her eyes on him, but that didn't matter, really. "Oh, well," she said. "I guess you're in one of your moods. Too much chili at lunch, I suppose. Spoiled your digestion."

He considered that thought. "Actually," he said, "I didn't eat chili. We went to the HoJo's. Saw you there, as a matter of fact."

He didn't look up, not even when the silence protracted itself for quite a while.

Then, "Bernard," his wife said at last, in a quite different voice, "if you've got something on your mind we've got to talk about, let's do it."

"Indeed we do have to talk," he said, finally looking down over the side of the Econoline at her. He gave her a smile. "But not just yet, if you don't mind. I don't want to do any talking at all until the mail gets where it's going."

"Mail? Bernard, I don't know what you're thinking, but, honestly, sometimes you make me crazy! What kind of mail are you talking about?"

He was busy dismantling the telescope. "It's a report I sent out," he explained, stowing the Questar in its case. "An important one, and besides it's the last I'm ever going to do for MacroDyneTristix, so I want it to go just right." By then he had climbed back down to the ground. He lifted the cased scope onto the right-hand driver's seat.

Sheila moved out of the way, staring at him. "The *last*? Bernard! Have you and Van—I mean—have you had some kind of fight or something?"

He climbed behind the wheel and smiled at her. "Not yet," he said, starting the engine. "I think that comes later. When he gets out of jail, I mean."

ELEVEN

THE PRESIDENT'S NEWS CONFERENCE

At last night's news conference, the President was questioned about the recent revelations concerning the disaster to the landing of the Seerseller expedition and the return of the *Algonquin 9* spacecraft and its Martians. Here is the exchange:

QUESTION: "Mr. President, Bernard Sampson has disclosed documents which seem to indicate that the landing systems for the Seerseller expedition were badly designed, and that the procedures for verifying them were bypassed. If the implications of those documents are correct, the accident on landing was a direct consequence of some questionable decisions. Of course, we know that that has led to the death of more than two hundred of the astronauts. What is your comment on this?"

THE PRESIDENT: "All of us were deeply grieved at the loss of those brave explorers. I am going to make sure that these charges are investigated to the bottom."

QUESTION: "Don't you have any comment on it now?"

THE PRESIDENT: "It wouldn't be proper for me to say anything until we find out what the investigations are going to show. After that, I'll have plenty to comment. You won't be able to shut me up!"

QUESTION: "There is another point. I would like to know how you respond to criticisms of the return of the Martians. Several scientists have said the trip will be fatal for them."

THE PRESIDENT: "There they go again."

QUESTION: "But isn't it true, Mr. President, that the evolution of life on Mars has caused them to be adapted to a lighter gravity, so that they can't stand the stresses of our own surface of the Earth, not to mention what will happen in the landing process?"

THE PRESIDENT: "Well, you know, I've always had my doubts about evolution."

QUESTION: "But what about their broken bones, Mr. President?"

THE PRESIDENT: "Naturally, we will take every precaution to preserve the health of our Martian visitors. They're pretty delicate, you see, and they require special handling. Well, what we've got for them, we've got what they call an exoskeleton, which was invented by a Dr. Leiber years ago for the use of people returning from the Moon."

QUESTION: "Is that what some reporters are calling the 'lobster suit'?"

THE PRESIDENT: "The scientists call it an exoskeleton. They say, by the way, that it will have valuable civilian applications, for people who have paralysis or anything like that. And that reminds me. This expedition is not only a wonderful scientific achievement, it is going to be extremely productive for the economic recovery of our country. I don't know if you're all aware of it, but there was a study made not long ago that showed a volume of over eighty million dollars in retail trade alone just from the Martian-related business in toys, records, things like that. That's not all, believe me. Don't forget, it's from the space program that we got things like the pacemaker, the home computer, and the Teflon frying pan. So when you question whether we should raise taxes to pay for the next Mars expedition and help balance the budget, I answer that we will have so much new business resulting from this and the other great strides we're making that we won't *need* to raise taxes. I guess that'll really upset our spendthrift Congress. But that's their problem."

TWELVE

TOO MUCH LOOSESTRIFE

When Solomon Sayre heard the rebroadcast of the president's news conference, he was driving his big gray battleship of a worn-out Lincoln convertible, ancient gas-guzzler with sketchy brakes and unreliable dashboard gauges, at eighty miles an hour in a fifty-five zone. He had the radio up to full blast. He didn't care much what was playing on it. He was terrified that he might pass out behind the wheel. The news broadcast woke him up. "—The shadowy figure of the mystery man, Van Poppliner," the announcer was saying, "may provide some answers to the question of why things were allowed to go so wrong with the Seerseller expedition. Senator Breckmeister's committee interviewed Poppliner for more than five hours in executive session today, but no word has been released on his testimony—" It was too bad about the Martians, Sol Sayre thought. He had a lot of sympathy for frail, hurting creatures whose lives had been disrupted, since he was one himself. But he thought that with only one part of his brain. Most of it was concentrated on keeping him awake and alive long enough to go where he needed to go.

It was four o'clock on a hot August morning. Except for eighteen-wheel trucks, he had the highway almost to himself. He needed it that way. He knew he was wobbling all around his lane, sometimes into the next one. He knew that if a cop car saw him the cops would stop him for certain. As far as he could see, that would have only one consequence. He would die. He would not be able to live through being pulled over, asked for his papers, and held there while the cop called his license in and wrote him a ticket. And that was only the best he could hope for. The worst was a lot worse. It was at least as likely that the cop would take him in right there on a charge of driving under the influence of an unlawful substance—if only that were true! But the cop wouldn't care that it wasn't. Then it would be the police station, the holding tank, and at least six or eight cold-turkey hours before he could get out to score what he needed.

So Solomon muttered to his foot, "Slow down! Slow down!" But his foot just pressed down harder on the gas, and the miles fled by.

"—The puzzle of the living Martians remains," the radio was saying. "Scientists have long maintained that no life was possible there, and until the accidental discovery on Christmas Eve the Seerseller expedition's own explorations seemed to confirm—"

Sol slammed on his brakes. He had almost missed the turnoff from the tollway. The huge old car swayed and the weary brakes were slow to respond, but then Solomon Sayre was going up the ramp into the city streets.

A miracle! No cop had turned up. And he had only a few blocks left to go. And, best of all, as Sol approached the diner, he saw that his candy man was still there, his back to the plate-glass window, scraping burnt food off his griddle.

That did it. Everything was going to be all right! For the first time in hours, Solomon Sayre felt almost good. He did not think he was going to vomit in the next minute. The sweat under his arms and in the hair of his temples didn't go away, but it didn't seem to be getting any worse, either.

He slid into a parking space in the nearly empty lot. He leaned back and stretched, actually took the time to stretch, before he reached to turn off the ignition. "—Most recent pictures received at the Jet Propulsion Laboratories," the radio was chattering on, "show still more detailed views of these creatures, which look as much like seals as anything else in human experience. Of course, scientists say they could not really be aquatic. This would be imposs—"

Sol grinned to himself as the voice squawked to silence. He kept on grinning as he pushed through the door into the diner.

There was a young couple having a bitter whispered fight in one booth; a trucker nursed a cup of coffee in another. Neither was close enough to the counter to be a problem.

"Hey, Razor," Sayre said to the man at the counter. "You been listening about the Martians?"

The candy man didn't answer. He looked at Sayre, then at the three other people in the diner. Without being told, he drew a cup of coffee.

"What you want, bro?" he asked softly.

In the same tone, Sayre said, "You know what I want, Razor. I've got the money." And he displayed the folded ten-dollar bills before he slipped them under the saucer of his coffee cup.

Then it was only a matter of waiting while Razor went through his routine. Turned his back. Chipped at the griddle a little. Yawned and stretched and disappeared into the kitchen for a moment. Came back and wiped the counter methodically, starting at the far end from Sayre. Displayed the little cellophane packets for a quarter of a second before he covered them with a plate containing a soggy cheese Danish. Whisked Sayre's cup and saucer away for a refill. When he put them back, the money was gone.

Sayre nibbled an edge of the Danish and took a couple of sips of the second cup of coffee. That was just theater. He didn't want either, but if he departed from the ritual Razor enforced, there would be no deal next time he came around.

Sayre dropped a dollar next to the plates and stood up. The little packets were safe in his coat, and the world looked hopeful again. On the way out he paused to say, "You didn't tell me what you thought about the Martians."

The candy man looked at him without expression. Then he said, "What the hell I need Martians for? You heads is weird enough already."

When Solomon Sayre reported for work the next morning, even Professor Mariano was talking about the news stories about the Martians, agitated as she always was, angrier than usual. Sayre was still coasting gently down the high slopes of that glorious fix. It was really a nice world, and he hated to see her unhappy in it. "You shouldn't put it down, Doc," he protested. "It's exciting. I mean, *Martians*. It's like all those old movies come true, you know?"

The professor looked at him, her eyes softening. Marietta Mariano was at least thirty years older than Sayre, he guessed. Probably right up against retirement age. He didn't treat her like a scientist or a boss. He treated her the way he treated all women, regardless of age, color, marital status, or physical appearance. He spoke to her and looked at her as though they had been lovers before and probably would be again. She seemed to like it. Women generally did, even though there wasn't any follow-through anymore.

Professor Mariano shooed the volunteers off to their jobs of welcoming visitors to the nature preserve or cataloguing plants and animals so far identified. She waved Sol into her private office. "Martians or no Martians," she said, "we've still got the wood-chip trails to border and the grass to mow in the arboretum. How's your back today?"

"Fine," he said. A lie. They both knew it was a lie, since Sayre's back would never be fine again, but there was enough junk left in his bloodstream so that, at least, it didn't make him want to scream. "Do I get a cup of coffee first?"

Of course, he did. He always did. She gave him coffee out of her automatic maker every morning, even the mornings when neither his back nor any other part of him was fine at all. And, like every morning, she looked him over carefully while he was drinking it. "Do you want a muffin?" she asked. He started to say no, but she was already putting it in the toaster oven. "You didn't get enough sleep," she charged over her shoulder. "You stayed up all night, listening to that stuff about the Martians, right?"

He grinned, confessing to the false charge. He had never known whether Marietta Mariano suspected the real one. He said deceitfully, "Well, hell, Doc, a thing like that doesn't happen every day."

"It happens a lot too often," she said firmly. "It's the same situation as the water hyacinth and the purple loosestrife. How do we know what pests they'll bring back with them from Mars? Now, Sol! You know you've got to get your rest and plenty of fresh air and exercise, or you'll be right back in the hospital."

"Promise I won't," he smiled. And meant it. Because if there was one thing Solomon Sayre was sure of, it was that the Veterans Administration hospitals had had their last shot at him. There was nothing they could do for his "intractable pain" that the candy man couldn't do better, and besides he didn't have to wear those funny-looking bathrobes.

What kept Sayre alive, with just enough left over to buy Razor's goods, was his hundred percent disability. It hadn't even come from a real war. That didn't make it easier. The invasion had been a walkover, tiny, little pukey island that found itself in the way of the American bulldozer. The official description of casualties was "very light." Maybe so, if you just looked at the numbers. But the small number of dead and wounded were just as dead, and just as wounded, as any of the casualties of Shiloh or Normandy. You didn't get a hundred percent disability for nothing. And for some of the things you got it for, a hundred percent disability was nowhere near enough. The burns were bad enough. The lacerations were a lot worse. But the thing that would be ruining Sol's life as long as that life lasted was what the crash of his troop carrier had done to his spine. Six times the surgeons had tried to relieve the pressure on his vertebrae. Six times he'd come out of the whole-body cast hurting worse than ever. "Doc," he said to Mariano, reaching over to pat the hand with the tendons that lay just beneath the skin and the age spots that seemed to spread over more of it every day, "this job is just what the doctor ordered. Better than that. Working for you makes it a pleasure."

She flushed and withdrew her hand. He had been talking to her bad ear, and she hadn't caught it all, but enough had come through to embarrass her. "The county doesn't pay you to drink coffee," she said sharply. "Take the muffin along, and get the chip spreader out. See if you can neaten up the paths on the west prairie before lunch."

"Sure thing, Doc." Then, rising, he paused to ask a question. "Are you really worried about the Martians?"

She looked suddenly angry—not, Sayre saw, at him. "I'm worried about *everything*," she said. "If you had any sense, you would be, too."

One time long ago, two hundred years and more, this whole part of the state was prairie, endless grasses and streams and, rarely, a clump of woods. It was the flattest country the world had ever seen. There were no great rivers or large lakes. There was a rippling sea of grass from horizon to horizon, and that was all.

The Indians didn't harm the prairie. They set fire to it once in a while to drive the buffalo to slaughter, but it was good for the prairie to burn now and then. The buffalo themselves lived off it and fed it with their dung and, ultimately, their decaying bones; the prairie and the buffalo were made for each other, and what little the Indians did didn't upset the balance. It was not until the Europeans came that the prairie began to vanish. It was plowed under to grow corn, cemented over to build condos, paved with freeways and interstates. There was nowhere in Illinois or Indiana or Iowa with as much as a thousand-acre stretch of original prairie left.

So the professor decided to re-create some.

As a full professor and department head at the university, she had connections. She used them. She begged eighteen hundred acres from one rich and childless landowner, bargained six hundred more from a real-estate developer who needed a tax break, lobbied some condemnation proceedings from the state to join the parcels together—and wound up with the John James Audubon Nature Preserve. It wasn't prairie, but it was all, for one reason or another, almost unbuilt, two squares miles of it to turn back into wilderness.

Well, not all of it.

There was a grove of fruit trees that had to be kept bearing because the crotchety old landowner had picked them as a boy—there went twenty acres. There was an arboretum that some previous philanthropist had created and given to the state, and the state made Dr. Mariano take it on as quid for the quo of decommissioning a two-lane farm road. And there were nature trails and native trees and an old farmhouse with old crops still being farmed by disgruntled tenants who knew they were zoo animals and didn't think they were getting enough out of it—they weren't at all what the professor had had in mind. But they were what the ghetto kids who came out from the core-city schools stared at longest, and without the core-city kids, the professor couldn't have gotten the federal grants that were still not enough to pay all the bills for all the things she wanted to do.

But what she could do was a lot. Under her orders, the volunteers savagely hacked down the imported English walnuts and the mulberry trees and planted native oak and birch. The remains of old flower gardens were steamed sterile. Prairie grasses and wildflowers were seeded. Within two years, it had begun to look almost as it had centuries earlier, and that was why Dr. Marietta Mariano gave up her full professorship and her tenure, taking early retirement to come to the John James Audubon Nature Preserve.

At noon Sol Sayre came back sweated and bearing bad news. "There are two new stands of loosestrife along the creek," he reported.

She looked up from the glass-sided beehive, where she was trying to poke bubble gum out of the ventilation holes, by which he knew they'd had another class trip in that morning. "Eat your lunch," she ordered glumly. "Then I'll come out with you and look."

"I didn't bring any lunch. I'm not hungry."

"Sol, Sol! You don't take care of—All right, then we go now," she said, giving up. But when they had come out of the West Woods Trail onto the prairie, where he had left the mower, she said, "Let's ride."

For Solomon Sayre the jolting his spine took on the mower and the jolting that walking gave it were a standoff. Both hurt. He debated trying to explain that to Dr. Mariano one more time, but decided against it: If she really knew what riding the power mower felt like for him, she would make him stop. There was just room for the old lady to stand behind him as he drove up the access road, slower than a walk, with plenty of time to look around. "Trees," she said fretfully. "We should put in some trees along the north line, so when they start building their houses there, we won't have to see them." But she wasn't really fretting about possible building outside the preserve. She was gazing off toward the wet prairie, where the whole shore was now patches of scarlet-purple and the same color was beginning to line the stream they were approaching. He felt her fingers dig into his shoulder.

She didn't say anything. She hopped off the mower, slipped out of her sandals, and, barefoot, climbed down to the muddy margins of the creek. There were twenty plants in the stand, and they hadn't been there a few weeks earlier. They were rather pretty, actually, Sol thought, chest high, with green stems and narrow leaves, and the reddish purple flowers ascending in the upper parts like a torch.

Professor Mariano snapped off one of the stalks and pulled a blossom apart. "Purple loosestrife," she acknowledged gloomily. "*Lythrum salicaria*. Good for nothing. Nobody eats it, and it drives other things out. Give me a hand."

Sol helped her up the bank. "I've seen bees visiting it for nectar," he said. "Butterflies, too."

"It will probably make them sick. And it doesn't *belong* here, Sol. It's an alien. Comes all the way from Asia somewhere."

"I could spray it," he offered.

"No!" Then, more temperately: "We don't want to use chemical herbicides in the preserve; you know that. Maybe I should get the volunteers to cut some of it out—but it'll just come back."

She perched on the edge of the riding-mower seat and shook her head. "You see why I'm not happy about the Martians? It's the same story all over the world. People bring in plants or fish or insects. They get to a place where they have no natural enemies, and so they become the enemy of everything that belongs there! Like the Hawaiian islands—"

Sol leaned patiently on the hood of the mower to listen to the familiar lecture. The water hyacinth in Florida. The rabbits in Australia. "And that rusty crayfish, *Orconectes rusticus*, you know what it's done in Wisconsin? You can't even swim in some of the lakes because it nips anything that moves; it eats everything, and then the lakes are dead. The elm trees in England, the American chestnut, the starlings in America—the African killer bees, the fire ants—"

"Don't get so excited, Doc," Solomon coaxed.

She put her hand on his shoulder. At first he thought it was a gesture of affection, but there was a lot of weight behind it. The whiteness of her face told him how close she was to exhaustion. Alarmed, he said, "Should I take you back to the cabin?"

"You might as well," she said, and sat silently for most of the rattly ride back along the access road. He didn't stop at the woods trail but continued around the loop to join with the main driveway. She didn't stop him.

When they were in the parking lot, the color had begun to return to her face. At the cabin steps she shook off his hand. "I'm all right now," she said. "How about you?"

"Oh, I'm fine, Doc," he grinned.

"Liar," she sighed. "But you might as well go back to work." She looked him up and down. "You're a good kid, Sol. I wish you could get a real job."

"I'm fine here, Dr. Mariano."

She nodded, not agreeing, but only showing that she had known he would say that. "I wish you'd meet some nice young women, though. You need a girlfriend, not some old bat like me."

He kept a smile on his face, though it wasn't easy. "I can take care of that when I want to," he said.

It was a partial truth. He could take care of the need, all right, because he didn't seem to have that need anymore. He had a different need, and a lot worse.

* * *

When Sayre had been called in to the final conference at the VA hospital, the Army doctors gave him the news straight. It was as though someone had written THE END across the story of his life.

It wasn't just his back. That was only painful. It was the other thing that made it impossible to see, anywhere in the future, anything that made life worth the trouble of living. "You've had," said the resident surgeon, "what we call a traumatic orchidectomy. It doesn't have anything to do with orchids, though." The man was apparently trying to work in some humor. "That means—"

"It means my balls were knocked off," said Sayre, nodding to show he understood. "I already know that. But isn't there some kind of implant, or hormones, or—"

The doctor was shaking his head. "Not in your case," he said regretfully. "You still do have some residual testicular tissue. It's enough for a certain amount of function. You could even father a child, perhaps."

"Oh, sure, *perhaps*," said Sayre. While he was still hoping desperately for a transplant that would put back what would never grow there again, he had been told just what he and any prospective mother would have to do in order for him to father a child. He could not imagine doing that.

"Anyway," said Dr. Hasti consolingly, "I'm afraid that, with your back the way it is, any normal sexual intercourse would be inordinately painful."

"Yeah," said Sayre, knowing that that was true enough because it already was inordinately painful. Only morphine made it bearable.

"In any case," Dr. Hasti said, "the other parts of the prognosis are not very good."

"I've been told," Sayre said.

"Yes. So you know that, although we could prescribe testosterone or some other steroids—"

"Yes, they'd probably kill me with cancer." Sayre was tiring of the conversation. What he wanted was to go off where no one could see his face and think about what the rest of his life would be like. "So

I've got this restricted regimen. No weight lifting. I'm going to have all kinds of glandular malfunctions. I'll probably faint if I try hard physical labor. My heart's going to need watching. I'll probably never be able to hold a full-time job."

"Oh, that's not *absolutely* certain."

"Sure it is, because nobody's going to hire me with the odds the way they are."

The doctor frowned. "You really should try not to be so negative, Corporal. You'd probably benefit from psychotherapy . . . maybe a few sessions with an analyst. . . ."

"I'll think about it," said Sayre, standing up. He was a corporal and the doctor a major, but he just turned his back and walked out. What could they do to him now? He went back to the ward. The next day he finished his separation papers, put on his civilian clothes, and limped out of the hospital into a very empty civilian life.

The one thing he did not have to worry about was money, he thought. He had his total disability pension, he had eighty dollars a month from an almost forgotten college insurance policy, and he had more than two thousand dollars in back pay in the bank.

And he had the pain.

Idle days and chronic pain added up to something new. Within the first few months, he had acquired something that changed his life in many ways: a habit.

One of the things *that* changed was that before very long he did have to begin to worry about money again, a lot.

The job at the nature preserve didn't pay much, but every little bit helped to come up with the money the candy man took. Also it helped to fill the days. Also Dr. Mariano was the best boss in the world to have.

The damaged veteran and the old professor got along extraordinarily well, though the differences between them were polar. Sayre was young. Mariano was past sixty. Sayre had quit college to go into the service. Mariano had three doctorates. Mariano was nearly blind in one eye and totally deaf in one ear. If you spoke to her from the wrong side, she would peer around with the good left eye for a bit, trying to figure out where the sounds were coming from, long before she decided that the sounds were a voice and the voice carried meaning that would perhaps repay the effort of deciphering it. Sayre, on the other hand, had 20/20 vision. He also had the hearing of a bat and a nose that could detect a woman's perfume half a block away. That was one of his problems. He was constantly being made aware of what he couldn't have. If he had needed an extra reason for seeking the pleasures of the needle, that would have been it. He didn't need extra reasons. He had two big ones.

First, there was the unremitting back pain that heroin would, for a while, chase away.

And then, after he had been on the heroin for a while, there was that considerably worse pain that came when he failed to score on time, and so might have to go a day too long without any.

That was not precisely pain. It was nastier than pain. It was misery. It was hurtful and obsessive; it involved vomiting and sweating and coughing. Most of all it involved the sure knowledge that if he could just score, it would be only a moment until he was well and happy again.

And then not very much longer until the pain crept back, and the shakes, and the terrible, burning, desperate *need*.

In the summertime the John James Audubon Nature Preserve didn't close until sundown. That was well after eight o'clock, but it was rare for any visitor to come after seven. It was rare for Professor Mariano to come back to the cabin after her quick and lonesome dinner, too, but when she did, she found Solomon Sayre with his chin propped in his hands at her desk, staring fixedly into the portable black-and-white TV she kept for weather warnings and the occasional major news event. "You're not being paid for overtime, Sol," she scolded fondly. "Go home. Let the volunteers close up."

He said absently, "Lucy's son has a temperature, so I told her I'd take care of it. I'm watching a special on the Martians."

"Martians," she sniffed and turned away. She rummaged through the library shelves for the *Native Taxa of the North American Plains*, hoping that volume six would identify which variant of Queen Anne's lace, *Daucus carota*, she had found in the parking lot of the Burger King where she had had her dinner.

"Everybody says they look like seals," said Sol Sayre from behind her. "I think they're more like that Australian thing, the platypus."

"*Ornithorhynchus anatinus*," Marietta Mariano said automatically. "No, not really, Sol. They don't have that duck bill, or webbed feet— well, they wouldn't have, would they, on Mars?" But she abandoned the search for the book to come over and stand behind him. She was looking less at the television screen than at her assistant. She didn't like the way he sounded: absentminded, edgy, depressed. He looked more than ever as though he hadn't had enough sleep. There were circles under his eyes, the pain lines deeper on his young face. She hoped he wasn't going to go through another of those bad times when, she guessed, the pain of his injuries flared up, or maybe just the realization of how bad they were came over him. She wanted to pat his shoulder. Instead, she said, "How much longer before those Martians get here?"

"Oh, a long time yet, I guess," Sayre said dreamily. "Another one died last night."

"Another Martian? That leaves, what, about five?"

"No, no. Another one of the crew died. A lot of them are pretty sick, you know."

Professor Mariano nodded. There had been all too much worry about the problems of the Martians and the astronauts, she thought, and not nearly enough about the problems of the Earth. "Oh," he said, "and the bees' vents were stuck up again. I cleared them out. I think it was a Hershey bar this time."

"Kids," she said, turning to look at the glass-walled, slab-sided hive across the room, where the insects crawled all over each other endlessly. "Serve us all right," she said, "if they interbreed with the African bees and sting us all to death—Sol! What's that?"

She had just noticed the potted, scarlet-bloomed plant by the window that had not been there a few hours before.

"Oh," Sayre said without turning, "I brought in a loosestrife specimen. I thought if I studied it, I could find something it was good for."

"You've been keeping yourself busy, haven't you? But it would be better," she said bitterly, "if you'd find a good way to kill it. It just doesn't belong here." She sighed, and mused. "Wouldn't it be wonderful if the kids would suddenly decide they could get high smoking it? Sneak in at night, and cut it all down? Get the Feds to spray it with paraquat or something, all over the country?" She laughed, pleased to have found something to cheer Sol up with . . . less pleased, a lot less pleased, when she saw that he wasn't smiling.

There weren't many smiles in Solomon Sayre just then, as he had a problem unsolved. Since he could not see a way to solve it, he tried to forget it. He kept himself busy with things that weren't his job or didn't need doing; when that didn't work, he plumped himself down before the television set and tried to let the Martians take his mind off his problem. He watched the film clips and the panel of experts—Carl Sagan and Ray Bradbury and some Russian whose name he didn't catch, speaking by satellite. He didn't always hear what they were saying, but he kept on watching. He watched even when the Martians were long gone and the station picked up the baseball game of the week in its fourth inning, with the Mariners leading Chicago five to nothing.

Baseball was not the answer to his problem. The problem was that the Lincoln's brakes had finally gone out altogether, and fixing them had taken his dope money. He had three dollars and forty cents in his pocket, and his next check was not due for two days.

Two days was an impossible length of time to wait.

Sol couldn't force himself to sit still any longer. Three dollars wasn't enough to score. It was just about gas money to get to his pusher. Sol wasn't even sure that he trusted himself to drive all the way into the city, the way he was feeling. But if he did, he thought, maybe Razor would just this once be reasonable.

He needed to get himself calmed down. . . .

Well, of course, that had just been a joke of the professor's, he told himself. All the same, he began stripping the leaves off the scarlet-flowered weed. He put them into the toaster oven Professor Mariano kept for heating up her hot dogs for lunch; when they began to smell toasted, he crumbled them into his hash pipe.

They did burn, at least. That was all. They tasted terrible and made him cough raspingly. When the pipeful was gone, his throat felt as though he had swallowed barbed wire, and of any sort of high, there was no sign at all—and the problem remained.

Sol had never, ever stolen anything from the nature preserve. It was his source of pride: He had never stolen at all for his habit, and never intended to.

Still, if he borrowed something and paid it back before anyone noticed it was gone. . . . And there was, he knew, a petty-cash box in the bottom drawer of Professor Mariano's desk.

It was locked. Patiently, Sol poked into the lock with a paper clip. It wouldn't open. Not that way, at least; when at last he forsook subtlety and stealth in favor of prying it open with a screwdriver, what was in it was twelve pennies, a Kennedy half-dollar, and an I.O.U. in the professor's handwriting for twenty-five dollars.

So there was no solution there.

There was no solution anywhere that Solomon Sayre could see. If there was even a hope, it lay in the compassion and human decency of a dealer in drugs.

Sol drove with great care in the heavy traffic, late commuters coming out of the city, suburbanites heading in for a night on the town. He took the long way, for he had no extra change for tolls, and his body was beginning to shake.

Fate was kind to him. There was no one in the diner but Razor, hunched over a cup of cold coffee at the end of the counter.

Razor was less kind.

"No credit, man," he said, not even looking up from the coffee.

"But I'm a good customer, man. You know I'm good for the money. The day after tomorrow—"

"Day after tomorrow you can come see me if you wants to," said Razor to the coffee cup.

"I can't wait till then," Sol explained. He was being very reasonable about the thing, he was sure, if only the dealer would see it. "Understand, man? The thing is, I can't make it till the day after tomorrow, you know? I'll just fall apart."

Razor looked at him at last. "Go get you some bread," he advised.

"Ah, no," Sol pleaded. "If I try mugging somebody or anything like that, they'll get me, sure. I'll be cold turkey in jail, you know? I'll die! I'll— I don't know what I'd do," he said desperately. "But what's going to happen if I just can't keep my mouth shut? I mean, like if they offer me a deal—"

The counterman stood up. He looked swiftly through the window at the empty parking lot. "What you sayin'?" he demanded softly. "You turn me in?"

"I didn't say that! I don't want to make any trouble, but—*please*," he said abjectly. "Look, I'll pay double. I swear I will."

The candy man studied him appraisingly. "Let's see that watch you got on," he said at last.

Sol could not force himself to drive all the way back to his room. He turned the Lincoln in at the nature preserve driveway, ran to unlock the gate, drove through without bothering to relock it behind him. In the cabin he switched on all the lights and flung the restroom door open. He rolled up his shirt and wrapped his arm in rubber tubing. The veins stood out like the ones on Professor Mariano's hands.

He had trouble finding a clear spot, but when the rush came, he slumped down beside the toilet bowl to welcome it.

All the colors of the world had changed around him. The stark little washroom was warm and loving; even the pink plastic toilet seat was a prettier shade than he remembered. Even his back didn't hurt anymore—oh, sure, he corrected himself, smiling, it *hurt*, but the pain certainly wasn't anything you could call *bad*. He sat there for some time, letting the warm numbness seep through him. Then he got up and walked, stiltlike, into the nature preserve office.

He caught a glimpse of the old Lincoln outside with the lights still on, and grinned; if he left it that way, he'd have a dead battery when he got in. It was also amusing that he had left his works in the washroom, where the first person to come in the next morning would find them. He reminded himself to take care of those details pretty soon. He laughed out loud, or thought he did, when he passed the poor bald loosestrife in the pot next to the beehive. Stripped the leaves off to smoke! What a dumb thing to do!

Then he stopped smiling. There was something new and very wrong.

The red-purple blossoms that climbed the stalk hadn't changed. The lowest part of the stem was still bare. But just under the flowers, something different had appeared. It was a tangle of green, lush and dense, almost like a bird's nest or a woven basket. And he could see, inside it, faintly writhing, something that had not been there before.

It was alive. It had the head of a rat, the slim, supple body of a weasel, the spindly legs of a newborn racehorse.

"A Martian," Sayre whispered, blinking. The professor had been right. He scrabbled through the litter on her desk until he found a pair of shears. He fell on the plant, hacking it off at the roots. He could feel the tiny thing writhing in its nest as, shuddering, he bore it to the toaster oven. Grinning like a berserker, he crammed it inside and set the control to BROIL. Fire would kill it! As it seared and popped inside, he could see the creature dashing itself against the smoky glass of the door.

Solomon Sayre, panting, took thought. If there was one, there might be more. He leaped to the window.

Sure enough, there was a whole new stand of purple loosestrife along the algae-green pond, just yards away—near enough so that he could see that each of them, too, had a swelling below the blossoms, swellings that pulsed like the belly of a pregnant woman.

Fire would kill them, too.

The only problem was technical, and he solved it at once. A flame thrower. What could he improvise to do the job? Inspired, godlike in his power, Sol dumped liquid fertilizer out of the sprayer, filled it with kerosene, plunged out into the night. He pumped the pressure high, ignited the spray with his cigarette lighter, hosed flame at the stand of vegetation.

It crisped and smoldered. He could hear the tiny infant Martians shricking their despairing fury as he torched them. When they were cinders, he hurried back into the cabin, certain of what he must do next. The world must be warned!

Professor Mariano had come in while he was outside, sitting at her desk, gazing at him with love and admiration. "I want a conference call," he snapped. "I want the heads of the Fish and Wildlife Service in every state—right away! Yes, and you'd better get the White House in on it, too!"

"Right away, Sol," she whispered, picking up the phone. He sat down, calm and confident, regarding her while she dialed. "You look wonderful," she said, and blushed as she began to speak into the phone. She looked wonderful, too, he saw, and he could not remember why he had ever thought she was really old. She had loosened her hair and put on a white dress with a red sash. The age lines were gone from her pretty, tender face.

"They're ready, Sol," she said, handing him the phone.

He knew exactly what to say. "This is a nationwide alert," he said. "Exotic species have been taken over by the Martians. The only defense is to burn them at once. All of them! All of the introduced species—water hyacinth, exotic birds and insects, anything that doesn't belong where it is. Burn them! There's no time to delay; start organizing flame-thrower crews at once!" He didn't ask if there were any questions. He didn't need to. These were resourceful, well-trained people. They understood at once, and there was no discussion. "At once," they said. Or: "Right, Mr. Sayre!" He could hear them all hanging up, click, click, clickety.

Then he heard one final voice: "Mr. Sayre, I won't keep you, but this is the President. I just wanted to say I think you're doing one heck of a job."

"Thank you, Mr. President," Sayre said, deeply moved.

"Oh, Sol," whispered Marietta Mariano, lifting her lips to his. "You've saved us all."

But even as he reached out for her, he stopped. Something was wrong. He could hear it.

Yes! The bees! The buzzing in the glass high-rise held a new and ominous note. He gave the woman a reckless grin. "Hold that thought," he called as he turned and leaped to the hive.

There was no doubt of it: The bees were turning into Martians, too.

He could see them, tiny little stilt-legged rat-things among the crawling, seething insect mass. Sol laughed out loud. For this he wouldn't even need fire; he clenched his fist and, with one sharp blow, shattered the glass. Furious insects flew out in all directions. More stayed inside, buzzing ominously, dangerously, as he reached in. He scooped the tiny bodies out by the handful, tossing them into the air regardless of stings. The important thing was to get at the tiny newborn Martians. They writhed away, but they could not escape. One by one he caught them between thumb and forefinger . . . and squeezed, *pop*.

When the last horror was dead, he wiped his fingers on the edge of the table and turned, smiling, to Marietta Mariano.

Her blue eyes were brimming with tears. "My poor darling," she whispered. "They've stung you a million times."

Godlike and triumphant, he reached out for her. He could see the angry red spots covering his arms, but he felt no pain at all. . . .

Not then, and not ever again.

When the first volunteer arrived to open the cabin the next morning, the first thing he noticed was that someone had been burning trash against the side of the building. There were scorch marks. The second thing was that the inside of the cabin was full of buzzing bees.

The third thing he saw was the body of Solomon Sayre.

By the time Professor Mariano arrived, the old face aged worse than ever with bitter weeping on the way, the police had been there, and the coroner. "It wasn't the bee stings, ma'am," said the policeman. "The medical examiner says they might have killed him, but he was already dead. Heroin. An overdose."

"Heroin!" Professor Mariano gasped. "Oh, my God! What a terrible accident."

The policeman shook his head. "The M.E.'s calling it homicide, ma'am. It was the pure stuff. Somebody didn't like him, so they gave him uncut, and he ODed on it." He hesitated, then. "Look at his face, though, ma'am? He's still smiling. It killed him, all right, but you can see he really was feeling fine when he died."

THIRTEEN

"OPRAH WINFREY"

WINFREY: The folks we have with us this morning are going to talk about the Martians. Now, I know all you people have been hearing about the Martians every minute since Christmas, but I think we've got some people here who can tell us about them from different points of view.

Starting on my far right there's Marchese Boccanegra—I hope I said that right, Marchese!—who's the author of *Ultimate Truth: The Amazing Riddle Behind the "Saucer" Flaps* and has been making all the headlines with his claims that the Martians have been many times before to the Earth. Next is Bill Wexler, who is president of the L-5 Society of Terre Haute, Indiana, and a former consultant on the Space Shuttle program, followed by The Amazing Randi, the famous stage magician who has devoted himself to exposing the people he calls frauds and charlatans. On my left is the celebrated scientist, Carl Sagan, and finally, Anthony Makepeace Moore, from his Eudorpan Astral Retreat.

I'm glad to see you all here today.

MOORE: I'm not glad, Miss Winfrey. You didn't tell me these other people were going to be on the program or I wouldn't have agreed to come.

SAGAN: I'm not thrilled to be with you, either, Mr. Moore. I must begin by stating that I believe the nonsensical claptrap of people like yourself does great harm to the scientific investigation of space.

RANDI: Why are you being so generous, Carl? It's worse than nonsense. It's plain, outright fraud.

WINFREY: Come on, gentlemen. I brought you all together because, one way or another, you all have a special interest in the Martians. I know you don't agree. That's why I asked you all. But the audience has a right to hear from each of you—starting with, I think, the least controversial of you, Bill Wexler. Bill, how do the Martians affect your movement to build L-5 habitats in space?

WEXLER: They're just one more proof that life can survive and flourish off our own planet. We in the habitat program have known that for years, ever since Dr. O'Neill, at Princeton, made the first detailed survey of the requirements for building a huge, self-sufficient home for human beings in orbit. Of course, the practical advantages are obvious. Solar-powered satellites, microwaving cheap electrical energy down to light our houses and run our industries on Earth, without pollution or fear of nuclear accidents. Space manufacturing on a vast scale. Relief from the overcrowded conditions of our cities —space gives us nearly infinite room to grow. A safe place for human beings to thrive even if nuclear war should—

WINFREY: Actually, what we're interested in this morning is the Martians.

WEXLER: I'm coming to that. Once you have L-5 habitats in space around the Earth, all you need to do is put motors on them and then you can go anywhere. If we had got started in 1965, when Professor O'Neill first conceived his plan, we'd have had some in orbit around Mars long ago. We'd have discovered these Martians long since. By now we would have known all about them, including whatever scientific knowledge they have to add to our own—

BOCCANEGRA: They don't have any. They haven't reached the theta level of consciousness.

WEXLER: I don't know anything about any theta level, but we should start now. We could have a habitat around Mars in eight years! With frequent shuttle landings to study everything there—and then Venus, Mercury, the Moons of Jupiter—

MOORE: Don't waste your time with Venus. It's dead. The Eudorpan masters reluctantly had to terminate its inhabitants eleven thousand years ago, because of the evil, materialistic direction their false science had taken.

RANDI: Oh, come on! Oprah, do we have to sit still for this?

BOCCANEGRA: Hear the voice of the professional skeptic! None are so blind as those who will not see! But truth will out. Mr. Randi, you know that Anthony Makepeace Moore and I have had strong disagreements in the past—

RANDI: Sure you did. You were cutting in on each other's flimflams.

BOCCANEGRA: That remark is below contempt. Hear me out, please. I want to take this opportunity to publicly acknowledge that Master Moore has helped us to see a truth so earthshaking and revelatory that this is a turning point in the affairs of the human spirit—and I have just found objective proof of his statements!

MOORE: I thank you for what you say, Dr. Boccanegra, though I must say I'm a bit surprised. I wasn't aware that you had become a student of Eudorpan enlightenment. What proofs do you mean?

SAGAN: Yes, let's hear it. I haven't had a good laugh in weeks.

BOCCANEGRA: You have all learned, I suppose, that by using his Eudorpan techniques of astral projection, Master Moore has achieved contact with the Old Minds of the previous Martian race—

RANDI: No, tell us about it. I haven't seen the *National Enquirer* this morning.

WINFREY: Wait a minute, Marchese. Are you telling me those dumb things have *minds*?

BOCCANEGRA: No, no, not those pitiful remnants the Seerseller expedition found. They are degenerate animals. I am talking about the *original* beings that inhabited not only Mars but our Moon, the Jovian moon Callisto, and even our own planet—

MOORE: Excuse me, Marchese. Are you confusing the Eudorpan Masters with these original beings?

BOCCANEGRA: Not at all, Master Moore. That is the wonderful news I have for you. By analysis at the theta level of reality I was able to locate one of the very Harmonic Centers used by these advanced beings during their sojourn on our own planet. It is on the banks of what we call the Mississippi River, although in their notation it was called the Ur-Papagat. They left a pictorial record, which I have seen with my own eyes.

MOORE: This is amazing, Marchese!

RANDI: This is crap, Marchese—excuse the expression, Oprah. What are you going to do now, sell tickets?

BOCCANEGRA: Certainly not. I am going to ask Master Moore to join me in a scientific investigation of these astonishing proofs of his theories—

MOORE: Of course I will, Marchese!

BOCCANEGRA:—as soon as we have arranged the financing for the necessary instruments to measure the electromagnetic, optical, and Kirlian properties of the relics.

RANDI: Oh, I get it. You're going to make a pitch for contributions for the "investigation," right?

WINFREY: Gentlemen, gentlemen! You'll all have a chance to speak, and maybe we should start taking questions from the audience—right after these messages.

FOURTEEN

IRIADESKA'S MARTIANS

Charlie Sanford had anticipated all along that he would be in strange places, doing strange things, because that was what public relations was like. But he hadn't expected to find himself in a narrow-bottomed boat with an outboard motor three sizes too big for it, roaring along a sludgy river in Southeast Asia, "inspecting" a plantation belonging to the Iriadeskan Army outside the capital city of Pnik. It was very hot. The fact that the Iriadeskans said it was 25 degrees did not alter the fact that it felt like pushing 90 in good old Fahrenheit, and soggy damp besides.

"Soon now!" yelled Major Doolathata in his ear, grinning encouragingly.

Sanford nodded, holding onto the windscreen as the driver swerved to cut through a floating green mat of water hyacinth. There was a Mindy Mars doll hanging from the windscreen, its plush fur as soaked with spray as Sanford himself. He had been surprised to see it there. The line had been introduced at the Toy Fair just a few months before. It wasn't even in the stores yet. So how had it reached this

Godforsaken part of the world so soon? And why did jolly Major Doolathata wink and glance meaningfully at it every time Sanford caught his eye?

"What I don't understand," Sanford shouted over the roar of the motor, "is why we're poking around out here when I'm supposed to get back to Pnik for my meeting?" He had arrived at the Pnik airport only at five that morning, thoroughly spaced out from the long plane ride with stops in Hawaii, Manila, and Singapore. Jet lag was not easy for Sanford, who hadn't really had much experience of long-distance travel. The flight had not only been interminable, twenty-seven hours of interminable, it had crossed ten time zones and the International Date Line. Sanford could not keep straight in his mind what day it was.

Major Doolathata thumped the boatman, who instantly cut the motor to a purr; Major Doolathata didn't like to have to raise his voice. "General Phenoboomgarat wishes you to do this," he explained. As he had before; and that was all the explanation, it seemed, that Sanford was going to get.

Sanford closed his eyes as the boat picked up speed again. It was better if he didn't look, anyway, because the boatman's driving made him very nervous. It would have been better still if, when this whole idea came up, he had simply said to the Old Man, "Sorry, Chief, but I don't know a thing about Iriadeska, and besides I'm right in the middle of the Fall promotion for the Pickle and Relish Packers Association"—that is, it would have been better in some respects, though it would very likely have meant that he would now be out of a job. And there weren't that many forty-thousand-dollar-a-year jobs for young public-relations executives just three years out of NYU.

"Charles," the Old Man had said benignly, "this is one of those once-in-a-lifetime chances. Grab it, boy! It's a big one for the agency, because it's our first real opportunity to go global. And it's a big one for you, because one of these days we're going to have an International Division, and who's going to be in front of you in the line to head it if you lick this one?"

That was big talk from the head of a seven-person agency, whose biggest previous accounts had been a fading screen star, a toy manufacturer, and the Pickle and Relish Packers Association. But it could happen! Midgets had become titans overnight in the PR field before, and the flunkies they employed had been suddenly carried to dizzying heights.

So Sanford had packed his bag and hopped his plane, and even gone along, bright-eyed and alert after no more than a few winks of sleep, to take this "orientation tour" of the manifold aspects of the institution he was, presumably, supposed to make lovable, namely the Iriadeskan Army.

It had been quite a surprise to discover what the Iriadeskan Army was like. It wasn't just an army. It was practially a conglomerate. Like any immense corporation, it had diversified. It wasn't just a fighting force—in fact, there was no good reason to believe it was any kind of a fighting force at all, because Iriadeska had never been in a war. It did possess tanks and cannons. But it was also the proprietor of a whole Fortune 400 string of business enterprises, plantations like the one he was sailing through, newspapers, radio and television broadcasting stations—even its own First, Second, and Third Military Bank and Trust Companies, all of them getting rich on American offshore deposits that would positively never be reported to any enforcement agency of the United States or anyone else with an urge to tax. The banks and the media companies had particularly interested the Old Man. "Let them know, Charles," he instructed, "that we control the advertising budgets for many of our clients, besides we give them financial advice on investments. Say, for instance, the pickle people ever decide to expand into Southeast Asia. There's no doubt they'd be spending a big buck on radio and TV and space—and why not on the Iriadeskan Army media?"

Of course, the Old Man's agency didn't really "control" much of anything. The shop lived on crumbs the big boys didn't bother to pick up. But no one in Iriadeska was likely to know that. Especially not that particular Iriadeskan who had walked in the door with this account, the military attaché of the Iriadeskan mission to the United

Nations. Sanford was quite certain that if the man had had that much smarts he would hardly have picked the Old Man's agency in the first place.

Sanford hadn't had much of a chance to spread the Old Man's gospel. He hadn't yet met anybody important enough to lie to. Major Doolathata had come to claim him at the airport, and ever since then Sanford had been exploring the rubber, sugar, and cocoa plantation the Iriadeskan Army called Camp Thungoratakma. He had watched a hundred tiny, wiry Iriadeskans in loincloths and rubber sandals slashing away at acre after acre of sugar cane, and hundreds more making their swift, spiral cuts in the extensively scarred trunks of the rubber trees, to catch the milky ooze that would ultimately be converted into automobile tires, hot-water bottles, and condoms for the world. He had putt-putted along miles of those smelly creeks, wincing as the boatman sliced through the tangles of weed and swatting at the swarms of insects, feeling the spot at the top of his head where the hair was just a tiny bit thin get hotter and redder every minute. He had—

"What?" he asked, startled. The boatman had cut the motor and Major Doolathata was speaking to him.

"I said," giggled the major, "there is one of our Martians."

Ahead of them, in the middle of a mat of water hyacinths, a broad, stupid head was gazing placidly at them. "What the hell is *that*?" Sanford demanded.

"It is what we call a chupri," the major announced. "It is called elsewhere manatee or dugong. It is said that the chupri is the original of the mermaid myth, although I do not personally think they closely resemble beautiful women, do you?"

He giggled again as Sanford shook his head, and added slyly, "Perhaps what they most closely resemble is something you are quite familiar with, Mr. Sanford."

"And what would that be?" Sanford asked absently, staring at the creature. The head, wide as a cow's, whiskered like a cat's, turned away from them and resumed munching the weeds. It certainly did not look like a mermaid. It was even uglier than a sea elephant, and less graceful. It was a lump of water-borne blubber the size of a compact car.

The major was carefully unlocking his shiny pigskin attaché case to pull out a limp, worn copy of *Advertising Age*. "You of course remember this, Mr. Sanford," he said pleasantly.

Mr. Sanford of course did. It wasn't something he would forget. It was the very first time in his life that his picture had made the front page of anything. To be sure, the little snapshot wasn't just him; his was a single face in a group photo of the agency's entire staff, posed at the Toy Fair where they introduced Mindy Mars and the rest of the line. The caption said, *Executives launch Mars spinoffs*, and it was true enough—even the word *executives*, because every employee of the agency was an executive, or at least had the title of Director of Something-or-Other or Project Manager for This-or-That—all but Christie, the receptionist, and she was just too pretty to be left out of the picture.

"Yes, that was the Toy Fair," Sanford said, remembering. They had all worked feverishly to get the Martian doll line ready for it; if you didn't exhibit at the Toy Fair you didn't get anything in the stores for Christmas. So they had all been co-opted, even Sanford, though it hadn't been his account. He was the one who stood over the artists while they airbrushed the immense blowup of a NASA photograph of a Martian that was the backdrop for the booth, with the rack of Mindy Mars and Max Mars dolls before them.

The major gave him another unfathomable wink and carefully put the paper away again. "We will say nothing more of this now," he warned. "Now we must hurry back to your appointment in Pnik."

At once the boatman jazzed up the outboard motor and though Sanford immediately asked what the sudden hurry was, the major only shrugged and winked again. Sanford craned his neck to stare after the dugong as the boat circled around and began its return dash. Something was stirring in his mind. What had it been, the major's incomprehensibly irrelevant remark about—

It clicked. He leaned over to the major and yelled, "It *does* look like a Martian!" And the major beamed, and then frowned warningly, shaking his head.

Baffled, Sanford watched the creature out of sight. Yes. Add the stiltlike legs that had been so much trouble to work into Mindy and Max (not too stiff! Children could poke their eyes out. But stiff enough to hold the damn thing) . . . add a few changes in the facial features, especially the eyes . . . yes, it did look like the Martians, a little bit.

And what possible difference did that make to anybody?

When they reached the dock he sprang ashore, looking around. There was nothing to see; no one was there to meet them. Major Doolathata erupted into a storm of furious, high-pitched Iriadeskan that sent the boatman off on an agitated run to the parking lot behind the palm trees. "The car will be here in a moment," he apologized. "These people! One simply can't depend on them."

"Yeah," Sanford said absently. He had a new puzzle. At the larger freight-loading pier a few yards downstream a boatload of farm workers was disembarking. As they stepped ashore in their loincloths each one marched past a long table heaped with articles of apparel. *Uniform* apparel. Each little man picked up in turn blouse, shorts, steel helmet, and boots, putting them on as he progressed, so that the farm workers at the river end of the table had metamorphosed by the time they reached its far end into active-duty soldiers of the Iriadeskan Army. They filed away through the trees toward dimly visible buses; and, although Sanford could not see clearly, it appeared that as each one boarded a bus he was issued an ugly little rapid-fire carbine.

The major was watching Sanford watch the men. "You see it," said Major Doolathata proudly. "Very tough troops, these men. It is an honor to command them."

Sanford offered, "I thought they were farm workers."

The major giggled. "Farm workers of course, surely. Also combat troops, for who would be better than soldiers to work in the fields of the Iriadeskan Army?"

Sanford smiled. It took some work, but he was making the effort, however irritating Major Doolathata was, to keep on good terms with the man. "And now, I suppose, they're going somewhere to practice close-order drill or something like that?"

"Something like that," Major Doolathata agreed. "Ah, here is your car. In just a short time now we will have you in Pnik for your meeting with General Phenoboomgarat."

It did not, however, work out that way.

When they reached the Fourth Armored Army's headquarters a female officer with colonel's insignia came out and engaged in a long, feverish conversation in Iriadeskan with the major. Then the major, looking angry, strode away, and the colonel turned to Sanford. "General Phenoboomgarat has been called away on urgent business," she explained in perfect, idiomatic American English. "I will take you to your hotel, where you can rest and enjoy an excellent lunch until you are called for."

One had to get used to Iriadeskan ways, Sanford thought with resignation. Anyway, a rest sounded good. Lunch sounded even better, because Sanford hadn't had time for breakfast and his befuddled metabolism was assuring him that, whatever number of clock hours or days had or had not elapsed, it was well time to eat again. "What's your name?" he asked as the car turned toward the riverfront.

"I don't think you could pronounce my name, Mr. Sanford," said the girl, "but you can call me Emily. Tell me. How are things in America? What's the new music? Are there any good new films?"

Neither of those were subjects Sanford had expected to come up in Iriadeska, but the colonel's face under the uniform cap was pretty, and putting on a military tunic had not kept her from adding to it with, Sanford's nose informed him, a charming hint of Chanel. Inside the car she seemed far less an alien military officer and far more an attractive young woman. Sanford did his best to tell her about the Madison Square Garden concert he had attended the month before, and what the reviewers said about the latest batch from Hollywood; and they were at the hotel before he was ready for it.

At the registration desk she was all officer again, firm with the clerk, peremptory with the head waiter of the hotel restaurant—all of it in

Iriadeskan, of course. Then she said to Sanford, "I will leave you here to enjoy your meal. All of your expenses will, of course, be met by the Iriadeskan Army, so do not allow them to ask you for any money. Not even tips! Especially not tips, because Americans always tip too much and then these people get sullen when they must serve an Iriadeskan."

"I would enjoy my meal more if you could keep me company," Sanford suggested; and when she smiled and shook her head, pressed a little harder: "I have so many questions about my responsibilities here—"

"Such as?"

"Well, there's this business about the Martians. I wondered—"

But she was suddenly stern. "Please be careful of your conversation here in the hotel! Everything will be explained, Mr. Sanford. Now I must return to my duties."

Sanford sighed and watched her leave, then allowed the head waiter to seat him.

The hotel dining room was vast, marbled, draped, and nearly empty. Sanford puzzled despairingly over the mimeographed menu for several minutes, trying to assess what might be edible among dishes like "twice-cooked fiathia with seven-moons rice" and "cinnamon perch, crayfish sauce." Then an altercation among the idling knot of waiters at the far end of the room at last produced a handsome menu the size of a newspaper page, in English and French.

It didn't end there, though. The waiter shook his head over Sanford's request for the breast of duck with Madagascar pepper sauce; no duck today, he indicated. Also no lamb cutlets with honey-flavored lamb gravy, also no poached filet of Iriadeskan mountain trout. When Sanford finally put his finger on the club sandwich à la Americain the waiter beamed in congratulation; the foreigner had at last struck on a winning choice.

Sanford had the good sense to order tea instead of coffee to go with the meal. The tea arrived in a pewter mug with the Lipton's tag hanging over the side; that, at least, was a known quantity. The club sandwich was less encouraging. One layer seemed to be a sort of egg salad, with unidentified red and brown things chopped into it. The other was meat on a bed of lettuce, but what the meat had been when alive Sanford could not determine.

Still, it was chewable, and not obviously decayed. Sanford's hunger overcame diffidence. He even began to relax. It was the first time in very many hours that that had been possible. What the future held was undecidable but at least, Sanford told himself, he was on an important job in a highly exotic place. He tried to remember if any of his jet-setting acquaintances had ever mentioned dropping in on Iriadeska and came up empty. If only he had brought a camera! It would have been worth doing to be able to say to a date, "Oh, listen, I've got these slides—temples, Buddhas, elephants. . . ." And he had actually seen all those things, even though briefly out of the window of a moving car. Maybe if he got this job well started there would be time for sightseeing. Time to get a better look at those funny idols with Abe Lincoln stovepipe hats—if idols were what they were, and not just ornamentation—and get out into the countryside again to see some of those elephants at work . . . maybe with Colonel Emily. . . .

He perceived he had company.

Two saffron-robed monks had entered the dining room, a skinny young one and an immensely fat older one, both holding their begging bowls before them. Six waiters materialized at once to bow to the monks, take their bowls, convoy them to Sanford's table, and race around to bring glasses, pitchers of ice water, even a vase of orchids. The monks seated themselves without invitation. The fat, old one beamed at Sanford, and the skinny young one said, in excellent English, "This is Am Sattaroothata. He bids you good morning."

"Good morning to you too," said Sanford uncertainly. Was he supposed to give them money? Would that be a terrible, unforgivable social blunder? Was this one of the categories Colonel Emily had meant to include under "tipping"?

The young monk went on, bringing the balls of his fingertips together as he spoke the name, "Am Sattaroothata is a very wise and holy man with many, many devoted followers. He is also the brother, on both sides, of General Phenoboomgarat. Furthermore, Am

Sattaroothata"—fingers pressed together—"wishes me to inform you that he is really not prejudiced against Americans at all."

Sanford was saved from having to respond to this piece of information by a pleased grunt from Am Sattaroothata. The waiters had come back, bringing the filled begging bowls. Actually, "filled" applied only to the fat monk's bowl. The younger one's contained only a few lentils, a dab of rice, and what might have been a single, thin strip of some kind of dried fish. Am Sattaroothata's, on the other hand, was a symphony. There were crisp stalks of sliced celery, carrot, and other crudités, all tastefully arranged around canapés delicately constructed of pâtés and tiny bright pink shrimp, topped with rosettes of cheese or scarlet pimientos or what certainly looked a great deal like caviar. Am Sattaroothata grunted to the young monk to proceed while he waded in.

"It was Am Sattaroothata," said the young monk, resolutely not looking at his superior's bowl, "who has chosen your firm to assist in our public-relations situation here in Pnik, Mr. Sanford. He was greatly disappointed in the failure of your predecessors to come to terms with the urgency of the matter."

"Now, wait a minute," cried Sanford, suddenly concerned. "What urgency? For that matter, what predecessors? No one said anything to me about having some other PR people here."

The young monk looked alarmed. He turned beseechingly toward Am Sattaroothata, fingers pressed so tightly together that Sanford could see the dark skin whitening around the fingernails. He whispered urgently in Iriadeskan at some length. Am Sattaroothata heard him out, then shrugged. As the younger monk returned to Sanford, Am Sattaroothata glanced casually over his shoulders at the cluster of hovering waiters. That was all it took. They whisked away his now empty bowl and returned it in seconds, wiped spotless, now with a wine bottle in it. Sanford had barely time to read the words *Mouton Rothschild* on the label before one waiter whisked it out of the bowl to uncork, while another set a long-stemmed crystal goblet before the monk and the remainder bore the empty bowl away.

While the wine waiter was pouring out a drop for Am Sattaroothata to taste, the other monk began to explain. "Six months ago, Mr. Sanford," he said, "even before this matter of the Martians came up—"

Explosion of wine in an angry bellow from Am Sattaroothata, and the younger monk looked up in agony. "It is not important about the Martians yet, Mr. Sanford," he said, cringing. "Allow me to say this in proper order. At that time it was decided that our valiant Iriadeskan Army, while ever unchallenged in battle, had failed to win the hearts and minds of the Iriadeskan people to the degree properly earned by their valor, constancy, diligence, and unflagging loyalty to the state." He glanced at his superior, who seemed to have settled down, and then, longingly, at the sparse and still untouched contents of his bowl. "So therefore, Mr. Sanford, an American public-relations firm was employed to help bring this message to our people, at a cost of many tens of thousands of rupiyit."

Am Sattaroothata, absently sipping his wine, gave a peremptory grunt. The young monk flinched and spoke faster. "To make a long story short, Mr. Sanford, two weeks ago, just when they were most needed, these other Americans resigned the account and left without notice, thus greatly inconveniencing our plans at a critical juncture—"

"Now, hold it right there," Sanford snapped, putting down the remains of his tasteless sandwich. "I want to know more about this other outfit, Mr.—say, what's your name, anyway?"

The young monk turned miserably to the other for instructions, got a negligent nod.

"I am Am Bhopru, Mr. Sanford," he said, "but my name is of no importance. May I proceed? Am Sattaroothata wishes me to explain to you at once your mission and the significant state purposes it will serve."

"Hell," said Sanford, but only in a mutter. The situation was not new. He had felt just this way, back in his freshman year in college, when he had for the first time tried using a computer to whip up a synoptic report on a marketing development in his first business-management course. The thing would give him all the information he wanted. But it would do it at its own pace and after its own style, and if he tried to shortcut its processes he simply fried the program. "Go ahead," he said sulkily, his attention diverted by the waiters hurrying back with Am Sattaroothata's bowl. It now contained what Sanford was quite sure was the breast of duck with Madagascar pepper sauce, flanked by perfectly steamed broccoli and zucchini, with two orchids tastefully laid across the rim. Sanford glared at the remains of his miserable sandwich in disgust, hardly hearing Am Bhopru's long-winded explanations.

The young monk was, after a fashion, answering his question. The previous PR team, it turned out, had come from one of MadAve's highest-powered public-relations firms. They had operated on the grand scale, starting with an all-out public-opinion polling survey. "That was completed within one week of commencement of operations," said Am Bhopru, "and you will be supplied, of course, with complete transcripts of their findings."

"Who did the polling?" asked Sanford.

"Oh, that was quite easy. Am Sattaroothata instructed fifty of his followers to seek enlightenment in this way."

Sanford shrugged; it was seldom a good idea to have interested parties do your polling, but he saw no point in bringing it up yet. And evidently there had been at least a sizeable effort. The monks had covered most of the neighborhoods of Pnik and even out into the fishing villages and farm communities and hill towns. "So the pulse of the Iriadeskan people has been taken," said Am Bhopru, and added proudly, "Of course, all of the data have been stored in our computer, and the printouts are here."

He pulled a thick sheaf of tractor-feed paper out of the recesses of his robe and passed it over the table. "Perhaps you will be good enough to look it over now," he said, and then, with an apologetic fingertip-touch to Am Sattaroothata, began greedily shoveling in the lentils and rice from his bowl.

Sanford struggled with the folded sheets. They were filled with tables and graphs and, although each page was neatly numbered, there was no sort of index to guide him in searching for some sort of summary

or overview. In any case, he ran out of time. He had barely begun
to read *Major Policy Issues, First Survey*, when Am Sattaroothata,
picking duck out of his teeth, signaled the waiters. Immediately they
flocked to take his bowl. It reappeared in a moment, scoured clean
and filled with petit fours and fresh pineapple chunks, but the fat
monk shook his head.

Am Bhopru gamely tried speaking while at the same time scooping
the last of his rice into his mouth, and managed, "Is time, Mr.
Sanford." (Chew, swallow.) "Is time for us to go to headquarters of
General Phenoboomgarat. A car is waiting." And he managed to
swallow the last mouthful and give his bowl a brisk wipe with his
napkin just as four waiters, two on each side, surrounded Am Sattaroothata and helped him, grunting, to his feet.

The car was a custom-stretched Cadillac, easily fourteen feet long.
The seating in it was according to rank. Am Sattaroothata got the
huge rear seat to sprawl in all by himself. A jump seat was pulled
down for Am Bhopru, while Sanford, with his ten yards of printout,
went up front, next to the uniformed driver.

Like every Asiatic city, Pnik's streets were densely packed with human beings using every form of transport possible. There were huge
tour buses, mostly empty, and garishly painted city buses, almost as
big. There were the converted flatbed trucks with wooden benches
installed that they called minibuses; there were taxicabs of the standard
worldwide sort, and those of the other, three-wheeled variety called
tuk-tuks, with their open seats and motorcycle engines. There were
real motorbikes and scooters; there were people on bicycles, usually
two on each, one impassively riding the handlebars; and, in and
around all the vehicles, there were pedestrians. Millions of pedestrians.
They dawdled at the open-fronted shops and ambled across the streets
and haggled with the hawkers' food stands along the curbs; they were
everywhere. Almost everywhere. Though the streets were narrow and
the traffic nearly solid, somehow the huge limousine purred through.
Channels of clear space opened around it, like water taxis slashing
through the mats of water hyacinth on the Choomli River. Sanford
could not tell exactly how that happened. The pedestrians did not

seem conscious of the car. They didn't even seem to look at it, and the soldier-chauffeur never blew his horn. But wherever he chose to turn, aisles of space appeared.

Sanford spent little time looking at the scenery. His big interest was in his bale of tractor-feed, and he flipped it clumsily back and forth as he rode, searching for answers, or at least clues. It was a gift of God that it should have been there for him . . . but there was so much of it! And not just text. There were pie charts and graphs and histograms, most of them in brilliant color; there were long tables of numerical data, and parenthetical summaries of the statistical tests, chi-squared and more sophisticated ones still, that had been carried out in support of the conclusions.

And there were conclusions.

When Sanford found them he sighed in relief. The relief didn't last. The conclusions were clear enough; his predecessors had measured Iriadeskan public opinion on many questions. It was the questions that were surprising.

The main issues polled were ten:

1. High taxes.
2. Increase in national debt.
3. Corruption in government.
4. Worsening balance of payments.
5. Urban crime and river/canal piracy.
6. Lack of appropriate employment for college graduates.
7. Iriadeskan government attitude toward Martians.
8. Failure to build additional temples.
9. Improper observance of major religious holidays.
10. Lack of sufficient funds to properly train and equip valorous soldiers of Glorious Iriadeskan Army.

Sanford gazed out the window, frowning. Peculiar! Not the first five questions, of course—they were the sort of thing the citizens of almost any country in the world, including his own, might be concerned about. But in the responses to the polls, all five of those were well down on the list of Iriadeskan worries! Even stranger, when the respondents were asked to rank their major concerns in order, the top of the charts, by a large margin, was concern that the Army wasn't getting enough money—followed closely by disapproval of the government's attitudes toward the Martians!

It was positively astonishing how often the Martians seemed to come up in this place—and positively annoying how little anyone seemed to want to talk about it.

Sanford swiveled around in his seat, waving the sheaf of papers. "Hey!" he cried. "What's all this Martian—"

He couldn't finish, because Am Bhopru leaned quickly forward and pressed a palm over Sanford's mouth; it smelled of fish and cloves and cigarette smoke, and it effectively cut Sanford off in the middle of a sentence. "Please!" the monk whispered urgently. "You must not speak now. Am Sattaroothata is meditating."

It didn't look like meditating to Sanford. The fat monk seemed sound asleep, and in fact Sanford could hear gentle snores coming from the shaved, lowered head. Fuming, Sanford turned back to the printouts.

Riffling through the sheets he found—if not exactly answers—at least supplementary data. There had not been a single poll. There had been, it seemed, one every ten days, and the ranking of matters of concern had changed markedly over the time involved.

There was, for instance, a graph showing the increase in concern over the Martian question that showed almost negligible interest a few months ago, gaining steadily at every sampling until it approached the number one money-for-the-Army question in importance. While the Army budget question had started strong, in third place after the two religious questions, and finished stronger, in fact all by itself at the top. You could understand that, in a way, thought Sanford, frowning to himself. The way the Army question was put was highly slanted; it forced an answer, which was bad polling practice. He was surprised that a reputable public-relations agency had phrased it that way, in violation of all established procedures . . . though, no doubt, they had been subject to a certain amount of pressure, since it was the Glorious Iriadeskan Army that had been their, as well as his own, employer. Certainly it meant that there was a substantial chance of error in the numbers generated. . . .

But not enough of a chance to alter the fact that Iriadeskans seemed very much to want more money given to their Army.

And that did not in any way explain the Martian vote.

Sanford folded the sheets and gazed unseeingly out at the hordes around him. Something drastic had been going on in Iriadeska. But what?

He tried to calculate. The earliest polls had been taken four months earlier. That took him back to June. Had something special happened with the Iriadeskan Army in June?

If so, he realized, no amount of cudgeling his brains would tell him what it had been, since he had barely heard of Iriadeska in June. Maybe someone would tell him if he asked the right questions, but that would have to wait until he was allowed to open his mouth.

All right, then, what about the Martians. Had something special happened with the Martians in June?

He couldn't think of anything. They had taken off in January. One of them had died a month later. The expedition was due to land fairly soon—within the next month or so, if he remembered correctly. But how could any of that account for a sudden surge of interest four months back, while they were doing nothing more interesting than dawdling through space on their interminable return flight?

There was one thing that could account for sudden interest in any subject. He knew what that was, because it was what he did for a living. It was called "publicity."

Had the Iriadeskan Army, for reasons not known, hired the PR firm to whip up Iriadeskan interest in the Martians as well as in itself? And, if so, for God's sake, *why*?

"Mr. Sanford?"

He turned, blinking. It was Am Bhopru, leaning forward to whisper urgently in his ear. "We are almost there," he said, contriving to watch worriedly the sleeping older monk while whispering to Sanford. "When we pass the sentries at the entrance to the compound, please be sure not to make any sudden movements."

Sudden movements?

Sanford had another of those nasty, shrinking feelings. What kind of place was he going to, where something might go wrong if he moved the wrong way? He blinked out the window. They were still moving through narrow streets, but most of the traffic was gone. No more buses of any kind, a handful of pedal-bicyclists scattering away out of sight as fast as they could go, pedestrians vanishing into buildings. The big Cadillac limousine had the streets almost to itself, except for an occasional hurrying tuk-tuk.

And, funnily, all the tuk-tuks seemed to have two things in common. They were all going in the same direction—toward the Army compound, along with Sanford's own vehicle. And every one of the tuk-tuk drivers had an identical expression of worry on his face, and identically carried a single passenger—an Iriadeskan Army soldier, and each one with one of those nasty carbines across his knees.

The young woman with the colonel's insignia on her uniform conducted Sanford wordlessly into the headquarters building. She did not respond to his greeting. She didn't even smile. She simply led the way to a door and threw it open. Pressing her fingertips together, she said, "General Tupalakuli and General Phenoboomgarat, this is Mr. Charles Sanford."

Sanford wondered if he should bow—or kneel, or crawl on his belly like a worm; he compromised by nodding his head briefly, looking at his employers. General Phenoboomgarat was short and skinny, General Tupalakuli was short and fat. They wore identical gold-braided officers' uniforms of the Iriadeskan Army and sat at identical teak desks the size of billiard tables. Each desk was angled slightly, so that they converged on the spot where Sanford was standing, in the center of the room. On a staff between them was the Iriadeskan flag, three broad bars of green, white, and violet, with twenty-seven stars that represented the twenty-seven islands of the Iriadeskan archipelago.

The colonel—had she said her name was Emily?—pressed her fingertips respectfully together before her breast and said to Sanford, "General Phenoboomgarat and General Tupalakuli welcome you to the cause of the Glorious Iriadeskan Army. General Tupalakuli and

General Phenoboomgarat wish you to know that you will be given every possible assistance in the accomplishment of your mission. General Phenoboomgarat and General Tupalakuli ask how long it will take you to draft your first proclamation, expressing the need of the Glorious Iriadeskan Army for a fifty-five percent increase in its annual budget, with escalator clauses for inflation?"

Sanford swallowed and glanced around. What he had not at first noticed was that there was another door to the room. It was half-open, and through it he could see the two monks, the fat one reclining on a love seat, the skinny one hovering nervously behind him. Am Sattaroothata beamed encouragingly at Sanford. Am Bhopru merely looked frightened at being present at this meeting taking place at the highest of all levels.

Sanford returned to Colonel Emily. He licked his lips and did his best with the question she had asked. "Well," he said, "if I had a typewriter and some paper, and someone to fill me in on the issues —maybe a couple of hours, I guess."

The colonel looked scandalized. She glanced at the two generals and lowered her voice, though neither of them showed any signs of comprehension, much less concern. "You do not have hours, Mr. Sanford! There are many, many proclamations and that is only the first. Can't you type fast? Remember, what you write I then have to translate into Iriadeskan and submit it to General Phe—General Tupalakuli and General Phenoboomgarat," she corrected herself, tardily remembering where she had been in the rotation to give each one equal eminence. "No, hours are out of the—"

She stopped before the word *question* because, evidently, there was even less time than she had thought. The phones on the desks of the two generals rang simultaneously. Each general picked up his phone and listened silently for a moment, then they gazed at each other. "Yom?" General Phenoboomgarat asked. "Yom," General Tupalakuli confirmed. They both said, "Yom!" into their telephones and slammed them down in unison.

"It is starting," the colonel whispered.

Outside, in the courtyard of the Army compound, there was a

sudden racket of engines starting, deep thudding diesels, yapping little putt-putts. In the room still a third door opened, and a lieutenant entered bearing a folded cloth. With an apologetic salute to each of the two generals, the lieutenant began to take down the Iriadeskan flag from its staff.

Sanford said desperately, "What's going on?"

The colonel glanced at the two generals, and then said, "Why, the Iriadeskan people are about to take back power from the corrupt bureaucrats under the wise leadership of General, uh, Phenoboomgarat and General Tupalakuli, of course. See for yourself." And she indicated the window looking out on the courtyard.

Dazedly, Sanford stared out at the scene. The throbbing basso-profundo motors belonged to tanks—big ones, at least twenty of them, with wicked-looking cannons snaking back and forth from their turrets as they began to grumble forward. The higher-pitched noises were tuk-tuks. There seemed to be hundreds of the little three-wheeled vehicles. Each one was driven by a soldier, with three more soldiers crammed into the passenger seat behind him, and all of them armed with the rapid-fire weapons.

"Oh, my God," Sanford whispered.

The colonel said crossly, "Now you see why things must be done at once. Please stand at attention!"

Sanford blinked at her. She was standing militarily erect. So were the two generals at their desks. Through the open door he could see Am Bhopru helping his fat superior to struggle to his feet, and all of them raising their right hands in salute.

The lieutenant had taken down the old flag and a new one hung in its place.

At first Sanford thought there had been no change; the broad bars were the same, and the design in the ensign was hidden in the folds of the cloth.

Then the lieutenant reverently pulled it taut, holding his salute.

The twenty-seven stars were gone. In their place, woven in threads of silver, was the image of—a manatee? A Mindy Mars doll?

No. It was the image of a seal-like creature with spindly legs like those of a newborn racehorse, just like the ones that were slowly coasting toward their landing on Earth in the returning spacecraft of the Seerseller expedition.

It was a Martian.

The typewriter was not a typewriter. It was a word processor, and the room it was in was not an office. It was a television studio. The TV station was located in the heart of the military compound, red lights flashing from the tops of its antennae. It was in the tallest building of the lot, surrounded by squat barracks and armories and headquarters buildings; it was a good seven stories tall, not counting the skeletal antenna structure that added another hundred feet.

Crossing the parade grounds to the television studio, Sanford and the colonel had had to dodge for their lives between the columns of ponderous tanks, sorting themselves into a line of march toward the main gate, with the supporting motorized infantry in their tuk-tuks racing their motors to take position behind the armor. Every vehicle bore a brand-new Iriadeskan flag, proudly displayed. And every flag bore the Martian design.

Sanford was full of questions. The colonel forbade him to ask them. "Later," she snapped. "First the proclamations! The march will begin at any moment, and we must have the broadcast ready!"

It wasn't easy. The word processor was a brand unfamiliar to Sanford. The colonel had to set it up for him and stand over him while he typed, grabbing at his hand when he seemed to be reaching for the key that would erase all he had done, or cause the program to suspend operations while it stored a backup record, or perhaps switch to some other mode entirely. But once he had the hang of it he typed fast.

This sort of thing was in the best traditions of his craft. Many were the times when the Old Man, or some other Old Man, had come beaming and gently deprecating into the copywriters' room at the close of a business day to announce there was a fire to be put out and they could all phone their wives to say that dinner would be late. Many was the stick of copy Sanford had hammered out under the gun of a newsbreak, or to counter a competitor's sudden thrust. It had never been quite like this, though. Never before had Sanford had to create powerful prose—powerful *translator-proof* prose, since he knew nothing of the Iriadeskan language his words were to be translated into, and could not risk word-play or jokes—on a subject of which he knew nothing, for an audience he had never encountered, on a machine he had never used before. When he had managed to hit a *Cancel* key a moment before the colonel's hand could stop him, and wiped out three lines, she gritted her teeth and pushed him away from the chair. "Just dictate," she ordered. "I will type. What you must say is that the New People's Reform Government, responding to the righteous needs and wishes of the Iriadeskan masses, has taken over the functions of the corruption-ridden and entrenched old power elite, for the purpose of inaugurating a new era of peace, prosperity, and reform for the proud Iriadeskan nation, under the wise leadership of the Glorious Iriadeskan Army."

"Hey," said Sanford, "that's fine the way it is. What do you need me for?"

"Just dictate," she ordered, and after a few false starts they had produced Communiqúe No. 1:

People of Iriadeska!
This is the dawn of a new day for Iriadeska! The New People's Reform Government, wisely responding to the just needs and aspirations of the Iriadeskan people, has kicked from office the petty bureaucrats and corrupt officials of the scandal-ridden and incompetent usurpers of power. This is the first day of the triumphant rebirth of the Iriadeskan nation, moving promptly and surely to a time of peace, prosperity, freedom, and reform for all Iriadeskans. Long live the Glorious Iriadeskan Nation and its beloved allies from afar!

"What's that about allies from afar?" Sanford asked, peering over the colonel's shoulder.

"Later, later," she said absently, beginning to translate it into Iriadeskan. He backed away to leave her to it, not dissatisfied. It wasn't sparkling prose. It wasn't even *his* prose, or most of it wasn't, because the colonel had edited as she typed. But it was, after all, a pretty fair first try for a man whose major recent work had been devoted principally to the task of persuading American consumers that no table was properly set for a meal without the presence of a jar of pickles and at least one kind of preserved condiment.

The colonel gnawed a knuckle as the printer zipped the words onto paper. Then, without speaking, she rushed out of the room with the copy.

Only minutes later, Sanford had the satisfaction of seeing Am Sattaroothata himself on the desk TV, reading the proclamation aloud in Iriadeskan. He listened attentively to the unfamiliar words that had come, at least partly, out of his own brain. It sounded, he decided, very Iriadeskan. When the old monk stopped reading he gazed benignly into the camera for a few minutes, while music played—no doubt the Iriadeskan national anthem.

Then the screen went black.

Tardily, Sanford wondered how the revolution was going. In the soundproofed TV studio there was no hint of what went on outside.

But there was a hall just outside the door, and a window at the end of the hall.

There was also a pair of Iriadeskan soldiers standing there with guns at the ready, Sanford discovered when he opened the door. They only glanced at him, though, and turned back to the stairwell, perhaps ready to repel any scandal-ridden and incompetent corrupt bureaucrats who might attack. Sanford walked cautiously to the window and glanced out at the courtyard.

He had supposed that the tank column had already left to fulfill its mission. It hadn't. All the tanks and tuk-tuks were still right there, just as before, except that now they were all motionless and their engines seemed to have been turned off.

The guards stiffened to present arms. Sanford turned apprehensively, just in time to see Colonel Emily appear on the stairs. "Oh, there you are," she said breathlessly. "I just came to tell you that there is a policy matter that must be decided. Make yourself comfortable. Study the former proclamations while you wait. I will return shortly." And she turned and hurried back out again.

"Shortly" turned out, in fact, to be rather longly. Sanford spent twenty minutes or so puzzling over the last batch of communiqués, issued by some previous "New People's Revolutionary Something-or-other Government," trying to find out just what he was expected to do. Many of them had to do with the questions his predecessors had polled—more money for the Army, jobs for the unemployed college graduates, temples, subsidies for young men when they put in their customary year of monkhood. But some were quite odd, notably one that said:

> Humble and reverential Iriadeskans!
> The Elephant is our Mother and our Beloved! All revere the Elephant for its wisdom, gentleness, and grace! In the symbol of the Elephant lies our strength and our glory. Let no one dare defame the precious Creature, for just as the Elephant is the loving preserver of Man, so will the Holy National Reform Enlightenment Movement be the loving servant, teacher, and ever-righteous guide to the reverential and obedient masses of the Iriadeskan people.

Perhaps, he decided, it sounded better in Iriadeskan, but it didn't seem to move him very much. And the colonel still had not returned.

Sanford risked another look out the hall window. Nothing had changed. Nothing looked as though it ever would change. The tanks seemed fixed to the parade ground as firmly as war memorials. The soldiers were squatting in groups about the courtyard, smoking fat yellow cigarettes and chatting desultorily among themselves.

And Sanford's physical exhaustion was beginning to catch up with him.

He glanced at his wristwatch, still on U.S.A. Eastern time. He despaired of trying to convert it to whatever they used in Iriadeska, but the watch told him unequivocally enough that it had been either twenty-nine or forty-one hours since he had boarded his first plane at

Kennedy, his head full of the Old Man's last-minute instructions. "The first thing you do," he had ordered, "is send me a full situation report. Don't leave out a thing, and don't let them put you on anything that will keep you from doing that *first*." Well, that certainly hadn't happened the way it was supposed to. Would there be trouble over that when he got back? Could he have done any different? The Old Man had gone on: "This could be The Big One, Charlie, so make sure I know what's what. I want to know everything there is to know about the situation in Irano—Iderian—"

"Iriadeska," Sanford had supplied. "Right, Chief!"

But yessing the Old Man and carrying out the Old Man's orders were two different things, and no one had said anything about Martians, elephants, or an armed revolution. What possible situation report could Sanford now file, assuming he would be allowed to file any, that would convey to the Old Man, sitting in the Old Man's big, bare office overlooking the noisy traffic of Fifty-seventh Street, just what sort of can of worms Sanford was being required to untangle on the steamy opposite side of the world? He wouldn't believe it! Sanford managed a wry grin, thinking of the Old Man's expression if he got such a report. . . . If a truthful report could be filed without once and for always breaching the mutual cozy agency-client relationship the Old Man prized. . . . If any report at all could be filed, anyway, without some potentially very unpleasant consequences to Sanford himself. . . .

He stiffened, staring down at the parade ground.

There in the floodlights, picking his way daintily among the troops and vehicles, was a short, skinny man in a general's uniform. Behind him were two Iriadeskan soldiers. Their carbines were at the ready, and as they followed they watched the general's every move.

If the man in the general's uniform was under arrest, as it certainly seemed he was, it did not appear to disturb his disdainful poise.

But it certainly disturbed Sanford's. It disturbed it quite a lot. Because, even at that distance, and with the lighting as chancy as it was, he was quite sure that the man being taken away under guard was the co-leader of this coup, or revolution, or spontaneous people's uprising against the corrupt bureaucrats, or whatever it was he had stumbled into. Specifically, it was General Tupalakuli.

Although there was no couch in the studio, the armchairs were not hopelessly uncomfortable. Certainly they were a lot better than the airplane seats Sanford had spent so much of his recent past in. When Colonel Emily at last returned he was fast asleep.

"Wake up, wake up," she said crossly, and Sanford did. She helped the process a little by providing coffee—what she called coffee, anyway. She had cups, and a jar of some Asiatic brand of instant, and a huge thermos of nearly boiling water.

By the time he had forced half of the first scalding cup down, Sanford was awake enough to ask questions. The answers he got, though, were not very illuminating. Yes, Emily admitted, the man under guard was in fact General Tupalakuli. Why was he arrested? Why? she parroted. He had revealed himself an enemy of the Iriadeskan masses; therefore, the New People's Reform Government had been forced to remove him from his position of trust. But that would not prevent the successful accomplishment of the coup, she explained. General Phenoboomgarat and his brother, the monk Am Sattaroothata, were even now engaged in high-level policy discussions that would in fact have the effect of strengthening still further the invincible New People's Reform Government—

And then she stopped and took a sip of coffee, watching Sanford over the rim of the cup, and finally grinned. "Well," she said, "that's more or less true. Actually it was mostly a question of leadership posts."

"Meaning what?" demanded Sanford.

"General Tupalakuli wanted his wife's uncle to be appointed Iriadeskan Ambassador to the United Nations, because it's in New York and he has always been fond of Broadway musicals. General Phenoboomgarat, however, had already promised it to his second son's mother-in-law's brother."

"Are you serious?" asked Sanford, startled. The colonel shrugged, and at last he laughed out loud. "When in Rome," he said, and thought for a minute. He frowned. "General Tupalakuli's wife's uncle sounds like a closer relative," he pointed out.

"Oh, surely. But there are other considerations. Mainly, General Phenoboomgarat's second son's mother-in-law's brother has three estates in California and part of a condo development in Connecticut. He wants to keep an eye on them. It's always useful to have something like that," she explained. "If a coup goes sour and somebody has to go into exile, it's nice to have somewhere to go to."

Sanford opened his mouth to speak, and then closed it again. He looked at her wonderingly, and caught her glancing at her watch. "These high-level discussions," he said. "How long are they likely to take?"

"At least a couple of hours yet," she told him. "Air Chief Marshal Pittikudaru has to helicopter in from his base at the Choomli River delta, but he won't leave until he is assured that the general of either the Fourth or the Seventh Paratroop Brigade is supporting the coup. And they're waiting to see if His Majesty is going to take a position."

"Will he?"

"His Majesty? Oh," she said thoughtfully, "probably not. He's got about as many relatives on one side as he has on the other. But no one is sure, because he's on a state visit to America and he hasn't yet said anything. If he turned out to be for us, or neutral, then everything can go ahead as planned—not counting General Tupalakuli, although then he might come back in. But if the king is against, then that's all different. It might mean almost anything. Probably at least somebody from the royal family may have to be included because, you see, General Tupalakuli's father-in-law used to be His Majesty's father's first prime minister, and so he was close to the court. On the other hand, His Majesty *does* have strong feelings now and then."

"So he might intervene for one side or the other?" Sanford offered, trying to keep up.

"No, no! Not for a *side*. His Majesty doesn't get into *politics*. He is—oh, I don't know how to explain this to you—the king is like supreme in matters of *tradition*, and *religion*, and, well, good taste, do you see?"

"I don't see," Sanford said despairingly. "Start from the beginning, won't you?"

Fortunately, Colonel Emily didn't take him at his word. Iriadeskan history went back seventeen hundred years, and all of them were full of plots, conspiracies, and coups d'etat. She went back only as far as World War II, when the then king had been an unusually popular —which was to say, fairly popular—and relatively secure monarch who had made one little mistake. He thought that when the Japanese took over from the French and British, who had divided Iriadeska between them for a couple of hundred years, the Japanese would stay. The 1945 surrender was a crushing blow. He didn't think the returning Europeans would like keeping him on the throne, and he was right. They didn't. So the collaborator king abdicated and spent the rest of his life, happily enough, in Antibes. A nephew was crowned. The boy had been at Oxford when the war broke out. He spent the entire war there, in the uniform of the RAF, safely assigned to ground duties. He had developed into a loyal subject of the British crown.

Unfortunately for the dynasty, that didn't work out either. Independence came. The young king didn't get deposed. He was simply required to turn the governance of Iriadeska over to a Council of Ministers. There it had remained ever since, with continual ebb and flow of members in and out as factions jockeyed for power. Or at least for plunder.

Iriadeska was not handicapped by many confusing notions of democracy. They did quite frequently have elections, but the candidates were always from the small list of the elite. No one not at least marginally a member of the Royal Family ever served as police chief or diplomat or military commander in Iriadeska, much less as a member of the Council of Ministers. However, that still left a large pool of available talent for every imaginable government office, because over the course of seventeen hundred years the Iriadeskan royal family had come to include many thousands of its citizens.

Still, it was an arithmetical fact that there were, altogether, something like twenty-odd million Iriadeskan nationals. Most of the millions were not related to royalty in any detectable way. They were the ones who chopped the cane, slashed the rubber trees, clerked in the banks for offshore trading, worked in the few factories, and staffed the tourist hotels, as well as doing everything else in Iriadeska that produced wealth. Some of them produced quite a lot of it. This was especially true among the Chinese community, where there were many privately owned wholesale establishments, brokerages, and shipping companies. None of these people, even the rich ones, could ever hold any really responsible role in the Iriadeskan government, but that did not make them unimportant. Indeed, the Iriadeskan government always had a very important part for these citizens to play, regardless of who made up the Iriadeskan government of that moment.

They could be taxed.

Sanford, listening to all this, shook his head, uncertain whether to laugh or lose his temper. He said, "So after forty years some people want a redistribution of the loot?"

Emily looked at him in puzzlement. "Forty years? What do you mean, forty years? It has been, let me see, yes, twenty-two months since the last coup attempt, not forty years. That was when two wing commanders of the Royal Iriadeskan Air Force and the Admiral of the Iriadeskan Navy combined to take over the government. They failed because they couldn't get any ground troops to occupy the Palace. In the last forty years there have been, let me see, oh, I think about thirty-three or thirty-four attempts."

"My God," said Sanford. "It sounds like a regular annual event, like the Rose Bowl Parade."

"I think," Emily said stiffly, "that our national struggles are quite a bit more important than that. Anyway, I'll bet more people are probably hurt in your parade."

"Really? Bloodless coups? How many of them are successful?"

"Ah, but don't you see? That's why you're here. None of them are, usually. So this time Am Sattaroothata persuaded General Phenoboomgarat that we could establish a stable regime with good public-relations management, so they hired you."

Briskly she rose, dumped the remnants of his coffee, and refilled his cup from the jar of instant and the thermos of still very hot water. "Can we now get back to work?" she asked. "Many of the communiqués can be used whichever way the discussions go, so let us write them."

"The one about the fifty-five percent raise in Army allocations?"

"Oh, yes," she agreed. "That and many others. Balancing the budget. Cutting the trade deficit. Limiting the police powers of arbitrary arrest and imprisonment to no more than six months without filing charges. And by all means something about finding work for college graduates; you have no idea how many of our people go off to Europe or America to study and have nothing to do when they come home. Why, I myself—"

She stopped, looking embarrassed. "Yes?" Sanford encouraged. "Were you one of those—or are you part American, with a name like Emily?"

She looked surprised. "My parents named me Arragingama-uluthiata, Mr. Sanford. But yes, I was one of those. When I was an English major at Bennington we put on a play. It was *Our Town*, by Thornton Wilder. I played the part of Emily, the young wife who dies and is buried in the graveyard, and as most of my college friends had difficulty in pronouncing Arragingama-uluthiata, they generally called me Emily. My years in Vermont made me quite fond of Americans, Mr. Sanford, and I have kept the name ever since."

"And when you came back to Iriadeska you couldn't get a job?" Sanford persisted.

"Not one for an English major specializing in the Lake Poets, no. In fact, nothing at all, at first." She looked around the Army television studio without enjoyment. "Then the opportunity came for a commission in the Army, and this sort of work. Which, actually, we had better get busy and do."

"Oh, right," said Sanford agreeably, not quite meaning it; it was distinctly more pleasurable to sit and talk with this rather pretty young woman, who mellowed considerably as you got to know her. "Explain one thing to me, though."

"Certainly, Mr. Sanford."

"Charlie, please?" She smiled and inclined her head. "It's about this elephant release. Communiqué Number Seven."

She took it from him and he watched her bend her head over it with pleasure. Actually, he was feeling fairly good, everything considered. The revolution did not seem to be turning violent. His short nap had revived him—or perhaps the coffee had; Emily had been making it progressively stronger, so that now it seemed she was barely dampening the crystals.

She looked up. "Yes," she said, "that was Air Chief Marshal Pittikudaru's idea, two coups ago. What about it?"

"I don't see what elephants have to do with revolutions," Sanford said apologetically.

"Because you aren't Iriadeskan. You do understand that this is an old proclamation? It has nothing to do with what's going on now."

"Well, yes, but still, elephants—"

"Elephants are very important in Iriadeska! That coup attempt adopted the symbol of the elephant because the elephant was the servant of man, just as the new government proposed to be the servant of the Iriadeskan people. They bought it, as a matter of fact, even though Marshal Pittikudaru himself pulled out of the attempt when the others wouldn't agree to make him an admiral as well. Only," she sighed, "some of the hill people thought elephants were holy. They didn't want them used in politics."

Sanford was surprised. "I didn't realize what people thought was that important to an, uh, excuse me, a more or less self-appointed government."

"Not what they *thought*," she explained. "What they *did*. The hill tribes made up most of the Eighth and Tenth Armored Divisions, and they all just ran off, tanks and all, until it was over. So it failed, and Admiral Pilatkatha and General Muntilasia are still in Switzerland over that one." She sighed and stretched. She added sorrowfully. "Anyway, His Majesty agreed with the hill people. And in matters of religion or good taste, what His Majesty says is, how would you say it? Conclusive. That's why we chose the Martians this time. No one thinks they're holy."

Sanford said doubtfully, "I still don't see the reasoning there. I mean for putting the Martians on the flag."

"Because they so closely resemble our chupri, of course. The chupri, or manatee, is strong, peaceful, kind, and gentle. It helps keep our canals and waterways clear of weed by grazing on water hyacinth. It is a friend to the Iriadeskans, just as our New People's Reform Movement will be, not to mention it is very newsworthy just now."

"I guess I didn't realize that Iriadeskans were so interested in space," Sanford apologized.

"In space? Oh, hardly at all. But that is what His Majesty is doing, you see. He is in America for that purpose."

"You said he was on a state tour!"

"Yes, exactly. He will address the United Nations tomorrow. Then he will visit Atlantic City, where he has investments in several casinos. Then he has been promised a day in Disney World, and then he goes to Cape Canaveral as a guest of your President to welcome the Seerseller expedition back to Earth. I mean," Emily said sharply, "if the *king* can travel twelve thousand miles to see the Martians come in, that makes them important, doesn't it?"

"I suppose. I don't know much about Martians," he apologized, and blinked when he saw the effect that had on her.

"You *what*?" she cried, scandalized.

"I said I don't know much about Martians," he repeated deprecatingly.

"But you—Your picture was on page one of the newspaper! Your agency chief claimed you were very familiar with the campaign—"

"Oh, you mean Max Mars and Mindy Mars. Yes, I did help out on that, but only for a week or two. And I don't know anything about Martians. That was just dolls, not the real thing."

"Holy shit," whispered the former Bennington student. Sanford blinked. "Oh, Charlie," she said sorrowfully, "do you have any idea what you're *saying*?"

He said defensively, "Well, I certainly never said anything to give anyone the idea that I was claiming to be an expert on Martians."

"What you claimed? What does *that* matter? Am Sattaroothata told General Phenoboomgarat to hire you because we needed a Martian expert. Do you know, do you have any idea at all, what it would mean to say that Am Sattaroothata was *wrong?*"

Sanford said apologetically, "Well, gosh, Emily, I'm sure it would be pretty embarrassing—"

"Embarrassing? *Embarrassing?* Oh, no, Charlie, it wouldn't be embarrassing. I'll tell you what it would be. It would be . . . it would be . . ."

Colonel Emily faltered in midtirade. She was listening. So, suddenly, was Sanford, because at long last, and even through the soundproofing of the television studio, there was something to listen to. The building itself was shaking with the steady seismic throb of the tanks.

They were on their way. For better or worse, the coup was launched at last.

From the top of the television tower the whole city of Pnik was spread out before them in the steamy Iriadeskan morning. Off to the west there was the River Choomli with its fringe of high-rise tourist hotels and the bright green mats of water hyacinth swirling upstream as the canal dams were opened for the morning traffic, flushing the weed out into the river. To the north the tall government buildings, all new, all shiny in the glass-sided style of every city in the world. To the east the old city with its temples and towers; glints of gold struck the eye as the sunlight bounced off gilded Buddhas and mortuary columns. To the south the airport, its jumbo jets and private planes all motionless. And in all directions, wherever you looked, it looked empty. When the assault column moved out of the compound it seemed to suck all the life of Pnik after it. There was no one in any street Sanford could see.

Nor was there any sound, either, not from the streets or from the airport with its interdicted planes. Least of all was there any sound of cannon fire, or tank engines, or screaming casualties, or any of the things twenty years of war movies had trained Sanford to expect. "Shouldn't they be fighting?" he asked Colonel Emily and she looked at him in some surprise.

"The attack is under way," she assured him, "probably. Anyway, Air Chief Marshal Pittikudaru has practically promised to overfly the Supreme Court building as soon as the Seventh Paratroop Brigade takes position around it. So we ought to see the airplanes from here, anyway."

"I don't," he told her, squinting.

"Well, I don't either!" she stormed at him. "We just have to be patient until we find out what's going on. And don't start again about radio contact; we don't keep in radio contact, because then everybody would listen in, since we're all on the same command frequencies."

"I was only trying to say—"

"Don't say it!" Then she peered over the parapet of the building. "That's funny," she said, mostly to herself.

Sanford gripped the hot tile edging of the parapet and leaned forward to see what she was looking at. There was something going on. Down on the parade ground a military figure, erect and sober in its braided uniform and cap, stood waiting. It was General Tupalakuli, and he was surrounded by a smart-looking squad of soldiers with carbines at the ready. From the opposite side of the quad another general stepped out, marching smartly toward him.

It was General Phenoboomgarat.

The whole comic-opera scenario suddenly turned ugly for Sanford, because it looked very much as though he were about to witness his first execution by firing squad. "He shouldn't kill him," he snapped at Emily. "He's his prisoner! He's entitled to the conventions of war, isn't he?"

She turned to look at him with uncomprehending eyes. "What in the world are you talking about?"

"That's a firing squad for General Tupalakuli, can't you see? Listen, this is carrying things too far! I want to—"

He did not finish saying what he wanted. On the quadrangle below a little drama was being acted out. General Tupalakuli saluted General Phenoboomgarat ceremoniously. General Phenoboomgarat returned the salute. The squad of armed men detached themselves from General Tupalakuli and re-formed in a hollow square around General Phenoboomgarat. They marched away with him . . . directly to the door of the military prison Tupalakuli had just left.

"Oh, *hell*," moaned Colonel Emily; and behind them on the roof a door opened. The same lieutenant who had changed flags in the room of the two generals, when the two generals seemed temporarily both to be on the same side, appeared again. He saluted Emily perfunctorily and went to the flagpole.

Down came the Martian-bearing flag of the New People's Reform Government. Up went the old twenty-seven-starred banner of the corrupt bloodsuckers and tyrants.

Sanford turned a horrified glance on Emily. "Does this mean what I think it means?" he demanded.

"What do you think it means?" she sobbed. "It means we lost."

The limousine was as big as ever, but now it was a lot more crowded. Am Sattaroothata and General Phenoboomgarat shared the back seat, Am Bhopru was in front, Emily and Sanford on the jump seats.

All around them, the city of Pnik was returning to its normal status. The metal shutters were raised again and the cubbyhole stores were doing their nickel-and-dime business in inches of fabric and ounces of meat or poultry. The tuk-tuks had civilian passengers again. Even a great gaudy tour bus rumbled ahead of them, its exhaust choking them, until it turned off to the Temple of the Ten Thousand Golden Buddhas.

General Phenoboomgarat was talking to Am Sattaroothata as though discussing the results of a recent tennis match. Sanford understood not a word, but Emily gave him a running translation. "The government promised to surrender as soon as the Air Force flew over the Supreme Court building," she said, "but Air Chief Marshal Pittikudaru was waiting for the Seventh Paratroop Brigade to surround the building, and the general didn't go because he'd heard a report that His Majesty had said it was insulting to the proud traditions of Iriadeska to put a child's toy on the flag."

"And did the king really say that?" Sanford asked.

"Oh, who knows? It's the kind of thing he might have said, and just *thinking* he could have said that was enough to make everybody think a second thought, because in matters of taste and religion—"

"I know," Sanford nodded. "His Majesty's word is, what did you say? Conclusive."

"Exactly," she said gloomily. "So General Phenoboomgarat released General Tupalakuli and turned the command of the troops over to him . . . and here we are."

"On the way to the airport and exile," Sanford finished. Emily nodded, pleased with his quick understanding. "Hoping we can sneak out of the country before anyone notices," he added, and she looked indignant.

"Sneak? Who is sneaking anywhere? The airport officials never require exit visas until twelve hours after a coup attempt. Otherwise," she explained, "how would the leaders get away?"

"Get away to where?"

She shrugged. "Wherever they're going. Am Sattaroothata, of course, will only have to stay away for a few months, until things quiet down—he said he wanted to visit his brokers in Singapore anyway. General Phenoboomgarat has a part interest in the Atlantic City casinos, along with His Majesty. That's probably where he'll go."

"And you?"

"Oh, I'll go to Atlantic City, too. No doubt they'll need some sort of personnel manager . . . and maybe I can go back to school and get my master's degree. What about yourself? Back to the agency?"

"If I still have a job," Sanford grumbled. "I haven't exactly covered myself with glory on this one."

Emily looked sympathetic. Sanford drank it up; sympathy wasn't either a success or a job, but it was the best he'd had that day.

Then Emily looked thoughtful. "Charlie," she said absently. "Does your agency have any casino accounts?"

"You mean gambling? Oh, no. I don't know anything about that, and I don't think the Old Man does, either, and besides he has some funny moral attitudes—"

He stopped, because she wasn't listening any more. Her fingertips pressed together, she was whispering deferentially to Am Sattaroothata and the general. They listened absently. Then the monk shrugged and the general said, as though the subject bored him, "Yom."

Emily bowed and turned back to Sanford. "Three hundred million dollars a year," she said, smiling.

"What?"

"That's the handle of our casinos. So there's money to spend on promotion, wouldn't you say? Enough money so that your employer might be interested in the account—with you handling it?"

Sanford said at once, "I think I could learn about casinos very rapidly."

"I think you could, too," Emily said. "I even suspect I might be able to help teach you."

FIFTEEN

NOTES FROM THE BRITISH INTERPLANETARY SOCIETY

From *Spaceflight*, The Secretary's Message

The Seerseller Martian expedition, now in the final stages of its return trip to Earth, has been so exhaustively covered in both *Spaceflight* and *The Journal of the British Interplanetary Society* that there would seem little that has been left to say about it. Certainly we all congratulate our colleagues across the Atlantic on their great triumph. Also certainly, we wish them all success in finding out just how some of the technical aspects were allowed to go so wrong.

But at this time our indefatigable Secretary wishes to discuss some tangential matters. He has unearthed some interesting historical material which demonstrates the remarkable correspondences, as well as the considerable differences, between Captain Seerseller's actual Manned Mars Mission now drawing to its close, and the plans and predictions made for similar projects in the earliest days of the Space Age.

The late Dr. Wernher Von Braun was perhaps the first to consider in detail the logistics and objectives of such a mission. Testifying before the United States Congress in August 1968, just one year after Neil Armstrong became the first human being to set foot on the Moon,

Dr. Von Braun stated that the lunar landing had been only a first step. The second step should be to walk on the surface of Mars, and he described for the congressmen how that could happen.

It would be a manned expedition, somewhat less ambitious than Captain Seerseller's, and it would take place within fifteen years of 1968. Dr. Von Braun's timetable called for a launch in November 1981, returning to Earth in August 1983. His proposal was greeted with enthusiasm by many members of the American Congress. Unfortunately their attention (and resources) were so deeply committed to events twelve thousand miles away, in Vietnam, rather than forty million miles away in space, that the project languished.

It was revived in 1978. Then the American National Aeronautics and Space Administration ("NASA") prepared an update of Dr. Von Braun's studies, in somewhat more detail. NASA envisioned a fleet of several ships, just as actually proved to be the case in the Seerseller mission. They were to be propelled by chemical rockets for initial thrust and landing, with solar-electric power used en route. (Still precisely the same as the Seerseller expedition.)

The 1978 NASA study, however, was still relatively small in scale. A total crew of six was envisaged, with three (all male) astronauts landing on the surface of Mars for a sixty-day tour of scientific study and exploration, while three others, also all male, were to remain in orbit. (In the event, Seerseller's party included one hundred and nine women and one hundred and sixty-seven men on takeoff, all of whom actually landed on the planet . . . although, tragically, only nineteen women and sixteen men have survived to this point in the return voyage.)

The physical specifications for the fleet were similarly scaled down in the 1978 NASA study. The total mass requirement for the 1978 plan was of the order of 1 million kilograms in orbit (as against just under 9.5 million kg for the Seerseller). And NASA's estimate of the solar-power requirement was for a 2-megawatt power array, as against the present fleet's 3.3 megawatts for the crew-carrying ship (and 4.3 mw for the cargo- and instrument-carrying ship which unfortunately crashed on landing).

Both the 1978 NASA plan and the Seerseller actuality included such features as a separate ship for instruments and supplies; assembly and fueling in Low Earth Orbit; and the use of a "heavy-lift" space shuttle to ferry materials from the surface of the Earth to LEO.

The total time for the 1978 mission was estimated by NASA at 600 to 700 days. The Seerseller time should finish out at just about 1,058 days, the difference, of course, being largely due to the greatly extended stay on the surface of Mars by Seerseller and his party.

Of course, there are some far greater differences between the imagined NASA expedition and the one we are just now seeing come to a close. The tragic crash of the landing rocket; the findings of widespread negligence and even coverup that are now beginning to appear—nothing like these, of course, was anticipated.

But the greatest difference still is all to the good. That is the wholly unexpected discovery of living and at least semi-intelligent native Martians! Neither Von Braun nor any other NASA scientist had dared forecast any such possibility—at least in public!

It now appears that the landing on Earth by the Seerseller expedition will take place at Cape Canaveral early in December of this year. A whole new runway is now being constructed to receive the touchdown. There will, of course, be the traditional huge NASA blowout, with dignitaries of all varieties present to welcome the returning Earthmen and their Martian passengers—and the final good news from your Secretary is that he has been invited to attend!

To be sure (the Secretary wishes to make known), he recognises that this honour is paid not just to him but to all the members of the British Interplanetary Society, which for well over half a century has ever been at the forefront of the drive to go into space. Nevertheless, assuming that his health permits (always an iffy question for what even our Secretary concedes is a somewhat aging human frame), he will certainly be there!

SIXTEEN

THE
MISSIONER

At five-fifty exactly the heralds began to race through the corridors of the old hotel, calling into each room as they passed, "Good morning! God bless you! Praise the Reverend!" As their eyes opened, each of the young men in Seth's room called back, in reverse order:

"Praise the Reverend! God bless you. Good morning."

Another blessed day had dawned for Seth. Just "Seth." It wasn't Seth Jones or Seth Robinson—it wasn't any more even Seth Marengeth, the name he had been born to. In the service of the Reverend you didn't use surnames, since all of you were, in reality, Reverend's very own and much-loved children. Praise the Reverend, Seth thought again automatically as he slid his feet over the side of the bunk, found slippers, and reached for his flannel modesty robe. (*Modesty* was what they called it, and modest it was—but in late November, in Reverend's blessed Sanctuary, it also kept the goose bumps away. Reverend did not believe in rejecting the weather God had sent.) Seth stood up to begin making his bed just as Jakob, nearest the hall, was already entering the bathroom and Jimmy, in between, was kneeling for morning prayer. By the time Seth had his covers neatly taut over the single pillow, Jakob was out of the bath and beginning to strip his own bunk and Jimmy was grabbing toothbrush and comb for his turn in the WC, while Seth slipped down to his knees.

"Oh, holy Reverend," he prayed, "save me from the temptations that assail me. Help me to overcome the wickedness of my old ways. Let me not fall by the wayside as my brothers and sisters march with you in the way of righteousness. Teach me to deny the flesh and exalt the spirit, holy Reverend, in His name and thine."

As always, the timing was exact. It was Seth's turn for the bathroom just as he finished reciting the words of grace and praise for Reverend. In six minutes exactly from the time the heralds first called in at the open door, all three of the young men who occupied Room 2143 of Reverend's Central Sanctuary were beside their beds, pulling on trousers before removing their robes, donning shirts, ties, and socks in perfect unison, like a Rockettes routine at the old Radio City Music Hall. By five after six they were part of the orderly, smiling line gathered before the elevators that would take them to the morning prayer breakfast.

It was a perfectly normal morning in the Central Sanctuary, except for one little thing. They discovered it as they walked politely in order into the great refectory hall.

Reverend wasn't there.

The great golden chair at the head of the Holy Table was empty. Where Reverend's holy work had called him no one at Seth's table seemed to know.

Time was when the Central Sanctuary was a worldly place—no, that didn't describe it—it was not only a *very* worldly place but even a really scandalous one. Before Reverend bought it and made it holy it had been one of those citadels of sin, a midtown hotel near the train station, a place where persons of all kinds sheltered for the night. A good many of those people were less interested in sheltering, it was said, than in practicing some of those peculiarly terrible vices that Reverend thundered against. Young girls had sold their bodies in these rooms! Married men and women illicitly bedded down in them with men and women other than the ones they were married to! Even worse, there were couples—half the listeners were blushing even before Reverend actually mentioned what came next—couples of the same gender who shared beds and practiced unnameable evil on each other's bodies. The rooms had held people who drank, and people who smoked tobacco and worse things. Up on the roof of the Central Sanctuary, where Reverend now had his broadcast studio so that his Sunday morning messages might go out to the entire listening world, there had been a "nightclub"—a place where scantily clad women pranced and lecherous comics used off-color language while saxophones and drums pounded out sensuous, obscene music for dancers clutching each other passionately. Sodom had held nothing wickeder than the old hotel!

All that was changed now, of course. What remained had been purified to the services of Reverend and the Lord. The great ground-floor ballroom, once rivaling the rooftop in the abandoned pursuit of vice, was now set up like the dining hall of a college or a monastery. Long trestle tables spanned what had once been the dance floor. Benches replaced the gold-backed chairs with embroidered seats that had once held drunken revelers. The dais where marijuana-smoking jazz musicians had blared jungle rhythms now held only the Holy Table itself.

More than four hundred of the Reverend's staunchest troops were fed in this refectory every day, and each night slept in the rooms overhead. The rooms were, of course, carefully segregated. Floors 8 to 17 were for females, 18 to 28 were male. But all the Reverend's followers ate in the same place. They even shared the same tables, girls on one side, boys on the other. Praise Reverend for that, thought Seth, as he eagerly studied the line of young women approaching to take their seats. Every one of them, he knew, was Reverend's blessed servitor, and they were all equal in Reverend's eyes. All the same, there was one female missioner Seth was more pleased to sit across from than the others.

Since seating was by the chance of any servitor's place in line, and since the order in the lines was mostly determined by the way the heralds dispatched elevators to each floor, the chance of pairing any two particular people was pretty scant. It was not likely that lasting attachments would be formed over the meal table. Seth might find any individual young woman across from him at any meal, and statistics said that it would probably be four months or more before she turned up there again. Four months, in the Sanctuary, was an eternity. The average stay of any servitor in any of Reverend's sanctuaries was rarely as much as a year, since there were always urgent needs to be met in some other city. So really, Seth knew, the statistical chance of having the one particular girl he wanted to see there this morning was almost nil. . . .

But statistics were obviously meant to be violated, for there she was! Sister Evangeline! She bowed her head almost at once and clasped her hands meekly in her lap, waiting for the signal to begin the meal. But before the head went down in the custody of the eyes she glanced briefly at Seth.

It was not an unfriendly glance at all. It made him bold.

"Good morning," he whispered, drawing a disapproving look from Jakob in the place next to him.

Evangeline must have felt the chill of the look. Obviously she didn't care. Regardless of rules, heedless of who might hear, she whispered back, "Good morning, Seth."

Seth felt a sudden flush of warmth and joy all over. He turned a smile on Jakob that warmed away the reproach on his roommate's face, and even smiled toward the herald at the head of the table, who was looking sternly at the breakfasters. Belatedly Seth realized that he and Evangeline were not the only whisperers at the table. In fact, the whole room was buzzing—very low-key, subdued buzzing, but still a thing that Seth had never before seen at a prayer breakfast. Oddly, the heralds were doing little to quell it. Unbelievably, Seth saw one of them pause in patrol around the room and bend to the ear of the table herald. Seth craned his neck, trying to hear . . . and managed to catch two words. One was *Reverend*. And the other was *Martians*.

* * *

To the best of Seth's recollection, he had never heard the word *Martians* spoken in the Sanctuary before, though the worldly papers were full of stories about them. Reverend was not against science. He was just against the more decadent applications of it. (Like air-conditioning, and like heating when it was not yet officially winter.) Reverend wasn't even against progress—probably—well, actually he had never mentioned progress at all.

The worldly world talked about the Martians a lot. They more than talked; Martians had become an industry as big as hula hoops or pet rocks. Down the street from the Sanctuary, Macy's department store had "Martian" furniture in its window. Street vendors hustled Martian dolls on Forty-second Street, right between the three-card monte dealers and the vendors of fake digital watches. The Air Force recruiting station had blowups of the *Algonquin* spacecraft, under the legend: "*Sustineo alas*—even on Mars!"

But in the *Sanctuary*?

But there it was. There had not been so much excitement in the Holy Sanctuary for months. Seth could not help but share it, because it was so unlike the servitors to take an interest in such worldly—well, not "worldly," exactly, but surely nonspiritual—matters as the half-dozen or so peculiar creatures that had been discovered on Mars and were now on their way back to Earth. He was almost wriggling with curiosity as one of the heralds at the Holy Table stood up and rang the silver prayer bell.

Dutifully the four hundred persons in the refectory repeated the morning prayer, their voices choiring in the words. Then the herald waved them to be seated but, instead of pronouncing the grace before meals, he tapped the bell again.

"My brothers and sisters in Reverend's service," he said, smiling, his soft voice carrying easily across the hushed hall, "there is good news for us this morning. Reverend is not here because he is even now on his way to Florida. He has been invited personally by the President of the United States to be present to welcome the space travelers and the Martian beings they bring with them when they return to Earth. Praise Reverend!" And all four hundred voices echoed *Praise Reverend!* "Bless the astronauts!" *Bless the astronauts!* "And bless the Martians!" *And bless the Martians* came the response—a little ragged, to be sure, since it was the first any of them had known that the Martians had souls to bless.

Eating was hurried and sparse that morning, because the whispering would not die down. Even the heads of table were doing it, or at least pretending not to notice when their charges broke silence in the meal. What an honor it was, to be sure!—not to Reverend, of course, because Reverend had no need of Earthly honors, but to the President and to the United States itself that Reverend should take time from his burden of cares to welcome these strange creatures from another planet and give them God's grace. Every face in the refectory was glowing with joy—even the faces of the almost worldly ones, who perhaps had been listening to radio or even reading worldly newspapers, and said that it was not merely Reverend who had been invited. No, they said wisely, there was a large ecumenical potpourri of Catholic bishops and born-again Baptist ministers and rabbis and Latter Day Saints and even an imam or two from the Muslim communities in New York and the West. None of the missioners thought that that mattered in the least. Reverend would carry the burden for all. "Oh, bless the Martians," whispered Seth across the table. He didn't look at Evangeline, but it was she who returned the whisper:

"Yes, and praise Reverend for blessing them!"

It was, all in all, one of the best days Seth had ever had, even compared with all those wonderful, blessed days since he had accepted that first bus-terminal invitation to attend one of Reverend's love-in dinners for the weary and heartsick. He had signed up to join Reverend's service before he left the table that night. His whole life had been joyous since then—well, *mostly* joyous; Reverend said that one must accept disappointments and difficulties as trials of faith, and even in Reverend's service one had such little setbacks now and then. But when he compared his life in Holy Sanctuary with the emptiness and futility of what had gone before, he knew in his heart that Reverend indeed spoke with the voice of God. Seth was almost absolutely, definitely sure of that.

He never doubted it at all . . . except now and then, when some profane outsider grabbed him and tried to tell him about Reverend's office buildings and mining stocks and two private DC-9s; but the doubts always passed.

There were no doubts in Seth's mind this morning. What a wonderful day this was turning out to be!

And when Seth took his place among the outside teams lining up for their day's assignments, it got even better. When the airport herald chose the missioners for Newark Airport that morning, Evangeline was the first he picked. Seth trembled—prayed—worried—and then, just as he had almost given up hope, the herald looked in his direction and said, "You, too, Brother Seth."

There was no doubt about it. This day was as nearly perfect as any day ever could be this side of Reverend's blessed Heaven. Newark Airport was the best assignment they could have drawn!

Of course, any missioning at all would be fine if he and Evangeline did it together, but some assignments were better than others. For instance, the sisters and brothers assigned to the Port Authority Bus Terminal or to the railroad stations had to walk to their destinations. So did the ones assigned to mission on Fifth Avenue or outside the midtown hotels, and, besides, at this time of year they had to compete with all those sidewalk Santas ringing their stupid bells. The Wall Street people took the subway. So did the teams for JFK and LaGuardia airports, although they would transfer to city buses along the way, and for the Kennedy people the trip would take more than an hour.

Newark was much the best. The Newark team contained seven missioners, because the terminals were so big. In the regular terminals you really had time to talk to the people you met. The buildings were sparsely used. You could walk along with the prospects, talking as you went. The old terminal was busier, and the people there always seemed in such a hurry that they were reluctant to take your flower and let you ask them if they were happy, really happy, in their lives. Still, the cut-rate airline in the old terminal attracted the very kind of young

people who were most likely to want to listen to Reverend's message
of hope.

But what was most important of all about Newark, in Seth's mind
that day, was that you went out there in one of Reverend's minivans,
two to a seat. And the person you shared a seat with might easily be
Evangeline!

No, there was no doubt at all in Seth's mind that this could easily
turn out to be the very happiest day of his life.

In the event, it wasn't quite all it could have been.

To begin with, when Seth presented himself for assignment everybody was talking about the Martians. It took a while for Thad, the
team herald, to remember that there was a message for Seth. "No, I
don't know what they want, but you'd better see them right away—
and hurry, because we leave in five minutes!"

It was the Bursary Herald who wanted to see Seth, and what he
wanted to talk about was Seth's recent inheritance. "Praise Reverend,"
the man said. "Brother Seth, have you heard from those lawyers?"

"No, Brother Herald," Seth said at once, though it was a silly
question. How could he have heard anything that the heralds would
not know about before he did?

"I think," the herald said wisely, "that if you don't get a letter in
the next two or three days you should telephone them. After all, if
your Aunt Ellen wanted you to have this money they have no right
to hold it up, do they? What was the amount you inherited again, a
little over sixty-eight hundred dollars?"

"There was also a silver tea service she wanted me to have."

"Oh, yes—and, oh, won't that tea service look grand at the Holy
Table! Reverend is certain to want to thank you for donating your
entire inheritance this way, Seth. I think he might even want to do
it in person! Perhaps right in the middle of a meal he will call you
up to the Holy Table, in front of everyone, and speak to you about
it personally!"

"Praise Reverend! I'll call the lawyers," Seth promised.

"Yes, that would be best. Let's say next Monday, if you haven't heard. I'll arrange a call from my quarters, so that I can be there to help you deal with them if they raise any impudent problems—you know how lawyers are!"

So that was short enough; but by the time Seth got out to the curb where the van was waiting the others were clustered around its door.

There was also a stranger there, a tall, red-faced man who looked like a football player ten years past his prime. He was certainly not any part of Reverend's servitors, but he was standing on the sidewalk watching them. The man was blocking Seth's way. As Seth dodged past with a civil, "Excuse me, sir," the red-faced man gave him a smile. Seth recognized the expression at once. It was the grin of contempt you got from the scoffing mundanes who had seen some of those vicious television programs about Reverend.

That experience wasn't uncommon. You got all kinds among the mundanes. Most of the New Yorkers who hurried past the hotel had no idea who was occupying it now, and wouldn't have cared if they had. But there were the others, the curious ones. There were the prurient-minded ones who were always trying to peer past the lobby door, or through the draped windows, to see who knew what? And every time you stepped out of the building on Reverend's holy work you were sure to see half a dozen gawkers and loafers studying you to see if you looked brainwashed or glassy-eyed. If they were tourists, they snapped your picture. If they were natives they snickered and turned away, with that wise-guy New York look that said they'd seen it all already, only better.

The red-faced man didn't fit either pattern. He was, Seth decided, a Class Three, the worst of all. He was one of the bigoted ones who hated Reverend and all his works, and would sometimes spit on you when you offered them a Peace Flower.

Seth stepped protectively between Evangeline and the man, but perhaps he had been wrong. The man turned away unconcernedly, and though Seth watched him stroll out of sight he didn't look back.

"Seth!" the team herald was calling impatiently. "We're all waiting!"

So Seth was last on the bus, and by then the seat next to Evangeline was taken. Disappointed, he crawled to the rear.

It was a pity that he was in the back, because the center seats were buzzing with conversation. "Reverend will be in the stand with the President of the United States and all sorts of foreign dignitaries," Sister Miranda announced, and Brother Everett declared: "He'll be on television! I bet they'll let us watch him!" And Evangeline asked —Seth was sure it was her voice, though her head was turned away —"But are these things *really* Martians?" and was drowned out by two or three of the others at once: "Of course they're real Martians! *Reverend* says they're Martians! Reverend wouldn't say that if it weren't positively so!"

It was as close as servitors ever came to quarreling, and the herald at the wheel did not let it go farther. Thad was not only in charge of the Newark Airport missioning team, he was an actual graduate of Reverend's leadership college, out among the farms of Sussex County, and thus certainly destined for a high place in the church. "Sing, brothers and sisters!" he cried, as they turned onto the line of cars waiting to get into the Lincoln Tunnel, and the sing-along ended all the talk.

Bravely Seth tried to join in Reverend's favorite old gospel hymns. It wasn't easy. He couldn't help yawning. Even a healthy man in his twenties can't go on forever on less than six hours' sleep a night. Long before they turned off the tunnel road to the free highway that led to the airport (there was no sense wasting Reverend's money on tolls that just went to support the wicked state of New Jersey), Seth's head dropped and his eyes were closed.

He woke with a start as the van slid into a space in the airport's underground parking garage. They were at Terminal Two. Evangeline was gone. All of the missioners were gone but Thad and himself, and Thad turned back from the steering wheel to look with disfavor at him. "Oh, Seth," he said, "you slept right through today's message from Reverend, didn't you?"

Half-dazed, Seth opened his mouth to answer, but Thad cut in and saved him from the temptation of a lie. "Of course you did," he said, pulling the cassette out of the dashboard player. "The message is about Mars, Seth. Reverend wants us to spread the good news that salvation is possible for anyone. Anyone at all! Any *thing*, even, Seth, because God's goodness is infinite. It extends to the Moon, to Mars, and to all the galaxies beyond. That's why Reverend himself has gone to greet these Martians and tell them of God's forgiveness and love. Have you got that, Seth? Do you know what to say in your missioning?"

"I think so, Brother Thad," Seth mumbled.

"Then go and tell it! You'll take the coffee shop, the ticketing areas, and any of the gates as far as the security checkpoints. I've got the baggage claim."

"Praise the Reverend," Seth said automatically, and slid out of the van to begin his work.

There was a time when Seth Marengeth was not a missioner for Reverend's goodness.

Seth's early life, in fact, showed very little interest in goodness at all. He was of the world worldly. In junior high he drank beer. As a senior he smoked pot. He thought college might be more interesting, because he majored in physics and astronomy and that was full of romantic implications for him, but it didn't work out that way. While he was flunking out of his junior year he tried ludes to soothe away the worries about what his father would say about his grades, and uppers to get through the cram sessions for the examinations he had no chance of passing anyway. That was when he discovered that he liked pills better than he liked going to college. His father tried to accept the fact that his son would not be a college graduate. He had trouble managing it, and Seth's father's acceptance wasn't enough anyway, for the real world turned out to be less forgiving. There didn't seem to be many good jobs for a youth with no college and no business experience, and it didn't seem to Seth that Dad and stepmother Grace much welcomed having him hanging around the house while he waited for something to happen.

He did get jobs of a kind, briefly. He tried MacDonald's and he tried the 7-Eleven, but actually they didn't seem a whole lot better than no jobs at all. Then he tried the Hare Krishnas.

That looked promising for a while. There was a lot he liked about the Hare Krishnas, but he couldn't quite give up the idea of ever eating meat again. The other thing he didn't like was the necessity of shaving his head. After he quit the Hare Krishnas he was wholly without direction. He might have tried things a good deal worse, if it hadn't been for the blessed day when he discovered the blessed Reverend.

That was (as Seth had to remind himself from time to time) a wonderful, blessed day! Reverend gave him a purpose to life and a reason for living it. More than that. Reverend gave him a home.

It was even better for Seth than for most of the brand-new converts who came in every day, all dewy-eyed and hopeful and wondering, because Seth turned out to be a kind of celebrity in the Holy Sanctuary.

It had nothing to do with Seth himself, really. It was his father's attitude that made Seth stand out. When, after the first week, Seth dutifully made his monitored phone call home to keep his parents from reporting him a missing person, he had been quite sure his father would throw a fit. His father surprised him. After the first moment's astonishment and dismay there was a silence at the other end—the kind of silence you get when someone has cupped the mouthpiece to talk things over with some other person. Then Seth's father came back on with, of all things, congratulations. It hadn't taken more than a minute for Dad and Grace to decide that, all things considered, maybe what Seth had done was as good a thing as he was ever likely to do.

So from that first week Seth was pointed out as something special in the Sanctuary. He was very nearly the only young man or woman there whose family didn't object—*really* object, sometimes even to the point of bringing lawsuits or hiring those evil deprogrammers who were whispered about in the minutes before evening prayer. So Seth was given early recognition by the heralds. They often put him on front-door duty. When middle-aged weeping Moms and blustering, bullying Dads came to demand the privilege of talking sense to their offspring, Seth, after politely refusing to permit an interview, was at least able to offer them his own father's phone number to call for reassurance.

Of course, Seth never knew exactly what his father might say, if any of them ever did call. But it did help get rid of the other parents.

What Seth's real mother might have said no one could tell, least of all Seth. He hadn't seen her since she took off with the husband of the woman next door, when Seth was three. He supposed that that event had changed his life. It had changed it religiously, anyway, because his father had had to stop being Catholic when he married Grace, who wouldn't stand for going to mass. The question of a Catholic upbringing had never come up in the Marengeth household anymore. It did come up as a topic of conversation in Holy Sanctuary, now and then. There were present followers of Reverend who had formerly been followers of *everything*, from Unitarians to born-again Baptists, and certainly a good many who had been Catholic—at least two, Seth knew, who had even thought about going for the priesthood before they discovered Reverend's equally orderly, but slightly less restrictive, way of life. Not to mention girls like Evangeline, who had insisted on going back for a teary, sobby three-hour conference with her old Presbyterian minister before she finally walked through the Sanctuary door. That was actually the first thing that had brought Seth and Evangeline together—or as much "together" as they could hope to be until, and unless, Reverend decreed something closer for them. Evangeline's father had been one of the Dads Seth had gently and politely turned away—not easily, because the man had been incandescent with rage: "Won't see me? What do you mean, she won't see me? I'm *Tim Beurdy*. I'm not some wimp to push around, and I'm her *father*." But Seth was firm, and ultimately the man had gone blustering away, and when he told Evangeline about it she had thanked him.

Seth smiled tenderly at the thought. How wonderfully steadfast Evangeline was! What a wonderful wife she would make for Seth . . . if only Reverend, in Reverend's unassailable wisdom, were to decide that that was what was to be.

There were plenty of people milling around in the airport for early flights, but that didn't mean that there were many good prospects for the missioners. Early-morning travelers were always in a hurry. Seth kept busy, but he didn't accomplish much, because he didn't have the right kind of raw material to work with. Charter-flight tourists moved in herds and huddled together against outsiders, because they were all terrified of not getting to the right gate or of failing to hear an announcement about where to pick up their free casino chips and nightclub vouchers. Businessmen with early appointments in another city wanted nothing but to get through the preliminary paperwork in their attaché cases; and those two classes were the principal kinds of people who took nine A.M. flights. By ten-thirty Seth had given away fewer than a dozen of the wilting Peace Flowers. He had less than ten dollars in his pocket to show for it, and not even one person had said, even untruthfully, that he was interested in attending a fellowship dinner.

There was, in fact, a moment then when there was literally no one in sight in the whole terminal—no one, anyway, but the items of fixed furniture like reservations clerks and security guards. It was no use offering any of them a Peace Flower. They had been hit on so many times before that they just shook their heads without even looking up.

Seth's feet were beginning to hurt.

What he should do, he knew, was to head for the coffee shop at the other end of the terminal. There might be someone, maybe even a good many someones, sitting there bored enough to strike up a conversation. What he *wanted* to do, though, was sit down and rest his feet.

That was one of the biggest no-nos in the business, he knew. It was not only against instructions from the heralds, it was actually, sort of, against the law. At least, it was the kind of thing the airport security guards picked up on. There was a narrow distinction between exercising the constitutionally protected right of freedom of religion and assembly, on one hand, and, on the other hand, plain loitering. Sitting down could erase that distinction.

What made things worse for Seth was that the nearest row of empty seats had coin-operated television sets in front of them, and somebody had left one of them going.

TV had once been Seth's principal way of getting through the interminable time between get-up and go-to-bed in those worldly days before Reverend. Now it was absent from his life almost entirely. Once in a while he got a brief peek at a set in a store window near the corner where he was missioning, but you never could hear the sound in those cases. A bummer. Even more rarely came those very infrequent occasions when a few lucky servitors were invited into the heralds' common room, to watch news, or maybe even reruns of "I Love Lucy" or "The Mary Tyler Moore Show," in that precious hour that heralds were allowed to have between dinner and evening devotions. Craning his neck, Seth could see that the program on the little coin-operated set was one of his old soaps. "All My Children," maybe, or "As the World Turns"—you couldn't tell which, really, unless you'd been keeping in touch, as characters came and went, and it had been many months since Seth had seen either.

Virtuously he turned away. His duty lay in the coffee shop, not in idling away the precious hours that belonged to Reverend!

Then, passing a row of unoccupied phone booths, he hesitated.

Seth wasn't exactly thinking about his Aunt Ellen's bequest. He had thought about it in detail when the news of her will reached him—had thought about it a lot, in fact, with Reverend's heralds helping him to clarify his thoughts. "The silver tea set she wanted you to have when you marry? Yes, Seth, that is very sweet, but when we marry we do not live in such a worldly way, do we? And the money—oh, Seth, how much good a sum like that can do in spreading Reverend's message of salvation to the weary world!"

"Praise Reverend," Seth had said; and that was the end of it. Almost the end of it, anyway. And the question was not really in his mind as he entered the phone booth, closed the door, and sat gratefully on the little seat. He was simply resting his feet for a moment, where no one could see.

It was almost without thought that he reached into his pocket, borrowed a quarter from the store he had collected for Reverend, and dialed a collect long-distance call.

The lawyer's office answered at once, and the lawyer himself was on the phone just seconds later. He had a pleasant, high-pitched voice, and he responded at once to Seth's tentative question. "Ah, yes, Mr. Marengeth. I'm glad to tell you that the surrogate court has approved the probate. We're just waiting for the official document. We should be able to distribute the bequests within a few days. Tell me, Mr. Marengeth, is there a tax question involved? Because I think we could get your inheritance to you before the end of the year, if that is an issue."

"No, it isn't a tax question."

"I see." There was a pause on the other end of the line. "Well, Mr. Marengeth, if you need a sum of money at once I believe there would be no impropriety in effecting at least a partial distribution. Certainly not for any sum up to a thousand dollars or so, if you would like that."

"Not yet," said Seth, and thanked the man, and hung up. He put the returned quarter back in his pocket and flexed his toes thoughtfully.

His feet no longer hurt; it was time to go back to Reverend's work. The coffee shop—

As a matter of fact, the coffee shop turned out to be full of prospects, and that kept him busy for a while. There was a party of Japanese tourists there. Although they didn't speak much English they were certainly not hostile. And when he came out of the shop a great Eastern widebody was beginning to load for Orlando, and another for Puerto Rico, and there were more people than he could talk to for a while. As he worked his way slowly down the lines waiting to go through the X-ray, then back into the terminal itself, the memory of the conversation with the lawyer faded from his mind.

His luck was running high. When he got to the waiting area there were three young people, A-frames strapped to their backs, gathered around one of the pay-TV sets.

They were watching a program about Mars.

Wonderful! "Have a flower," Seth said genially, and in the same breath, "Going down to watch the Martians come in?"

When the shorter-haired of the two girls in the group smiled, "You better believe it!" Seth was on safe ground.

"I'll bet you're not aware," he challenged, "that the President of the United States has personally invited Reverend to welcome the Martians. The President! I don't know how you feel about our President—" they didn't give him a clue, so he took the safe middle ground, "but whatever you think of him, it's the best thing he could have done. Reverend is going to bring those poor, lost Martian souls God's message of love and grace and forgiveness." He was already pinning a flower on the fringed vest of the third person, a bearded but peaceful-looking male. "We all need that, don't we?" he asked. It was one of the say-yes rhetorical questions that you asked to get the prospects in a yes-saying frame of mind, and he didn't wait for an answer. "What are you going to do, camp out across the Banana River and watch the spaceship come in? Gosh, that sounds wonderful. Well, let me give you an address. If you want some fine, home-cooked food and a nice place to stay, Reverend has a Sanctuary in Orlando. You'd all be really welcome. Nobody will hassle you. You don't have to pay a thing, and you don't have to do anything; it's just a nice, clean place with good food and a lot of friendly people—what can you lose?"

The final boarding call came then. But all three took the address, and all three had listened. And when they had gone, Seth saw that the Mars program was still playing on the television set.

That was a temptation that surpassed even his soap operas! Seth found it hard to resist.

There had been a time in Seth's life when space travel occupied as much of his thoughts, and love, as Reverend did now—well, not really that much, maybe; but all the same a lot. As a child he had been the biggest space fan on the block. He had read every story the school library could produce for him about Mars and the Moon and all the wonders of the universe. The interest hadn't survived as such total dedication, but it had never left him entirely, either. Seth had still been in the world, three years earlier, when the Seerseller expedition's two great spaceships pulled themselves out of Low Earth Orbit and headed for the red planet. He had thrilled to the wondrous sight. He had wished with all his heart that he could be on it. He had even thought briefly of taking one more shot at college—finish up those physics and astronomy courses, anything that might give Seth Marengeth, too, a shot at getting accepted on one of those wonderful expeditions of discovery and adventure.

He hadn't really done that, of course. But he still remembered the awe and delight of watching those two great ships of the Seerseller expedition at their launch, sliding each in turn out of its orbit in stately procession, with the swelling, almost invisible plumes of ionized gas shoving them gently and irrevocably toward Mars.

When the expedition's instrument and supply ship crashed on landing it was a stabbing and unhealed personal disaster.

Seth's last thoughts of becoming an astronaut died with that ship. What was the point? Things were obviously just as screwed up on Mars as on Earth.

Still, Seth remembered that magic. He stood irresolute before the television set. It was a remote broadcast from the Cape itself. Seth could see the great, broad landing strip the remaining ship would come down on behind the network commentator, as the man described the arrangements for the next day's welcoming.

That decided Seth. The welcoming! Of course! Wasn't Reverend himself going to be among the great and famous there to welcome the space travelers? So no one could possibly object, he thought, if he took a moment to see what the worldly announcer might have to say about Reverend's presence. . . .

In that he was wrong. He had just sunk into the cramped little chair when Thad's reproachful voice told him so from behind: "Oh, Seth, what are you doing?"

Seth got up quickly. "I thought I might see Reverend himself—"

"You will certainly see Reverend himself," said Thad, "at the proper time, in the proper place. This isn't it."

"I'm sorry," Seth apologized. The herald accepted it without comment, only saying:

"It's time for lunch."

And then, as they turned away to pick up the others for the twenty minutes allowed for eating the sandwiches in the van, he added, "I'm changing the assignments around for this afternoon. I have to go back to the Sanctuary for more books after lunch. Sister Evangeline will take my place with you here at Terminal Two."

Rarely had Seth joined in the grace prayer before the meal so wholeheartedly.

It was a short lunch hour, of course. Missioners never took more than twenty minutes to eat. None of them wanted to. Reverend's heralds had many times made it clear that every moment on this earth was a special and irreplaceable gift from God. None of those moments was to be wasted on worldly things like dawdling over a meal. But never before had twenty minutes gone so fast. Or so tenderly, for Evangeline's fingers touched Seth's as she passed the mustard, and Seth's very pores joyfully soaked in the warmth that came from her body, right there in the seat next to him—and the whole promising afternoon still lay ahead!

The missioners gave their reports as they ate. Thad carefully counted up the love offerings from each in the sight of all, so all could sign the tally slips that would go in to the offertory heralds at the Sanctuary. When he came to Seth's his mouth dropped open and his eyes widened. "Seth! You've got eighty-three *dollars* here," he gasped. "This is a fifty-dollar bill!"

"That's right. I think the blessed donor was Japanese," Seth said proudly, aware of Evangeline's admiration. "His English wasn't very good, but I'm sure he said he wanted me to take it for Reverend's work."

"I don't see any Japanese name on your list," Thad complained. "How often do you see someone with that much grace for giving, Seth? Such a person should be remembered and thanked—a letter from Reverend himself, maybe."

"He didn't understand what I was talking about when I asked him for his name," Seth explained. He thought of adding, but didn't, that the man hadn't seemed too sure of the denomination of the bill when he pulled it off a roll. "And then he had to hurry to catch his plane."

Thad pursed his lips, then decided to be rewarding. "You've done well, Seth," he said, "although next time Reverend would want you to make a greater effort about the name."

He turned back to his tallies. Evangeline whispered, "I've never brought in a love offering like that, Seth." And Bruno, the nineteen-year-old, said enviously:

"Did you tell them the Reverend's message about the Martians, Seth? I tried, but people just laughed at me."

"Of course I did. I explained that even Martians are worthy of God's grace, although Christ came to our planet first, to give His life to redeem us."

"Reverend didn't say that," Thad said, looking up sharply from his tallies.

"No, but it stands to reason," Bruno argued, swiftly switching his loyalties, "because how could you think the Redeemer would take the form of one of those dumb-looking animals?"

And that was good, too—oh, everything was good on this very good day! Because Thad thundered at the boy, "Animals? But how can they be animals, when Reverend himself says they have souls? He said they can be saved; therefore they have souls. Therefore they are not animals, because what does Reverend teach us is the difference between animals and people?"

"People have souls," Bruno said sullenly. "Okay, if they aren't animals, what are they?"

"They are Martians," Thad said severely, and that explained it all.

And while Bruno was being chastened, and the others were listening in fascination, Evangeline got up to begin collecting the waxed paper and the plastic cups that had contained Kool-Aid, and Seth leaped to help her. Though their hands touched more than ever, the herald was too involved with Bruno to notice.

Seth, on the other hand, certainly noticed each touch. He noticed them most acutely. He noticed with the nerve endings in the tips of his fingers, because every touch made them tingle; and he noticed, with his blissful mind, that Evangeline did not try to prevent any one of those touches.

On as blessed a day as this, anything was possible!

It was even possible that the secret plans Seth had been turning over in his mind might actually become real. This was Thursday, Seth thought. On Saturday he would have his weekly one-on-one talk with the herald who was his spiritual adviser. The herald, Andrew, had himself once brought up the consideration that, sooner or later, Seth would ultimately need to marry—not for Seth's own sake, to be sure, and certainly not for any reason of lust or passion, but because it would be Reverend's wish. Reverend explained that, too. He taught that marriage was a blessed state, in no way incompatible with faith and devotion to the higher realm—of course, provided it were brought about in the proper way. Reverend had defined what the proper way was. It was his practice to decide when his followers should marry, and whom.

That was unarguable, of course. But certainly there would be nothing sinful if Seth were to mention to Andrew that he felt the call—and that he had observed that Sister Evangeline was a decent and devoted young woman. . . .

Planning and dreaming lasted Seth all the way back to Terminal Two. As the van left them and disappeared toward Terminal One Evangeline offered him a sisterly blessing on his missioning. When Seth, blinking out of his wonderful daydreams, opened his mouth to return it, the roar of another car's motor drowned his voice, and all the dreams were blasted away.

A big, black limousine raced up to them, tires screeching.

It skidded to a stop at the curb. Three men jumped out. One shoved Seth brutally away, while the other two grabbed the girl.

There wasn't any doubt in Seth's mind about what was happening. Any missioner would recognize the situation at once; they had been warned and warned that it might happen to any one, at any time.

Deprogrammers. And while the men were trying to drag Evangeline, struggling and screaming, into the car, Seth was leaping on the back of the nearest one, shouting for help at the top of his voice. "Kidnappers!" he roared. "Anybody! Help! Call the police!"

The men were huge and strong, and there were three of them. But Evangeline was fighting them as hard as she could, back against the open door of the limousine, kicking and scratching at them, while Seth was wrestling on the ground with the big, red-faced one he had seen outside the Sanctuary. Of course, the two young people couldn't win. They were matched against professionals, men who made their living by snatching youths from the Moonies and the Hare Krishnas and the Scientologists and battering at them for days on end until their will was broken and they agreed to come back to their families. But, big as they were, the men didn't want to break any bones. . . . And then, a miracle!—a rusty old station wagon nosed around the corner, and four young Army recruits on their way to some new training station jumped out and ran toward them.

That did it. The men swore and shoved Evangeline and Seth away and leaped back into the limousine before the soldiers reached him. "What was that?" shouted one of the soldiers, and another cried:

"I got the license number. Let's go find a cop!"

And it was all Evangeline and Seth could do to persuade the recruits that, really, it was all right, and the police shouldn't be involved (because Reverend's instructions on that were very clear) . . . and that what they really needed to do was to get to a telephone and report back to Sanctuary what had happened. . . .

If, that is, one of the soldiers would lend them some coins for the phone.

When Thad and the other airport missioners had been contacted and come hurrying back Seth and Evangeline climbed thankfully back into the van, and they all joined in an exultant sing to praise Reverend, and praise God, and praise the glory of service in the Lord's work. Then Thad and a senior herald named Wendell excused themselves for a moment, while the others begged Seth and Evangeline to tell them everything, every last thing, about what the deprogrammers had done, and said, and wanted.

When Thad came back he opened the door and peered in. He looked serious. Seth automatically almost loosened his hold on Evangeline's hand, then belligerently tightened it again; but that wasn't what was on the herald's mind. "You have done very well, Seth," he said. "Reverend is very pleased."

"You mean Reverend knows about it already?" Seth marveled.

"Reverend knows everything," Thad said severely. "He wishes to reward you for your courage and dedication. Also, it's a good idea to get Sister Evangeline out of this area for a while. Wendell?"

Wendell leaned in the door, looking frostily at Seth. He handed a couple of airline ticket envelopes to him. "There you are, Seth," said Thad kindly. "The two of you are going on the next flight to Florida."

"Florida?" Seth repeated, blinking in surprise.

"Of course, Florida! It's the best place for you right now, and besides missioners are needed there for the welcome to the Martians. You're going to serve Reverend at the Cape!"

SEVENTEEN

Time Magazine: "WE WAIT WITH EAGERNESS AND JOY"

Captain Seerseller, this is the President speaking.

Captain Seerseller, I want to tell you that all America, indeed all the world, is praying for you as you make the final approach to come home to the Earth we all love. We salute your heroic leadership and extend a warm hand of welcome to your very special passengers.

Captain Seerseller, we wait with eagerness and joy to welcome you home.

When Herbert George Wells's fictional Martians came to England in 1897 they brought heat rays, vampirelike bloodsucking of their enslaved human "cows," and total destruction of all the works of Man (and then they produced another wave of panic, 41 years later in America, through the famed radio broadcast of that other Welles, Orson). Not so the latest immigrants from the Red Planet. Our newest Martian arrivals are named Alexander, Bob, Christopher, Doris, Edward, and Gretel, and what they are bringing us, pundits say, is a much-needed shot in the economic arm, a dazzling spectacle for the enthralled multitudes and—can it be possible?—a new sense of national purpose.

Start by adding up the dollars that have appeared, as if by magic, in our stagnating economy: The biggest and newest jolt is the $42 billion in new appropriations for the revitalized American space program. Santa Claus has come early to Houston, Orange County, and Huntsville, Alabama. Add in six new feature films on Mars and its Martians, with a total announced production budget of $225 million. A burgeoning toy, game, and doll industry with third-quarter retail sales alone of $380 million or more, and Christmas yet to come— Darlin' Doris competes with Mindy Mars for the hottest item in the Christmas trade.

But, scientists say, that may be just the beginning. Food chemists are eager to get their hands on samples of the "algal froth"—the soup of living funguslike organisms—that the Martians have survived on for eons unknown. Can these grow on Earth? There is no apparent reason why not, the agronomists say, and see in them a possible cheap, effective, and permanent solution to recurring famines in the hard-hit underdeveloped areas of our own hungry old world. Then there are the, as yet unknown, lessons to be learned from whatever science and technology the ancient Martian race possessed. What discoveries may there be here? No Earthling yet can say. Surely the current slow, sweet-tempered cave dwellers have little to teach us in the way of fast-track, high-technology science; but the signs are there to say that someone, once, had the skills to dig vast catacombs and warrens. The "Martian Macy's" seems to have held manufactured goods—once. That means that, once, there must have been factories and industries to produce them in processes which, since they arose with no possible contact with their Earthly equivalents, almost certainly embodied different kinds of technologies. And, among the discoverable lore of that vanished people, perhaps there are lessons our own idling workshops can employ to start the machines buzzing again.

But all that is for Christmases yet to come. What brightens our current approaching Yuletide festivities is the vast and multifaceted welcome we Earth creatures are preparing for our cosmic brothers.

In Pasadena, California, five giant effigies of the Martian voyagers are being sculpted out of 456,000 rosebuds for the forthcoming Rose Bowl Parade. In Hannibal, Missouri, two ancient enemies, Marchese Boccanegra and Anthony Makepeace Moore, have buried the hatchet in a joint "scientific" (and very profitable) exploitation of what they claim are Ur-Martian relics here on Earth. Even the Bishop of Rome has entered the Mars Mania as in his weekly 500-word column he chides us with, "It is worth noting that the Martians have survived for many centuries, it seems, without the prospect of overpopulation and without recourse to artificial methods of birth control or to the murder of unborn children we call abortion." But surpassing even the thunder of His Holiness is the glorious spectacle and drama that will be acted out on the Cape on Friday next as, for the first time in human history, Earth welcomes visitors from another planet.

And who will be there, as the President promised, to welcome the wanderers? For openers, there are the ones who received the gilt-edged invitation to the VIP stands on the Cape itself. There are sixty-one thousand of them, and carpenters are still nailing together the seats that will hold them as they watch the touchdown. The nearest of them will be two miles from the landing strip, where 104 ambassadors, 26 heads of state, 31 Nobel laureates, 460 members of Congress, and 1,115 of their wives, husbands, parents, children and siblings, 11,400 clergyman of every denomination, 3,200 university professors, 850 stars of stage, screen, TV, and recordings, 19,800 press and broadcast media people, and 33,914 other Very Important People will greet the incoming explorers, giving a new and much broader definition to the term "very important."

This says nothing about the estimated 50,000 Australians, 500,000 Hawaiians, and 115,000 people in Mexico, extreme south Texas, and the western coast of Florida who will have some chance of seeing the ship as it blazes through reentry and slices through its descending course in the air just prior to landing. Nor does it account for the million-plus (no one really knows how many) tent-trailer-and-sleeping-bag visitors whose advance patrols are already beginning to take up squatters' rights on the shore of the Banana River, across from the

Cape itself, and it certainly does not include the hundreds of millions—it is possible that it may even reach into the billions—who will observe the spectacle in their bedrooms, living rooms, or friendly neighborhood saloons on the world's television screens.

What a difference a year makes! Twelve months ago this week, Congressman Phil Ingram was trying to get Mars cut right out of the budget. Harking back to the dying moan of the inconclusive Select Committee hearings on the causes of the supply-ship disaster, Ingram opined then, "The disaster to the Seerseller expedition underscores the inexcusable waste of spending money on this foolish fancy. I will never vote for a single dollar for such bloody boondoggles again." Maybe so; but last week he was listed as co-sponsor of the $42 billion Mars-Is-Heaven spending bill. Even the vultures of Senator Breckmeister's Select Committee itself greeted whistle-blower Sampson's revelations of alleged corruption and cover-up with only tepid screams and lawyer talk about the statute of limitations. If there is any bad news about Mars these days, no one wants to hear it.

What the world wants to hear is that the Martians have landed safely, and so have their human discoverers. Old Broadway is sprucing itself up for the biggest ticker-tape parade since Lindbergh's arrival from Paris in 1927, and even now the worried Department of Sanitation crews are installing additional trash baskets and painting red traffic lines all along the parade route, to match the color of the Martians' home planet.

Herbert George Wells may not have been so far off in his vision of conquest from the Red Planet. In a telephone poll taken for *Time* last Thursday, more people knew Alexander, Bob, Christopher, Doris, Edward, and Gretel than knew the names of their own senators. The Martians have not only won the tribute of *Time*'s cover this week, they have conquered us all.

EIGHTEEN

ACROSS
THE RIVER

The whole world wanted to see the Martians come in, and a lot of them were doing it.

By the time the *Algonquin* 9 had entered the parking orbit, getting ready for the landing at the Cape, the Earth's networks had killed their regular programming. All over the sun's third planet, television sets were tuned in to the preparations to welcome the guests from the fourth. On London's Oxford Street and the Champs Elysées of Paris, afternoon shoppers stopped at store windows to peer at the pictures from the Cape. Fur-hatted workers going home on the trolleybuses of Moscow, and sun-tanned ones on those of Capetown, kept track of the ships' positions with little transistor radios. Children in the homes of Tokyo salarymen fell asleep in front of their television sets, and children in Perth, allowed to stay up past their bedtimes, gazed crankily up at the sky.

That was the electronic audience. There was more. For those who could possibly make it to the Cape in the flesh, radio and television just weren't good enough. The place to be was one shore or another of the Banana River, and everyone with wheels and gas, and time enough to make the trip, had been heading there for days.

Reverend's Holy Sanctuary in Orlando had emptied itself out by six in the morning. By a quarter of eight the Sanctuary's four packed vans crept through the traffic to the riverfront. Forty-two tirelessly smiling missioners, Seth Marangeth and Evangeline Beurdy among them, spilled out of Reverend's buses and began to spread out among the welcoming crowds on the Banana River shore.

Seth was thrilled. He had almost forgotten about the deprogrammers, about the conversation with the estate lawyer, even, almost, about his hopes for Evangeline. He took a deep breath of the sultry Florida morning air, gazing across the water at the distant Kennedy Space Center. "You're not here to dawdle!" the herald in charge of his group called. "Get on with the Reverend's work!"

"Praise the Reverend," Seth said automatically, but took one last look at the huge buildings and spiky launch towers. It was all so *wonderful*.

It was a pity that everything was so small and so far away. But here he was in Florida! Waiting for the Martians to arrive! There were palm trees! There were bright, tropical vines, somehow surviving where the feet of the hundreds of thousands had missed crushing them flat . . . and there was Evangeline, touching his hand and smiling at him before she turned toward her own assigned post on the beach.

The riverbank was an instant city, half a million people in the crowd already counted and the number going up. The vehicles kept crawling in through the choked roads—campers, popup trailers, vans, sometimes just the family car with a car bed in the back seat for Baby and blankets in the trunk for Mom and Pop. There were kids of every age in the happy mob, from newborns still at the breast to late teenagers with sleeping bags and ghetto-blaster radios. Almost everyone seemed to have a battery TV to keep in touch with what was going on across the river—and portable cookstoves, and field glasses, and ice chests filled with beer and soda.

Among them moved pairs of Florida state police in their Smokey the Bear hats, doing their best to keep the snatch-and-run thieves restrained and the beer-guzzlers quiet. Police surveillance was not the only thing the State of Florida had provided to welcome the flood of space fans. The visitors were a lot of trouble for the state, but they were really welcome, too. They were big business. Every one of those hundreds of thousands of out-of-state people, it was calculated, would drop an average of eighty-five dollars in Floridian gas stations, 7-Elevens, and Burger Kings. So the state had brought in water trucks and police communications vans and at least three portable first-aid centers. Hundreds of Port-a-Johns were scattered about the riverfront, with lines of people already shifting uncomfortably from foot to foot in front of each. There were corrals for lost kids. There were even perky little girl guides from the Florida Tourist Bureau with white pillbox hats and red, white, and blue shorts, moving about the crowd to answer any questions about lodging or roads or anything else that one of those eighty-five-dollar visitors might want to ask.

Seth looked enviously at a man on top of an Econoline van, sitting peaceably in the sun and watching the screen of a portable television set. Seth could hear the voice of Peter Jennings, killing time at the broadcast command center as they waited for something to happen. "—the *Algonquin* 9 has three more low-Earth orbits to complete before the geometry is right for its landing here at the Cape," he was saying. "When it lands, the first person to greet it will be the President of the United States. Then all the astronauts will be taken immediately to the debriefing chamber, where NASA's doctors will give them a quick examination to make sure they are in good enough shape for the festivities that will follow. At the same time, specially trained teams of exobiologists will board the *Algonquin* to begin the delicate job of bringing the Martians out into the specially prepared mobile habitats that will be waiting for them. But for now, all any of them can do—all we can do ourselves—is just wait."

No one seemed to mind the delay. It was a day none of them wanted to end.

Yawning, the earliest risers (or the latest to sleep) in Los Angeles and Seattle and Mexico City were already tuning in to the pictures from the Cape. In New York City offices were beginning to open, but only the most disciplined of the people who worked in them were without TVs or transistor radios. In Atlantic City, New Jersey—

In Atlantic City's $40 million Jubilee Casino the Executive Vice-President was having an argument with her boss, the Chairman of the Board.

For the sake of her husband, standing by her side, the argument was in English. "I'm only asking you to turn the television sets on for three hours," Emily Sanford, the former Colonel Arragingama-uluthiata of the Glorious Iriadeskan Army, said forcefully. "It is an historic occasion."

The former General (now simply Mister) Phenoboomgarat said, "Do you know that in three hours we can lose more than forty-five thousand dollars net profit from the slot machines alone? What is more historic than forty-five thousand U.S. dollars?"

"Harrah's is showing the landings," Emily said. "The Diamond Horseshoe may be, too. Do you want our players to go down the Boardwalk to Harrah's? or Trump's?"

Phenoboomgarat flinched. He looked at her husband. "What does our director of public relations say?"

Charlie Sanford replied promptly, "Do it. Don't forget, it's still morning. We're only running at about eighteen percent capacity, and—" He hesitated, then finished doggedly: "And it's real *Martians*, Uncle Phenoboomgarat. Please? I would like to see us do the right thing."

The former general hesitated. Then his mind made up, he said simply, "Yom." He thought a moment longer and added, "That will be all right, but it is to be in the slot-machine rooms only. After all, the players can easily enough pull down a lever or two while they watch the landings on the television—and it is, as you say, my dear Arragingama-uluthiata, a very historic occasion."

As Reverend's heralds always explained in the training sessions, to make a contact required only five seconds for the approach, five seconds to pin a Peace Flower on the prospect's breast, ten seconds at most to find out if the prospect was willing to talk. In the worst of times a missioner could make three contacts a minute, and it was a statistical fact that, on average, eight contacts out of every hundred would respond in some favorable way—taking, again on average, about seven minutes each to collect the donation, make an appointment to visit a sanctuary, or sell a book. What it added up to was that in every hour an active missioner, with a good crowd, should have made some twenty-five contacts, with at least four or five scores.

But after the first hour Seth had given away only four Peace Flowers and had no love offerings at all. No one was really interested. Almost everyone was willing to talk—to him, to each other, to anyone—but what they wanted to talk about was only Martians.

When he completed the circuit of his assigned space he found himself back near the white Econoline van. Approaching the vehicle from the other side, he saw that someone had painted a picture of Mars's great dead volcano, Olympus Mons, on the wall of the van. It was beautiful, Seth thought enviously.

The man who owned the van was lifting something out of the back door. He looked around at Seth. "Give me a hand?" he asked amiably.

What Seth should have done was offer him a flower. He didn't. He put the little bunch of flowers down in the shade of the van and took the heavy little case from the man. It was, Seth saw, a Questar telescope. When the man had climbed the little metal ladder to the roof and was reaching down for the case, Seth asked eagerly, "Can I help you set it up?"

"Sure," said the man. "Come on up. My name's Bernard Sampson."

There was something about the tone of his voice as he said it, as though he expected to be recognized, that made Seth pore through his memory. It took a while. Missioners did not keep up on the latest news of worldly concerns, but as the man was locking the telescope to its mount Seth made the connection.

"Oh!" he said, startled. "But you're *famous*." He waved an arm at the distant VIP grandstands wonderingly. "Why aren't you over there with all the other important people?"

"Whistle-blowers don't get invited to parties," Sampson said. He didn't sound angry, or even offended; he simply stated it as a fact. "They were glad enough to have me testify about faking the documentation for the Mars expedition, but after that was all over I got unpopular." It didn't seem to bother him. He swiveled the Questar to look across the river, then looked up, grinning. "Here, would you like a look?"

"Oh, yes!" Seth was surprised to see that the image was upside-down, but it only took a minute to recover from the disorientation. The great stands across the river were still nearly empty. There was no real reason for the VIPs to arrive early. They didn't have to elbow each other for position; their seats were reserved. The most important of the Very Important People, he saw, were still arriving, in limousines and even in helicopters spiraling down to a landing site just behind the stands.

From the tiny portable television set Dan Rather was saying, "—now we take you to the *Algonquin 9* as the crew prepares for reentry." And as Seth lifted his face from the eyepiece he got a glimpse of the palm-sized picture on the television screen, two men floating at odd angles as they checked the foamed cradle where one of the Martians uncomplainingly lay, its mournful eyes gazing at the camera.

"Bastards," Sampson said unmaliciously. "Do you know why they're holding up the landing? They're waiting until everybody's out of bed in California, so the voters won't miss seeing what their taxes have paid for. There'll be two more orbits after this one."

"Can we see them go by through the telescope?" Seth asked eagerly.

"I'm afraid not. They don't come anywhere near here until the final pass—oh, *hell*," he finished, gazing down the shore. A big blue Turner Broadcasting System truck was moving slowly down the lane the police had kept open for vehicles. Strolling spectators moved casually out of its way, trying to wave and grin into the cameras on its roof that were panning the crowd.

"What's the matter, Mr. Sampson?"

Sampson said unhappily, "Listen, will you stay up here for a minute while I, uh, go down inside the van?"

"Of course," Seth said; but Sampson was already on his way.

He didn't move quite fast enough. Someone on the TV truck's roof had spotted him, and it stopped before he could get all the way down the ladder. A good-looking black man jumped out, microphone in hand, while the roof cameras zoomed in on him.

"Bernard Sampson?" said the TV man. "I'm from the World's Greatest News Network. Could you say a few words for our audience?"

"I'd rather not—" Sampson began, but the man was already speaking into the microphone. "I have here Dr. Bernard Sampson, who made the headlines last summer with his revelations about the falsification of data on the original landing of Captain Seerseller and his crew." Then, looking invitingly toward Sampson: "I'm sure this is a proud moment for you, Dr. Sampson—"

Sampson turned and gazed into the cameras. "As a matter of fact," he said, "it is. I'm proud as hell. Not for me, I mean," he added quickly. "For the whole human race."

"I'm surprised to see you on this side of the river," the television man went on. "Why aren't you in the VIP stands?"

"The company's better here," Sampson said, smiling up at Seth. "Well, there's another reason, too. No offense, but I was hoping to stay away from the TV cameras for a change. I had enough of them when I was testifying."

The newsman nodded and said, "We won't make this any harder on you than we have to. Can you tell us what is going to happen as a result of your testimony?" Sampson shrugged. "Or about where your partner is now?"

"My *former* partner," Sampson said without heat, "is supposed to be in Europe somewhere, trying not to get extradited. Along with my *former* wife. I don't expect to see either of them again."

"And what do you expect, Dr. Sampson?"

"Well—I've been granted a position at Northwestern University, heading a special institute on Martian science. That starts on the first of the year, and I've been interviewing candidates."

"We all wish you the best of luck," the newsman said warmly. "Now we'll let you get back to your relaxation."

And, as the truck moved off, Sampson climbed back to the roof. He looked curiously at Seth. "Is something the matter?" he asked.

"No. Not really. Only—," Seth hesitated. He really did not understand exactly what was going on in his mind at that moment; all sorts of contradictory impulses were fluttering around there. And the thing he wanted to say to Sampson was so utterly at odds with all the plans he had made for the rest of his life—

He said it anyway. "Dr. Sampson? What kind of candidates are you interviewing, exactly?"

Even in the lobby of the Athens InterContinental there was a television set showing the excitement at the Cape. It didn't have much of an audience, though. Most of the guests were in the bar, having their predinner aperitifs.

Vladimir Malzhenitser glanced at the TV on his way to tell the concierge that he was ready for the couple who had engaged his services for the evening. Malzhenitser was in his happiest mood of months. It was really true, this time, that his luck had changed! These tourists weren't just Americans, they were *Washington, D.C.* Americans, and definitely in some way involved with the space program! So it was not too late. Even though the *Algonquin 9* was getting ready to land, there would be big doings in the American space effort, and the luck of meeting these two might yet make up for all the evil fortune that had gone before.

Well content, Malzhenitser strolled over to the lobby television set. He saw a black man who looked almost familiar speaking out of it, saying, "As all of my constituents know, the space program has never had a better friend in Congress than me—" And realized that he had never seen that man before, but had definitely seen his brother. The forty-five-dollar check that had arrived just a week earlier was the last he had heard from the real-estate man, but the letter with it had been cordial enough, though clear that the development program was now complete and there would be no more "royalties." Malzhenitser shrugged philosophically. At least it had cost him nothing, really, and there was still hope that the real-estate man's brother might actually intercede for him—along with, he schemed, the couple he was about to give his most special private tour of Athens that very night—

He turned as the hotel manager hurried toward him, softly calling his name. "Mr. Seriakis," Malzhenitser said. "A pleasure to see you. I am waiting for two of your guests, Mr. and Mrs. William White—"

But the manager's face was gloomy, and the man was shaking his head. "Checked out," he said. "Gone."

"Checked *out*?" Malzhenitser gasped. "But no, that isn't possible, we had a definite engagement—"

"They didn't check out voluntarily," Seriakis said sadly. "They were taken into custody one hour ago. And their names were not Mr. and Mrs. William White, Malzhenitser. They were Mr. Van Poppliner and Mrs. Bernard Sampson. Imagine! Here in my hotel! Do you recognize those names?"

Malzhenitser stared at him in horror. "Poppliner? The crook? The one who falsified the scientific studies?"

"Exactly," the manager said heavily. "So they will not be joining you this evening, Malzhenitser. Do not waste your time waiting. Go home."

And then, when he reached his room, thinking nothing further could happen on this day, there was one surprise left. The landlady grumpily climbed the stairs to give him a box from the American Embassy. From the Embassy! For him personally, and with the seal of the United States of America on the label! Was it still, even now, possible . . . ?

And when Malzhenitser, almost daring to hope, got the stiff wrappings open . . . a set of drinking glasses, engraved with a picture of the *Algonquin* 9 against a background of the planet Mars, and a note on the stationery of the United States House of Representatives. It was signed by Walter Thurgood Thatcher, Esq., Representative, 24th District, State of Illinois:

Dear Mr. Malzhenitser:
I'm truly sorry to say that we will not be able to alter the decision of the U. S. Immigration and Naturalization Service in regard to

your application for a visa. But, knowing your interest in our space program, I thought you might enjoy having this memento of the occasion.

Please accept my very best wishes for a Merry Christmas and the Happiest of New Years.

Very sincerely yours,
Walter Thurgood Thatcher

Even though it was December, the sun was getting hot at the Cape. Seth looked around for heralds, but none were in sight, so he shucked the long-sleeved white shirt. "Are you serious about quitting the Reverend?" Sampson asked him.

Seth said unhappily, "I wish I knew for sure."

Sampson nodded and handed him a plastic bottle of sunscreen. "Better put this on," he advised. A swell of sound from the crowd made him look quickly at the television screen; all four networks at once had announced that *Algonquin* was on its last orbit. "Not long now," Sampson grinned. And then, "Seth? Do you mind if I ask why you got hooked up with the Reverend in the first place?"

Seth thought it over. Then he said slowly, "I was looking for a purpose to my life, Dr. Sampson."

"And you found it?"

Seth wrinkled his brow. "Not exactly." He thought a moment longer, gazing out at the crowds in the hot sun. "Almost, though. I'll tell you what I did find. I found a lot of people who were trying to figure things out, just as I was. It was really nice, being with people who wanted to be decent."

"There are a lot of decent people around who don't join up with people like the Reverend."

"I know that. I guess I just didn't run into them." He shook his head and corrected himself. "Or when I did I just didn't think of them that way. I thought they were wimps, I guess."

"But when you're in the cult—," Sampson began, and then stopped in the middle of the sentence. He grinned at Seth. "I'm not criticizing you," he said. "A lot of us make mistakes. You're lucky. You're still young when you find out you made one—I mean," he added hastily, "if you do decide that's what it was."

He was embarrassedly silent for a moment. Then his eyes widened. He said, looking past Seth's shoulder: "That pretty girl that's waving this way over there—is she calling to you?"

And, of course, it was Evangeline, looking flushed, and excited, and very happy; and Seth noticed even in that first glance that Evangeline wasn't carrying her Peace Flowers anymore either.

On board *Algonquin 9* Captain Seerseller hauled himself one more time through the cluttered, smelly chambers of the ship, checking the stowage of the weary, uncomplaining Martians and the restraining belts of the even more weary human survivors of his crew. The humans were relatively uncomplaining too, now—relative to what they had been for the past few years, and Sharon bas Ramirez even reached up to give him a forgiving kiss. "We're almost home, anyway," she murmured. "One more hour—"

"One more hour," muttered Manuel Andrew Applegate from beside her, "is about all I can stand! Jesus! What will it be like to be *clean* again?"

The captain blinked. Until Applegate said that Seerseller had almost forgotten the incredible, the pervasive, the very nearly health-threatening stench that he had lived with all these months since they took off from the surface of Mars. It was part people and part Martians and part worn-out machines and electrical stinks, and most of all it was decay. If only the refrigeration system hadn't gone irreparably sour six weeks from Earth—

But it had. There would be hell to pay over that, too, Seerseller thought. Not just that. Once they were back on Earth there would be a lot of hell, for a lot of reasons. Seerseller had listened with total concentration to the radio reports of the hearings on Earth, and he dared hope that, with the falsification of data clearly pinned on someone else, at least that charge would not be waiting for him when he landed.

It was not enough. There would be plenty more. It was his expedition, after all. He was the captain. Captains weren't supposed to take other people's words for whether their computations and flight plans were right. Captains were supposed to double-check everything, *everything*, and if anything went wrong it was captains whose asses were in a cleft stick afterwards.

Seerseller sighed, no longer noticing the stink.

He became aware of Sharon bas Ramirez stirring beside him. "What?" he demanded, seeing her loosening her belt. "What is it?"

"Can't you hear? They're calling from the storage hold. Christopher's pulled himself out of his packing again!" And when he had jumped back to the Martians' quarters it was true; Christopher had succeeded in disentangling himself from the layers of foamed plastic that were meant to preserve him from the stresses of reentry. They'd given up on the water tanks because the Martians had splashed so much of it into the ship's air; the foam was their last resort. Christopher's front legs were still caught, though the rest of him floated free. He hung upside-down, gazing at Captain Seerseller with those mild, satisfied eyes: And the female, Gretel, had begun the same infuriating job. "Oh, hell," Seerseller groaned. "They were all right a minute ago! Well, Sharon, you'll just have to take them out and repack them both."

"Why me?" Sharon demanded, looking persecuted.

"Well, you don't expect me to do it, do you?" the captain asked reasonably. "Get the cargo team to help you. And hurry up about it, we don't have much time left!"

Seerseller scuttled back to his control seat in case he needed to make another transmission to the Cape. But they were out of direct contact range, and he couldn't stay away. When he came back the stink was worse than ever. It was a pity that, in order to cushion the Martians completely against all the stresses of reentry, it had not turned out to be practical to make allowances for their natural bodily functions. The foam plastic was soiled with excrement, and the people repacking the Martians had not avoided getting smeared with it. "Oh,

Christ," Captain Seerseller groaned. "Look at you! How's that going to look when we get out of the ship, with TV cameras everywhere, and the President, and everything?"

"If you think you can do it better, why don't you try it yourself?" Sharon asked bitterly. "Otherwise just stay out of the way!"

Seerseller was glad enough to do that, as best he could in the cramped space. All the Martians were lowing mournfully to each other and stirring in their wrappings. Christopher and Gretel, freed from their bonds while the crew strove to reline their cradles, were clutching each other as they floated. But there was something about the way they licked and groomed each other that made Seerseller look more closely.

Christopher was throwing one long leg over Gretel. "Stop that!" the captain shouted. "You, make the dirty little things stop! Can't you see they're trying to make love?"

The landing was only twenty minutes away now, and all over the Cape—both sides of the river—and almost everywhere else on Earth people were forgetting their private concerns to whisper to each other and watch, and feel their pulses beginning to throb with excitement.

Seth and Evangeline, however, were in a private world of their own. They were sitting on the edge of the roof of Bernard Sampson's van, dangling their feet, and whispering to each other while Sampson tried not to listen behind them.

"You know," Evangeline said seriously, "you were very brave with the deprogrammers, Seth. I never thanked you properly."

"Those bastards," he growled. He hadn't meant to swear; he just couldn't help himself at the thought of them daring to lay hands on Evangeline.

She didn't seem to notice. "The thing is," she said soberly, "they didn't do it by themselves. It's Dad who sent them. I probably should have talked to them—"

"But they were *kidnapping* you! Anyway, you know what they would have said. They'd just try to talk you out of Reverend's service."

"Seth," she said in a very serious way, "I made up my own mind to come with Reverend. I'll make up my own mind when I want to leave."

Seth sat up straight, looking at her. "Are you—"

She didn't wait for him to speak, but continued on her own thought. "Seth, Dad always treats me like a five-year-old. I guess he can't help it. I guess it's just the way he has of loving me. But I couldn't stand it; I had to get away. So I joined with Reverend—"

"To escape an impossible situation at home, right?" Seth nodded.

She looked at him. "Yes, but then. . . . Well, when you come right down to it, Seth, how does Reverend treat us? Maybe not even like five-year-olds! Oh, Seth. I do love all those good brothers and sisters. They're the sweetest, kindest people in the world. But they're all like *children*, Seth, and maybe I want to finish growing up."

Seth took a deep breath. He reached for Evangeline's hand before he spoke. "Evangeline? When you talk about loving your brothers, did you, maybe, have anybody in particular in mind?"

She looked at him for a long moment. Then, as she opened her mouth to speak, there was another sudden mutter from the crowd. Behind them, Bernard Sampson said apologetically, "It's just another report from the *Algonquin*. They're almost across the Pacific; the coast of Mexico's in sight. They'll be here in a few minutes."

"Thank you," Evangeline said politely, and then turned back to Seth. "What were we saying?" she asked.

Twenty-eight hundred miles away, in downtown Los Angeles, Sam Harcourt was standing in a fast-food line in the Arco Shopping Center, waiting for a chili dog with everything. He heard the muttering from the dozens of TV sets scattered around the underground mall. He couldn't help hearing. But he didn't listen. Sam Harcourt had more important things on his mind.

Inspiration had struck again. Nobody ever went downtown in LA, of course, but Sam made an exception. This trip was to research his great new idea about Martians living underground and erupting into a shopping center very like Arco. It was, Sam knew with absolute certainty, a *very* good idea, although Oleg had refused to handle it.

But that only proved what a dope the agent was. He would, Sam was certain, change his mind in a hot minute when he saw the sketch for a treatment Sam was going to prepare, as soon as he finished getting the feel of Arco.

Even a genius had to eat, though. When Sam Harcourt had his chili dog he looked around for a place to eat it. All the little tables at the fast-food places were full, mostly with people watching the overhead television screens from Florida. Sam disdained them. He knew a place, and it was only steps away.

A minute later Sam was sitting down in front of the mall's radio broadcast booth.

There wasn't much competition for seats there. All the people who were willing to idle in front of some electronic entertainment were doing so at TV sets. Of course, even the talk on this little FM radio show was about the Martians. Since the whole program was relayed on loudspeakers outside the glass wall, Sam couldn't help hearing a little bit of it.

Sam knew the host of the show. His name was Johnny Trumpet, once a jazz-band musician, now a talk-show host specializing in antifluoridation, people who had written books about Communist spies, and women urging the Right to Life. Today's guests, Sam saw through the glass wall, were a little odder than usual. One was a bald, plump man in a lavender robe, and next to him a man in stark black and white, clutching a gold-headed cane.

An electric shock ran through him. He knew them, too! In fact— though nothing before this minute could have persuaded him to say so aloud—it was these very men who had helped germinate the great idea about Martians living underground on Earth. He scowled at them. What were they doing in Los Angeles? Why weren't they busy in their caves somewhere? Was there any chance that one of them might hear about Sam's idea and, who the hell knew, start some crazy, baseless legal business about where the idea came from?

He gazed at them with suspicion and hatred . . . and then, a moment later, out of nowhere or out of that wonderful Somewhere whence all truly great, BO-smash ideas came, the capper that would make his own idea absolutely bankable hit him between the eyes.

Thirty seconds later Sam was in a phone booth a few yards away, keeping his eye on the door to the studio as he phoned his agent. "Oleg, that you? Oleg, listen! You know that Martians-under-the-Earth story you couldn't figure out a way to sell?"

"Oh, Sam," said his agent's weary voice. "Sam, Sam. When are you going to wake up? The Martians are *here*, Sam. Practically. Nobody's gonna want low-budget sci-fi about them, it's too late for any of that. When are you going to see that when something's over it's over?"

"It isn't over, Oleg, not with the concept I've got. It hasn't even *begun* yet. Oleg. Listen. We forget about theater release, okay? We go for made-for-TV. Of course," he went on, catching fire from himself, "after the TV, which is maybe a miniseries anyway, there's theater release in Canada and the rest of the world and then, who knows, maybe even in the USA—"

"*Sam.*"

"All right, all right! Just listen! Those two guys, Marchese Boccanegra and What's-His-Face Something Moore. We get them as *hosts* for the show. See what we've got there? Name recognition! Scientific authority for whatever we say! We put them on, all weird-looking the way they are, and—"

"Sam!" Oleg shouted. "Hold it! Don't you ever listen when I'm talking to you?"

"I'm listening," Sam said, subsiding.

"Then listen to this! Those two, they're has-beens, Sam. Everybody knows that. They're fakes! Johnny Carson doesn't even do them in the monologue any more. Who wants to have a couple of hosts that everybody laughs at?"

"They're not laughing in the studio right now, Oleg," Sam protested gamely. "Do you hear what I'm saying? They're in there promoting right now, on Johnny Trumpet's radio show; you could tune in yourself!"

The agent's voice was weary. "Sam, Sam. What do you mean, they're promoting? The 'Today' show is promoting. Donahue is promoting. The CBS nightly news is promoting. Being on some five-watt FM station broadcasting out of a cellar, that isn't promoting. Go away, Sam. Why don't you try going straight?"

And Sam, after he glumly hung up, did for one instant think about going straight. There was certainly *something* here. You could see it. You could almost smell it. This was, he perceived, some kind of a big deal for ordinary people in the world, people who did not, in any way he could see, have a single dime to make out of whether Martians landed or not.

He gazed uncomprehendingly at the people around him, so uplifted, so generously thrilled. He wondered. Was it possible to capture that —that—what would you call it?—that *pure* emotion? In a film script? In a TV series? Even, maybe, just so he could feel a little of it himself?

But the fact was, he didn't know how.

On Sampson's tiny TV screen they were seeing one last-minute pan around the great VIP stands. They stood there together, the three of them, Seth and Evangeline with their arms around each other's waists, and Sampson smiling beside them. "That's *him!*" Evangeline cried, and Seth saw that it was true: It was just a quick flash, but there was Reverend himself, sitting alone in the stand while all around him were jumping up to scan the sky. And he was eating a hot dog. He didn't look holy. He didn't even look like someone you would buy a used car from, much less your hopes of eternal salvation; he looked like an elderly little man who hadn't quite caught on to what all the excitement was about.

"Poor old Reverend," Evangeline said soberly.

Seth looked tenderly down at her. And then he bent his neck and whispered into her ear, "I want to marry you, Evangeline."

Evangeline looked up at him. She didn't seem surprised. She was gazing at him with affection, and a certain amount of amusement, too. "Dear Seth," she said, "do you know that until yesterday we never spent as much as five minutes talking to each other?"

"I don't need any more time. I know. And Dr. Sampson says he'll give me a part-time job at his Institute while I finish school . . . and I've got sixty-eight hundred dollars coming from my Aunt Ellen's estate. Not counting the silver tea service. It isn't really sterling, you know, but it's about triple-plated, really heavy stuff—"

He stopped, realizing she was laughing at him.

It seemed like a friendly kind of laugh. One might even think of it as a loving one. But before he could find out exactly what she meant by it there was a roar from the crowd. Everyone near a radio or portable TV had got the word at once: "They're coming in!"

And on Bernard Sampson's tiny screen they could see *Algonquin 9*, a tiny bright spot in the bright, thin cirrus clouds in the sky, somewhere over the Gulf of Mexico.

"It's on its way, folks!" shouted the voice of Tom Brokaw. "The Kennedy Space Center estimates seven minutes to touchdown on the new runway specially built for the occasion!"

Sampson, Seth, and Evangeline were all hugging each other. Seth was surprised to see that Dr. Sampson's cheeks were wet. He dabbed at his face, grinning. "You know," he said apologetically, "it's really funny to see all these people, all so happy. . . . I mean, you know how people are. They all have their own worries and little secrets and meannesses . . . and then something like this comes along. And then, somehow, for just a moment. . . ."

"I know," Evangeline said. "People aren't so bad, after all, are they?"

Across the river, the President of the United States pushed the makeup woman's hands away. "Enough, enough," he grumbled as he got up from her chair.

"Just one more minute with your hair," she begged, but he shook his head.

"It's showtime," he said, looking around the room wistfully. It was his very own retreat under the great grandstands, with his teletype and his red phone and his four waiting aides. He hated to leave it, but there wasn't any choice. He had to be outside in his place when the door of the spaceship opened. Outside were the Secret Service men and the newspeople. Outside was the grandstand where fifty of the Very Most Important of the Very Important People were already sitting in the Presidential Box. He glanced at the television monitor, showing the *Algonquin* 9 now on its turnaround glide back to the Cape.

"So now we've got Martians to go with the Cubans and the Haitians and the Vietnamese and the Russian Jews," he said wryly. "That damn Seerseller! First he fucks up his whole mission, and then he brings these creeps back for us to deal with. I ought to court-martial the son of a bitch. Why couldn't he just leave them where they were?"

The Martian called Christopher felt the sickening lurches of the spacecraft as it battered its way back into Earth's atmosphere. They were painful and frightening to him, but he endured them with the tranquility of a thousand generations whose principal task had been to endure.

He thought wistfully of that brief moment when he and the female the Earth people called Gretel had been touching each other. It did not occur to Christopher that what he and Gretel had been doing would have seemed objectionable to the Earth people. Why should it? He did wonder, mildly, why they had all been kept strapped apart for so long. He thought that was quite uncivilized. How could the Earth beings expect them to get along when deprived of the chance to communicate with each other? Did they expect the Martians to communicate by sound alone?—and lose the great nuanced vocabulary of stroke and touch, of grooming and of sexual pleasure, of sniffing smell and licking taste? Christopher did wonder a bit about that, but he didn't wonder much. Martians were not wondering beings.

The kind of beings Martians were, of course, was patient ones. They had no choice about that. Whatever their long-ago ancestors had been, the ones that dug the tunnels and tried to make their surroundings fit their needs, these late descendants were a different breed. Impatience had been selected out of them long ago. Impatience did no one any good. Impatience would not make their algal froth grow one moment sooner, for the rhythm of their lives depended entirely on the slow float of food from the bottoms of their vertical seas to the surface, where they could skim it off for food. That was all there was to "earning a living" among the Martians. They didn't have to build houses because they no longer lived in houses; they manufactured nothing because they used nothing. So they had plenty of time for the things they valued, which were the long, huddled conversations—one on one, or in groups of three, four, a dozen—with the bleats and moans coming from no one cared which, and the poking tickles and serious pokes, and inquiring nibbles and affectionate licks. Humans might have understood this, if they had tried. Sometimes humans, too— especially young ones, or lovers, or colleagues—would talk a night away and think those the best moments of their lives. But then humans had to return to the hard reality of school or work. The Martians had nothing they needed to return to. The best moments of their lives were all of them . . . except when, as on this interminable voyage, the human beings kept them too far apart to touch or taste, barely able to hear or smell, and so quite unable to converse of the really interesting things.

It was a pity, really.

It was also quite unexpected. That first human who had entered into their tunnels had seemed to understand how civilized intercourse was carried on. He had accepted the snuggling embraces of the Martians who had found him. He had even paid them the compliment of dying in their arms. Why weren't the others more like him?

They were taking turns at the Questar now, and in his ten seconds Seth could see the faint glimmer of sunlight reflected from the stubby wings of the *Algonquin 9* as it turned. He didn't mind giving the telescope back to Bernard Sampson. The TV had a better picture now, anyway. There wasn't any plume of rocket exhaust. *Algonquin 9* was a glider now. The captain was nursing his velocity, cautiously reducing it with flaps and spoilers as the great bright ship completed its turn to come in.

As it touched down a great shapeless noise came from the million people at the Cape. It wasn't a shout, not even a gasp or a sigh. It was pure white noise, without form or content. It was the sound of a million lungs exhaling satisfaction at once.

The spacecraft landed straight and true. As it plunged through the thirty deceleration webs along the runway it sent fragments of plastic net and cable flying about. Some of them were still trailing from the ship as it came to a perfect stop, no more than a hundred yards from the great red X painted on the runway. Already the chase trucks were gaining on it. In a moment the crews were there with their hoses, spraying cooling foam and misting water over the retrorockets to purge away the last noxious vapors.

The noise from the crowd was deafening now. It was wave on wave of cheering, louder than the takeoff blast of a rocket, and it didn't stop. It went on steadily while the foamers and the misters did their work, and Seth discovered that he was cheering too.

He broke off when he felt Evangeline's hands on his shoulders, and realized she was murmuring in his ear. "What?" he bawled, half turning to look at her.

She said, "I said, I've always wanted a really nice silver tea set in my home."

He kissed her, and hardly saw the President's open limousine as it drove up, and the ground crews trundled the wheeled steps to the spacecraft's port. And then they both, arms around each other's waists, joined in the joyous shout as, slowly, the spacecraft door opened and warily Captain Seerseller poked his head out to see what welcome he was going to get.

Algonquin 9 was home.

In the suburbs of Chicago the dozen distinguished patrons of the John James Audubon Nature Reserve were all applauding too. Dr. Marietta Mariano, wiping a tear from her face, did not. She simply stood there behind them, moistly smiling. It would be half an hour at least, she knew, before any of them would be willing to turn off the set and get back to the important ceremonial of the day, the official opening of the Solomon Sayre Memorial Trail.

On the television set the President was pinning the Medal of Freedom on the stained, filthy tunic of Captain Seerseller. "—This heroic feat of American skill and daring," the President was proclaiming, "deserves the prayers and gratitude of every one of us, even of every person in the human race—" He seemed to be just warming up. Dr. Mariano judged there would be at least ten more minutes of the President, then heaven knew what else before the guests were willing to do what they had come here for. It would be quite a while yet.

But she was willing to wait. The trail was finished. It bore Sol's name. He would not entirely be forgotten. And Sol, she knew, would have loved it, as he would have loved this whole wonderful day.

Dr. Marietta Mariano was at peace.

And, wonderfully, for this one day at least, so was the whole world.

NINETEEN

THE DAY
AFTER THE DAY
THE MARTIANS
CAME

There were two cots in every room of the motel in Cocoa Beach, besides the usual number of beds. Mr. Mandala, the manager, was trying to get them all taken out at once.

It wasn't easy to do that, because a lot of the rooms were still occupied. For twelve hours the million out-of-state people who had streamed into Florida to help welcome the Martians had been streaming out again. They were filling every highway, overloading every train and plane and bus. Still there just wasn't transportation enough for all those people at once. The Tom Brokaws, the Senators, the foreign heads of state were all long gone in their private planes and charters, but then they hadn't been staying at Mr. Mandala's motel in the first place. The ones who had come there were the sound-crew people and the third-string reporters or the ones from third-rate outfits, the ones who were lucky to have found any bed at all. All of them knew that they had to wait their turn for transportation home.

Mr. Mandala's toughest problem was figuring out what to do with the extra cots he had installed for the overflow. He was trying to persuade his black bellmen to clean out the trunk room and store the cots in that. They were resisting. "Now, please, Mr. Mandala," the bell captain said, speaking loudly over the noise in the lounge, where some of the leftover newsmen were waiting patiently for their rides, "you know we'd do that thing for you if we could. But it cannot be, because we don't have any more room there on account of it's full of all that hurricane stuff you told us to save."

"We can't throw that out, Ernest. There could be another hurricane any time and we'd need those tarps and lamps and things."

Ernest nodded. "That's surely true, Mr. Mandala, but the cots won't fit in there now."

"Then where are we going to put them, Ernest?" Mr. Mandala demanded.

"You could send them back, Mr. Mandala."

"No! Oh, no. I can't do that. I had to pay cash for them, that was the only way I could get the things. They won't refund the money."

"You already made your money out of them, Mr. Mandala. Throw them on out."

Mr. Mandala gave him a look of distress. "You're arguing with me, Ernest," he complained. "I told you to quit arguing with me." He drummed his fingers on the reception desk and gazed angrily around the lobby. There were at least forty people still taking up his space in it, talking, reading, playing cards, dozing. Some were watching the lobby TV, which was showing reruns of yesterday's landing and all the other scenes of the Seerseller expedition that everyone had seen a hundred times before. On the screen the Martian named Doris was gazing uncomprehendingly into the camera and weeping large, gelatinous tears.

Mr. Mandala turned in time to see that the bell captain was also gazing at the picture. "Now, you quit that, Ernest," he ordered. "I don't pay you to watch television. Get those cots out and stack them in the indoor swimming pool."

"The guests won't like not being able to use the pool then, Mr. Mandala."

"The guests don't *have* to use the indoor pool. Put a sign on it saying it's closed for maintenance. Guests can be just as happy in the outdoor one, can't they? I mean, this is Florida, isn't it? So you get along, Ernest. You too, B.G.," he ordered the other bellman.

Gloomily, he watched them retreat through the service hall. He wished he could get rid of the crowd of leftover guests in the lounge as easily. They didn't have to be in the lounge. There were plenty of places they could be. They could just as well be sitting outdoors in the sunshine instead of cluttering up his lobby. In Mr. Mandala's opinion they could be even better buying drinks at the lobby bar, or eating in the motel coffee shop, but he knew that none of them was likely to be doing that. Now that the landing was over they were on their own time; no more expense accounts.

According to the registration slips they were nearly all from newspapers, radio, and TV stations and networks. Hardly any of them were paying their own way. Nearly every reservation had specified billing to NBC or the *Washington Post* or some foreign network—Mr. Mandala scowled at the thought of all that extra bookkeeping—not to mention that every instruction had stipulated that bar bills were not to be included, so all the restaurant checks had to be gone over one by one.

Mr. Mandala was pleased with the dollar volume all these guests had represented, but the dollars had dried up. Now he wished they would leave.

On the television screen the great parade down Broadway—no, Mr. Mandala reminded himself, down "Henry Steegman Boulevard"—was over. The heroic astronauts, or at least the ones well enough to endure it, had been whisked away to a ceremonial luncheon with the mayor of New York and the cardinal of the diocese. While the networks were waiting for the speeches to begin they were filling with live shots of the exterior of the Kennedy Space Center, where the Martians were spending their first full night on Earth under the observation of NASA's best specialists in the as yet nonexistent science of exobiology. When their man on the scene ran out of things like that the broadcast switched to the old, and never very good, clips of the *Algonquin 8* instrument ship as it had crashed on landing long ago. No one was watching.

That disaster simply didn't seem relevant any more, but when the shot changed to one of the Martians, looking like a sorrowful dachshund with elongated seal flippers for limbs, one of the poker players stirred and cried: "Hey, I've got a Martian joke!"

"Oh, hell," somebody groaned. "Another one?"

"But this one's good," the player insisted. "Listen. Why doesn't a Martian go for a swim in the Atlantic Ocean?"

"It's your bet," the dealer said. Nobody else said anything.

"Because he'd leave a ring around it!" the reporter said, folding his cards and looking around. No one laughed, not even Mr. Mandala. Privately he thought some of the jokes they'd been telling were pretty good, but he was beginning to get tired of them. So were the reporters in the lobby . . . as well as getting fairly tired of each other.

Mr. Mandala leaned against the reception counter, chin in his hands, gazing at the television screen. He wondered why, really, a million people had come to the Cape to see those things and hundreds of millions of others had been glued to their television screens. Who would really care about the fact that this Henry Steegman guy had discovered some kind of animal on Mars? When the landing date was first set and the owners had put the rates up for the occasion Mr. Mandala would not have been surprised to find they didn't get any takers. He found out how wrong he was when the reservations began to flood in. Mr. Mandala was pleased about that, but when you had said that much you had said everything about the Martians that really mattered to him.

On the television screen the picture went to black and was replaced by the legend, *Bulletin from ABC News*.

The poker game paused momentarily. The lounge was almost quiet as an invisible announcer read a news release from NASA: "Dr. Hugo Bache, the Texas A & M professor of veterinary medicine called in by the National Aeronautics and Space Administration, has issued a preliminary report that has just been released by Colonel Eric T. 'Happy' Wingerter, speaking for NASA."

A wire-service man yelled, "Turn it up!" There was a convulsive movement around the television set. The sound vanished entirely for a second, then blasted out:

"—Martians are vertebrate, warm-blooded, and apparently mammalian. A superficial examination indicates a generally low level of metabolism, although Dr. Bache states that it is possible that this is in some measure the result of their difficult and confined voyage through 137,000,000 miles of space in the specimen compartment of the *Algonquin 9* spacecraft. The splints applied to the Martian called 'Gretel' appear under X-rays to be producing satisfactory healing, and there is no, repeat no, evidence of any communicable disease, although standard quarantine precautions are still—"

"Hell he says," cried a microphone boom handler from CBS News. "We had an interview with somebody at the Mayo Clinic that said—"

"Shut up," bellowed a dozen voices, and the TV became audible again:

"—take you now to the scene." The picture showed a room almost like Mission Control at Houston, or at least the control room of a TV studio. White-suited technicians were studying boards, listening on headphones, tending tape machines, watching screens where sine waves flickered and coursed. And beyond them was a huge glass wall, and on the other side of the wall—

"It's the zoo!" a voice cried.

"It isn't a zoo, it's just where the Martians are kept," someone else corrected, and half a dozen voices at once shouted:

"Shut up!" From the television set the veterinarian's voice was saying:

"—blood and biopsy samples have been taken painlessly, by medical technicians wearing germ-free suits with antibacterial coatings. By means of slings on wheeled frames the Martians are able to move about their enclosure quite freely in spite of their greatly increased weight, and a pool, containing their own algaelike food, is kept at the same temperature as their so-called oceans, so they can swim and reduce the gravity stresses still further. . . ."

The veterinarian didn't have to say all of that. The picture showed the Martians through the glass wall, wheeling themselves stolidly around on canvas slings under their bellies. A medic in a suit with a hood was inserting a rectal thermometer into one of them, stroking it to calm it down. The thing was gazing at him wonderingly, then seemed to try to throw a leg over him.

The picture ended there. As the special bulletin announcer wrapped up, one of the voices from the poker game said, "They're horny little devils anyway, you have to give them that." Then the voice of the announcer, weary but game, found its place in the standby script and resumed its recap of the previous half-dozen stories. The poker game started up again as the anchorman was describing the news conference with Dr. Sam Sullivan, of the Linguistics Institute at the University of Indiana, and his conclusions that the sounds the Martians made might indeed be a degenerate form of some sort of language.

"What a lot of crap," Mr. Mandala muttered to the credit-card printer. "Language, for God's sake!" For anyone could see that they were only animals. Then he turned resentfully toward the noise of laughter. "Could you hold the noise down, please?" he called.

The reporters didn't even look at him. "Yeah, sure," one of them called over his shoulder, "but wait a minute. I got one. What's a Martian high rise?"

"I give up," said a red-haired girl from Ms.

"Twenty-seven floors of basement apartments!"

"All right," the girl said over the snickers, "but I've got one, too. What is a Martian female's religious injunction that requires her to keep her eyes closed during sexual intercourse?" She waited a bit, then gave the punchline: "God forbid she should see her husband enjoying himself!"

"Are we playing poker or not?" one of the players growled, but they were too many for him. The jokes came from all directions. "Who won the Martian beauty contest? . . . Nobody!" "How do you get a Martian female to give up sex? . . . Marry her!" Mr. Mandala found himself laughing out loud at that one, and when one of the reporters came to him for a light he gave the man a whole book of matches. "Ta," the man said, puffing his pipe alight. "Be glad when you've seen the last of us, won't you?"

"Well, we'll be glad to see you all come back some day," Mr. Mandala said with his very best imitation of geniality. Actually his smile was real, because the man was dropping his keys on the desk, and behind him a woman was lugging a garment bag and an overnight case toward them. Two more checkouts; two fewer people around to waste his time. The man turned to the woman as Mr. Mandala searched for his file folder. "Going back to Chicago now?" he asked. When she nodded, he went on: "Jokes aside, don't you think this was a pretty great experience?"

She looked at him appraisingly. "How's that?"

"Why, all these people, you know," the reporter said. "The way they all became, how would you describe it, well, almost civil to each other? Do you know the Florida police reported only four arrests all day, out of all those people on the riverside?"

"That was probably just sloppy police work," the woman said.

"No, really," the man insisted. "There was something special there. I could sense a sort of—call it brotherhood. Something like that. Didn't you feel it?"

"I felt *nothing*," the woman said decisively. "What are you, a dreamer? You've seen this kind of sudden glow before. A kid gets pulled out of a well or a paraplegic flies across the Atlantic and, jeez, everybody goes all mushy for a minute. Then it's over. It never lasts. Tomorrow they'll all be cutting each other's throats again—and look, Mister Cashier Clerk, check me out, will you, because my car's waiting outside for me right now."

On the television screen the tape of the landing began to run again, for the fourth time that hour. Mr. Mandala stared vacantly at it, yawning. One of the poker players was telling a long, complicated story about the Martian equivalent of a bar mitzvah. Mr. Mandala gazed at the man with dislike. Mr. Mandala didn't particularly like Jewish people, but he had learned very thoroughly that it didn't pay a hotel manager to show any prejudice against them. Or against Cubans or Orientals or for that matter even against blacks, or at least not against the blacks who turned up with confirmed reservations and valid credit cards. The ones who worked for him were, of course, another story.

But somewhere in Mr. Mandala's incurious and mostly inactive brain was a hazy feeling that you shouldn't tell jokes that put Martians on a par with, even, Jews. Martians weren't *human*, were they? What was all the fuss about? He gazed at the creatures on the screen, now given over to a roll call of the Martian survivors, and could not imagine anyone *caring* about them. They did not look worth caring about as the file tape showed them sluggishly crawling around their pen in the *Algonquin 9* on their long, weak limbs, like a stretched seal's flippers, their great long eyes dull.

"Stupid-looking little buggers," a cameraman remarked to the pipe smoker from Thames Television. "You know what I heard? I heard the reason Captain Seerseller made them stay in the back of the ship was the way they smelled."

"They probably don't even notice each other's pong when they're home on Mars," the Thames man said judiciously. "Thin air, you know."

"Notice it? I bet they love it!" The cameraman dropped a dollar bill on the desk in front of Mr. Mandala. "Can I have change for the Coke machine?"

Mr. Mandala counted out quarters silently, though he wasn't even sure the man was a registered guest. It had not occurred to him that the Martians would smell bad, but that was only because he hadn't given it much thought. If he had considered the question at all, that was what he would have thought.

Mr. Mandala fished out some quarters for himself and followed the newsman to the Coke machine. The picture on the TV screen had changed to clips taken by the Seerseller expedition, back on Mars itself. It showed the queer, angular underground cave, with its shelves and pillars, that they called "the Martian department store," and then it changed to show the angular tunnels and caverns the Martians lived in. "I don't know," said the cameraman at last, studying the picture. "Would you say they're intelligent?"

"Difficult to say, exactly," the Thames man replied, taking the pipe out of his mouth for the purpose. He looked like the Englishman he was, like, in fact, every American's idea of an English squire, with a red, broad face. "They do build habitations," he pointed out.

"So do gorillas, kind of," said the cameraman, who had once gone with a crew to photograph some of the vanishing silverbacks.

"No doubt, no doubt," the Thames man agreed. Then he brightened. "Oh, I have one," he said. "That brought it to mind. Once there was—let me see, at home we usually tell this about the Irish— yes, I have it. Once there was a spaceship that went to Mars, the next one after your *Algonquin*, I suppose you could say, and at any rate when they get there they find all the Martians caught smallpox or something from Seerseller's lot. The whole race has been wiped out, all but one old female. These fellows who're here, they're dead too. All but the one she. Well, the Greenpeace people and all those are terribly upset, and so they demand the United Nations pass an anti-genocide law and do something to restore the Martian race, do you see? So the Americans vote two hundred million dollars for reparations, and they use it to hire a human man who's willing to be bred to this one surviving Martian female."

"Cripes," said a man from *Time*, looking at the Martian on the screen as he listened.

"Yes, exactly. So they've found old Paddy O'Shaughnessy, down on his luck and pissed out of his mind, and they say to him, 'See here, Paddy, just go into that cage there. You'll find this female and all you've got to do is render her pregnant, do you see?' And O'Shaughnessy says, 'Faith, and what's in it for meself?' and they offer him, oh, thousands of pounds. And of course he agrees like a shot. But then he opens the door of the cage and he sees what the female looks like, and he backs clear out." The Thames Television man squeezed the Coke can in half and tossed it into a basket, grimacing to show Paddy's expression of revulsion. " 'Holy saints above,' he says, 'I never counted on anything like this. It'd be like making love to a grizzly bear,' he says. Then—"

"We had a fellow here wrestled grizzly bears," one of the card players remarked. "Remember him? Maximilian Morgenstern, his name was. Whatever became of him?"

"He lost," someone else said.

"Now, hold on there," the Thames man said irritably. "Do you want to hear this one or not? Anyway, he doesn't want to do it. 'But it's thousands of pounds, Paddy,' they tell him, urging him on. They wave a bottle of the creature at him, and he looks at it and licks his lips. Then, 'Oh, very well,' he says, 'but only on one condition.' 'And what condition is that?' they ask him, and he says, 'You've got to promise me that the children will be raised in the church.' "

"Yeah, I heard that one," said the cameraman. And he finished his own Coke and bent the can in half and tossed it at the basket. He missed.

"Ernest!" Mr. Mandala shouted angrily. Such sloppiness from these no longer welcome guests was more than he could stand. It took five minutes before Ernest showed up, followed closely by the other bellman, B.G. Both of them were looking aggrieved. "I told you a hundred times to keep the lobby cleaned up," Mr. Mandala scolded. "Look at that! Cans all over the place! Ashtrays full!"

"Mr. Mandala, we've been lugging those cots down into the pool area—"

"*First* you clean up this mess. *Then* you finish with the cots. What's taking you so long, anyway?" He stopped, aware that he had raised his voice. Some of the newspeople were looking at him. Ernest and B.G. bent to the task of picking up the cans, their faces glancing up at him sidewise, one dark plum and one Arabian sand.

Mr. Mandala stared them all down. He pointed to the lobby clock. "Checkout time," he called, self-righteous, annoyed. "Any guest who has not yet completed his checking out, please do so now."

Then he was busy enough for a while as the laggards came up to settle their bills. Two big trucks pulled up, filled with cameras and lights and the NBC peacock bright on their sides, and half a dozen of the guests went out to squeeze in next to the drivers. Then Ernest, finished with tidying up, called from the doorway, "Airport bus!" and he and B.G.

were jumping to get the bags on the bus. They moved a lot faster when they were hustling suitcases, Mr. Mandala reflected. Of course, that was the high spot of their day, because that was when the tips came in.

And then, with the log jam broken, the rest of the guests were picked up by their friends at the better motels, or decided to take a chance on the traffic, or simply disappeared, and the motel reverted to its usual state of peace.

Peace was something worth having, Mr. Mandala decided, and so he himself came out from behind the desk, cruising the now empty lobby and picking up the odd twisted cigarette pack from a settee or the empty soft-drink can out of an ashtray. "You can take your lunch break now," he told B.G., and to Ernest, "Care for a Coke?"

"Don't mind if I do," the bellman said neutrally. When Mr. Mandala got them out of the machine he popped the tab for Ernest himself before handing the can over. If there was one thing Mr. Mandala knew, it was how to get along with the blacks. Firm, fair, and friendly—always firm and fair, and friendly now and then to show that, really, you could treat them like ordinary human beings.

"What a bunch of weirdos," he commented, referring to their departed guests, but also to the foolish million who had spent their time off on the banks of the Banana River. "Such a lot of commotion about nothing. And did you hear all those old jokes?"

"I did hear one good one, Mr. Mandala," Ernest said, looking at him obliquely over the rim of the Coke can. "You want to hear it? It's, what do you call a seven-foot Martian with a spear?"

"Oh, hell, Ernest, everybody knows that one. You call him 'sir,' right? That's just what I mean. You'd think there'd be some new jokes, but all I heard was the old ones. Only instead of telling them about the Poles and the Jews and the Catholics and—and everybody, they were just telling them about the Martians. You know what I think, Ernest? I think that those Martians coming here aren't going to make a nickel's worth of difference to anybody."

Ernest finished his Coke. "Hate to disagree with you, Mr. Mandala," he said mildly, "but I think it's going to make a difference to some people. Going to make a *damn* big difference to me."

TWENTY

HUDDLING

At least the group was together now, for the first time in longer than they had any way of remembering. The crushing gravity was a permanent, aching, frightening drain. Nevertheless all the Martians had climbed out of their slings. Painfully they had crept across the sterile floor to the margin of their pool. They lay in its shallows, huddling together in a knot of legs and heads and bodies.

They knew they were not alone. They could not see through the one-way glass wall, and they had no clear idea at all of what was happening on its other side—the linguists and the code-breakers, with their computers and their frequency analyzers, trying to make sense of the ways the Martians communicated with each other; the exomedics, the exobiologists, the exopsychologists, the exoeverythings who were puzzling over every sound and movement. They did know that human people were there, because they could feel the dim warmth of their bodies even through the glass, but they didn't care about it. That didn't matter. What mattered was that they were all together, and huddling, and touching.

"Oof," grunted the Martian called Edward. "What a distending, griping place this is!" The only audible part of the remark was the "oof." A deliberate swelling of his belly, a grimace, a flick of his tongue toward nothing in particular and a small, gentle breaking of wind completed the thought.

Gretel, her splinted legs stiffly poked outside the group, licked him, then herself, then moaned. It meant: "I feel sorry for you—and for me, too!" There was a flurry of licking and tickling as everyone agreed. They talked that matter over for a while, crooning and writhing and poking each other, but there really was nothing to say that hadn't been said, and the subject was not pleasant.

Bob offered to help Gretel get the hard, stuck-on things off her legs again, but Alexander pointed out that the humans would just put them back on, and Gretel licked him to thank him for his offer but to decline it. There was a period of silence until Gretel, always cheerful, began to reminisce about the last time she had eaten, and all the group chimed in with their own pleased recollections—of eating, of sleeping in each other's embrace, of making love, of all the joyful things they loved to talk about. Slowly the Martians began to feel happy again. In spite of fear, in spite of the cruelly crushing gravity, in spite of the bright lights all around them, they were at peace; for they were huddling and communicating, and wasn't that what life was all about?

They had almost dropped off to sleep when Alexander shook himself and said drowsily, "Poor humans. We never see them huddling. I wonder how many of them it takes to carry on a real conversation?"

The question was interesting enough to rouse the group, a little. They poked and fondled each other inquiringly for a moment before Doris lifted her head. She licked a pair of the nearest flanks, sighed, wriggled a limb, and blew a soft, sweet breath successively into the faces of each of the others. They understood her at once. She was saying: "Probably none at all, since they don't seem to have much to communicate."

OUTSTANDING
SCIENCE
FICTION

FROM ST. MARTIN'S PRESS